THE HOUSE OF THE EGO
THE COMPLETE CABALISTIC CASES
OF SEMI DUAL, VOLUME 3

THE
ARGOSY
LIBRARY

THE HOUSE OF
THE EGO
THE COMPLETE CASES OF SEMI
DUAL, VOLUME 3

J.U. GIESY &
JUNIUS B. SMITH

COVER BY
W.B. KING

POPULAR PUBLICATIONS · 2021

TABLE OF CONTENTS

THE HOUSE OF THE EGO

1

THE BROTHER OF THE SERPENT

LOOKING BACK AT it now, I can see how the tremendous ingenuity of Semi Dual seized upon each episode in the affair and pieced together, bit by bit, the elements of a complete incident in the train of our experiences.

At the time, though, even I, who, knew him best, did not know how deeply he had gone into it, nor that he had worked steadily in his own peculiar fashion from the first, while the police and I bungled along in ours; so that at the end he was but awaiting for the proper time to strike.

The beginning of the matter was in itself commonplace enough, as are many things the ending of which proves startling in the extreme.

One afternoon Smithson, city editor of the *Record*, summoned me from my desk in the local room and asked: "Glace, what is the House of Ego?"

"The brain, at a guess," I replied.

Smithson shook his head.

"Cut that highbrow stuff," he grinned. "I'm not asking you a psychological conundrum. I'm asking what you know about a place out on Park Drive which bears that label in letters a foot high."

"I get you now," I said, smiling, and sat down in Smithson's other chair. "You mean that red brick, set back from the street among a lot of trees. I don't know what it is, Smithson. I've seen it, and I've also seen some pretty swell conveyances lined up in front of the place, and I've seen some expensively dressed women, both going in and coming out of the house. There's one thing I can add, however, under your twelve-inch letters, if one looks closely, you'll see the further legend, 'Swami Bhutia, Director.'"

"Let's see," said Smithson. 'Swami is a sort of title, isn't it-sort of a professor of—what?"

"Occult philosophy," I replied.

"And the name Bhutia is Hindu, I suppose?"

"Probably—Sanskrit originally. I've an idea this chap is an exponent of some cult of Oriental mysticism—a Yogi."

Smithson smiled his crooked smile.

" 'S'nough!" He said. "I reckon you're the fellow for the job, son. I've an idea there's a Sunday story in that chap and his hang-out. Suppose you go out there and write him up?"

"All right," I accepted.

"And *write* him up," said Smithson.

I grinned as I got out of the chair and turned to leave. I knew that Smithson was referring to that other time when he had first sent me to Semi Dual for an interview to be used as a Sunday feature.

I didn't get the Sunday story, but, thanks to Dual's assistance, I scared my first great scoop for the *Record* and won the friendship of Smithson, who up to that time had not thought much of me as a reporter. I lighted my cigarette and tossed the match into a tray on the editor's desk.

"I'll do it," I said.

I think, if I'd known what was going to happen, I'd have faked the interview.

As it was, I went back to my table, picked my hat off the back of my chair, and left the office. I took a cross-town car which would carry me to Park Drive, the thoroughfare of fashionable residence which had steadfastly refused to allow the traction company to lay rails along it, and settled myself into a seat.

And then, all at once, I grinned.

Smithson's last words had brought back that other time I had started forth at his bidding. Then instead of going for a car-ride, I had walked up the street to the Urania, our largest office-building, and taken a cage to the top.

For Semi Dual lived on the roof and in the tower of the Urania. That alone would serve to indicate that the man was peculiar—a personality apart from the mass. On the roof he had constructed a beautiful garden, full of flowers and shrubs, with a fountain in its midst. In spring and summer this lay open to the skies of heaven. In winter it yet stayed green under a dome of yellow green glass which Dual had built above it, converting it in a veritable conservatory where the plants he loved defied the killing blasts.

In the tower itself he had fitted up his own living quarters along lines of rich elegance which I have never seen excelled. There he dwelt with his one servant, Henri, and there he pursued his studies of the higher forces of the universe, which enabled him to perform acts of sapience which I have never equaled by any other living man.

These quarters of his were reached by a magnificent staircase of marble and bronze leading upward from the twentieth floor of the building, crowned at the top by an annunciator-plate of inlaid glass, which rang a chime of bells in the tower and announced the arrival of any approaching guest.

Now, as the car took me rapidly toward my destination, I recalled the peculiar emotions with which I had first mounted those stairs and placed a foot upon that inlaid plate where glass letters spelled a warning to those who came with selfish or unworthy motive. I recalled my first meeting with the tall, gray-eyed, olive-complexioned man who was now my friend, and I wondered what sort of an individual I was going to see to-day.

That was, of course, but natural, for Dual himself was what many people called an "occultist," believing in telepathy, astrology, chirography, subconscious analysis, and such kindred abstruse subjects, which he constantly used, in those instances where he endeavored to straighten out some of the tangles in the lives of men.

Now the name of the man I was going to interview suggested that he, too, was an exponent of the so-called occult. I felt a keen interest in being enabled to compare the two men.

The car was now approaching the crossing of the drive, and I pushed the bell, rose, and swung off the rear platform as we slowed. I had alighted some little way from my destination, and, turning, I walked along the street toward the House of the Ego itself.

Such was the beginning of the peculiar experiences which immediately followed in rapid succession and taught me a new lesson in the things which men will do.

The house itself was set back at a considerable distance from the street at the end of a rolling sweep of lawn, dotted here and there with the dark cones of evergreens, and was reached by a long cement walk. Several great elms, planted about it, threw it into a shade, out of which the white caps above; its windows gleamed like the highlights in a picture.

It was built in the old square architecture of a past generation, with high narrow windows and a massive front porch reached by some four steps from the walk. No doubt it had once been a residence of wealth, but recently I knew it had been standing empty until some months ago, when suddenly the gilt sign which now topped the porch had appeared.

To-day as I approached it I saw that there were some dozen automobiles and carriages lined up to the curb at either side of the entrance to the grounds. Of the former most were electrics or chauffeur-driven limousines. The carriages were those of people who employed liveried coachmen, as attested by the figures yawning on the boxes while waiting their employers' return. Whatever the object and mission of the House of the Ego, I decided that it was not lacking patronage of the better sort.

I turned in at the gateway and went up the walk, ascended the steps to the porch, and put my finger on the button of a very modern and palpably new bell. Scarcely had its reverberation started when the door opened, and I stared at the figure of a dark, little man in a long, yellow robe and a yellow turban, who stood bowing before me.

"Whom seek ye, stranger?" said he the next instant.

I sized him up and concluded that he was only the doorman. I gave him my card and watched him while he appeared to read it.

"I would like to see Swami Bhutia," I explained.

He retreated crabwise backward and bowed again.

"Enter—please," he suggested.

I came through the door and it swung silently shut behind me on well-concealed springs. The little man straightened and smiled upon me.

"The master is at the present assisting those who are seeking to invoke the light," he announced.

I gathered that Bhutia was busy. I glanced about for a chair. It was in my mind to wait. Then for the first time I noticed the hall in which I stood.

It was hung in what looked like black velvet, embroidered and embossed in gold thread in all sorts of allegorical designs. Even the carpeting was of black, with a heavy pile. It was a nice, cheerful sort of place! I decided that I wouldn't sit down, after all, and turned back to the little man in yellow.

Almost at once he started to speak:

"Pairhaps it would eventually transpire that the honorable stranger would desire to acquire merit by sitting at the feet of the master while he invokes the light upon lesser souls?"

"Oh, then, it isn't a private seance?" I remarked.

"The light is the light," observed my Swarthy guide. "The light shines for all. Come."

He turned and went swiftly before me, leading me through a sort of dividing portière of the same black stuff into a passage which was plainly a continuation of the hall. This, too, was hung in somber trappings and lighted by amber-colored globes set on stands, their orange glow serving but to make the walls more dusky. The passage was narrower, and I came to the conclusion that a part of the original hall had been walled off.

I felt confirmed in my suspicions when my guide turned a corner and started along another passage, which my sense of direction told me was the other side of the old wall. I followed along, and presently came to a door covered by a curtain, which he held ajar while he signed me to enter.

I slipped past its folds and he dropped them into place, leaving me standing in a darkened room. I strove to look about me, and presently, when my eyes had accustomed themselves to the lack of illumination in a measure. I saw that I was not alone.

Numerous persons were seated beyond me, grouped in a sort of semi-circle before a raised platform or dais, upon which glowed a misty, clearly defined globe of light. It was of an opalescent quality, and seemed to pale and brighten in a slow rhythm as I watched it. Dimly I perceived a chair a little way before me, tiptoed to it, and sat down.

I turned my eyes toward the light on the dais once more now: I saw a figure behind it. As near as I could make it out it was that of a man sitting cross-legged, his body clothed in a loose robe of the same tawny color as that worn by the little man who had brought me to the room. Upon his head was a turban of similar material, and below it his face seemed stating straight at me.

It was brown and oblongly oval, with high cheek-bones and thin lips and a high, overhanging forehead, and his eyes, in the half light from the glowing globe, seemed utterly dark like deep pits, at the bottom of which something glinted with a transient refraction of light.

So far as I could see, he sat there without movement, his hands clasped before him—long, slim, prehensile, almost effeminate in their slender lines.

And even as I sensed all this, he opened his lips and began to speak in a low, penetrating tone:

"Once again, spirits who come seeking the light of knowledge-once again breathe ye the breath. Clasping thy hands before ye, fasten thy eyes on the light which glows and pulses, and breathe deeply, inflating the chest until each and every cell is flooded with the luminance of the spirit of light. Hold ye the thought that the light is flooding your being, driving out all that is evil, all of sickness, all of disease, all of doubt. Breathe in the light—breathe in the light. Now, while one may count to seven. Hold it—hold the light, through seven pulsations, and as you let it depart again, know that it takes with it all impurity within ye and breathe forth the word 'Peace.'"

"Peace," hissed a figure before me in a long-drawn exhalation. "Peace," echoed a sibilant volley of articulation from the other figures in the room.

By now I could see better, and I let my eyes wander from the figure of Bhutia, the master, to that of his pupils.

They were for the most part women. Some of them were old, more of them middle-aged, and one or two mere girls. But whatever their age, I could sense that they were people of means. There was something about them which subtly suggested wealth, even if I had not seen the line of carriages and autos in front of the house.

There were one or two men, but to these I gave little notice except to mark the preponderance of women, who seemed to be seeking the light in a darkened room.

That was the whimsical idea which came to life and caused me to smile. There they were sitting with clasped hands, counting seven and breathing in, counting seven and holding their breaths, counting seven while they hissed "Peace," with their eyes on an opalescent sphere. Some way it all struck me as bizarre and unreasonable that any one should expect to gain spiritual advancement in a place like that.

If they wanted light, why, I asked myself, didn't they get out where it was and drink their fill of it in a natural way. Anyway, the whole place impressed me badly. I found myself contrasting its gloomy vestibule and its darkened chamber of rites with the light, the openness, the high position of Dual's abode, and by a natural step I compared the saturnine face of the man on the dais with the open countenance of my friend, lighted by his deep gray eyes.

"Once more." The Swami was speaking again. "Once more breathe in the light."

My eyes came back to him and wandered again to the pulsing light in the globe, and then suddenly a cold chill went tingling and trickling up over my scalp and down along my spine. I had seen something which up to now I had missed.

Behind and a little to one side of the light there was a moving something, like a swaying metronome. It stood upon the dais, not far from the opalescent glass of the globe, and, like it, was of a sort of dirty gray from where I sat. Back and forth it swung, back and forth in perfect time to the rise and fall of the lamp in the globe, and all at once I felt very glad that I occupied a back seat, for the thing I was looking at was something I had read of and seen pictured, but never before met—a monster specimen of the cobra, deadliest of snakes.

The dirty gray pendulum, swaying back and forth beside the pulsing light, was the belly of the serpent.

I shivered without any voluntary control of the action. The room was hot, yet I felt cold. Also I felt a great sense of disgust with the place in which I sat, with its darkened windows, its black-draped walls. Its ruling cross-legged spirit, and the audience which sat before me in rapt attention to his every word and act.

Suddenly I felt that he was in fact the brother to the serpent which he made a companion and part of his rites, and with it equally unclean. However, I made up my mind to see the thing through. And then I noticed that the light in the luminous globe was paling. It still pulsed and throbbed, but with each rise and fall it grew fainter.

Presently it faded out and left us in almost a total darkness, out of which came Bhutiai's voice. "The lesson is finished. Think well, ponder upon it. Return at the appointed time. Peace be unto thee now and forever— peace."

The lights flashed up and the audience rose and began to file out of the room. Looking about I judged that it had once been the parlor or drawing-room of the old house, now converted to the Swami's purpose. Like the approaches, it was hung in black, embroidered in gold. The stand which held the light seemed to be of ebony blackness. Only the robes of Bhutia and the gold embroidery broke the color scheme.

I gave my attention to the people as they passed out. As I had supposed, they were those of fashion and wealth. They passed me in silence, with compressed lips and intent expressions. Some way they impressed me as souls escaping from an ordeal rather than as ones illumined with any sort of light. And then the voice of Bhutia called me back to attention:

"And now, strange soul yonder, approach and tell me what ye seek."

2

SEMI DUAL PROMISES AID

I TURNED TOWARD him, where he had risen and come forward to the edge of the dais, beside the dead, misty glass of his extinguished light, on the other side of which the cobra had sunk down on its coils.

"How about your little play fellow?" I asked.

Bhutia smiled.

"Kwali?" he said. "Oh, you need have no fear of Kwali. See?"

He put out a hand toward the snake as he spoke.

It drew back as he approached it, lifted its head, and hissed sharply. Bhutia only smiled and opened his hand to seize it. The serpent suddenly dropped its crest and sought to dart under his hand, and he closed his fingers upon it, raised it and dropped it lightly into a covered basket.

"Now?" he suggested, with a smile still spreading his thin lips.

"I feel safer with Kwali in bed," I accepted as I rose and advanced toward him. "The fact is, Swami, I never have liked snakes. If you can spare me a few minutes I will explain the reason for my call."

He nodded and again seated himself tailor fashion on the dais, waving me to a chair.

"Perhaps I should not have come in here, save that your servant suggested it," I began.

He answered me in the words of the little man.

"The light is the light. The light shines for all."

"That should make our interview easier," I responded. "I am Glace, of the *Record*. I wish you would give me a little talk on your religion or philosophy, in order that we may publish an article about it; unless, of course, you have objections thereto."

Bhutia's eyes twinkled.

"I am not of those who—what is it you chaps say?—hide my light under a bushel. I am a teacher of the way of attainment, the development of the Ego. Those who wish may come and receive. However"—he rose and stepped from the dais—"if we are to converse of me and my endeavors to spread the wisdom, suppose we adjourn to other quarters. This room is well for the purposes of instruction and concentration of the mind, with the world shut out, but scarcely needful for a talk with a modern representative of the press."

I was perfectly willing to follow his suggestion, and rose with him. The man was proving a surprise to me by the evidences of education shown in his tones and the absence of any foreign accent in his pronunciation. I began to hope that my interview would prove pleasant, after all.

He led me out of the room and along the passage until we came to the back of the hall, where the little man had brought me around the corner. Here, instead of following back along the passage; he lifted a curtain and threw open a concealed door, drew back and motioned me to enter.

The transition was from darkness to light. If the passage

I left was gloomy and depressing, the room I now entered was equally flooded with the mellowed brilliance of the outer day.

To add to the effect, it was furnished with absolute magnificence. A splendid Indian rug covered the floor. In the midst of it stood a massive desk of carved teak-wood inlaid in mother-of-pearl, and furnished with what appeared to be a gold-mounted desk-pad and writing equipment. Chairs, tables, and taborets of teak and other rare woods stood about the apartment, the walls of which were hung in tapestries of red and blue and gold.

I felt as though I had suddenly been transported from a dungeon-cell to an Oriental palace, and no doubt some of my surprise showed in my face, for Bhutia smiled again as he followed me in and allowed the door to close.

"Not the hermit's cell you expected, perhaps, Mr. Glace?" he remarked.

"Hardly," I confessed.

"Sit down," said Bhutia. "Asceticism is not necessarily a part of advancement to every one, my dear sir. If you care to smoke, there are cigarettes and cigars on that taboret close by your hand for your liking."

I took a cigarette and sank into a chair. Bhutia took a seat at the desk and looked across, with an unspoken invitation for me to begin.

"I take it that you are a Hindu?" I began.

He nodded a "Yes."

"But," I said, "I thought men of your cult generally remained in India, or even in monasteries?"

"I am one of those chosen to spread the Truth," replied Bhutia. "Therefore, that I might be qualified, I was educated at the University of Calcutta, and afterward at Oxford in England, before taking up my mission."

"And just what form of philosophy do you teach?" I inquired.

"Gnani Yoga—what is commonly called the Yoga of Wisdom. Gnani is derived from the Sanskrit Gna, to know. It is the path of attainment which appeals most to men and women of intellectual temperament—souls who are attracted to metaphysical reasoning and speculation. Not, of course, that one has to be a skilled metaphysician to understand or avail himself of its teachings. It is designed to reach those who have outgrown the childish explanations of the great truths of life and desire to know the esoteric side of Truth.

"People to-day continually ask: 'Whence am I—whither do I go?;' Gnani Yoga is the Yoga of the 'Why.' Heretofore men have sought the answer to the 'Why' from the outside, when in reality it lies inside themselves. The Spirit has involved all the truth of the universe. We must seek in the Spirit to evolute the truth for our own comprehension."

"This is an East Indian religion, is it not?" I asked as he paused.

"All great religions have had their birth in India," Bhutia replied. "Today, as in the past, the conditions for deep thought are more favorable in India than in your western world of materialistic principles. Yet the Yogi will apply to all and every class of mankind."

He smiled.

"In fact, we have false gods who are legion in the East, while in the West you have only one—Material Wealth."

"And the object of your creed and its teachings is what—Swami?"

"The development of the Spirit—the Ego—the I. In other words, the unfoldment of the soul, in order that it may have more of the three attributes of the cause of universal activity—what we call the Absolute and others call Nature. Allah, God—that it may know more, have more power—be able to master space and matter—in other words, develop itself."

"Then that is why you call this the 'House of the Ego'?"

"Of course, Mr. Glace."

"Do you have many students?"

"There are many who desire to learn," Bhutia said. "Oh, yes, many wish to learn to master the principles I teach."

"Can you give me some idea of what one has to do—has to subscribe to-in order to enter your class?" I pursued.

"They subscribe to nothing," said Bhutia. "As to what they have to do, they must purify their minds and make them receptive for the germs of the Truth. The first thing we ask is that they lay aside all former prejudices, dogmas, preconceived beliefs, suggestions, poured into their minds in childhood, suggested thoughts or opinions, and such rubbish as litters the house of the mind.

"This is done in order that the mind, freed from the restraint of these tenets, may I grasp the presentation of the Truth without interference. We believe that a mind so cleansed will intuitively seize upon the Truth and recognize it as such. In this way we pick our classes. If one is unable to give up the old beliefs, or, having done so, does not apprehend the Truth when it is presented, we know that such a one is unready to receive the divine pabulum of attainment. But should the Spirit experience a filling satisfaction, we are certain that that one is ready. For that one the Truth is his for the taking."

"Then the Spirit proves its own fitness to advance, or the contrary, with you, I take it?"

"Exactly. You have caught the idea precisely, Mr. Glace."

"But what of those unfit?"

Bhutia laughed slightly.

"They have heard the Truth, and the truth never dies, Mr. Glace," he said. "Some day they will see it again. Eternity is long."

"So I have heard," I remarked. "Now, a few moments ago you used the words, 'The Absolute—Nature-Allah—God.' What is your conception of the Deity?"

"The primary and continual cause of all things here and elsewhere," Bhutia replied. "All existence, conscious or otherwise, is an emanation from the Absolute."

"And what," I asked, "were you making them do this afternoon?"

"That," said the Swami, "was a lesson in pranayama—the control of and absorption of prana by the power of chitta."

"I beg pardon," I interrupted. "Really I don't get those terms."

"Of course not," he returned quickly. "Let me try to explain. Prana is in our teachings the name for the force which energizes matter and causes motion or activity. Chitta is the name for the form of energy which causes mental activity—a higher form of energy than prana. Pranayama is the art of controlling and using prana by force of mind. By force of will one may charge himself with the energy of prana and store up that force in his being for his own future use."

"Then," I said, struck by an idea in his words, "you believe in the mental healing of diseases?"

"Is there anything new in that?" he challenged. "Your own cult, celled Christian Science, advocates the same thing."

"But is it a part of your Creed?"

"It is embodied in the belief of all students of the Truth, Mr. Glace," Bhutia declared.

"And you would perform it by the force of chitta operating through prana or upon it?" I suggested, twisting my tongue around the new words.

"The operation of chitta would cause the prana to enter and cleanse the system of all sickness," Bhutia explained.

"Very interesting. I'd like to go into it further some time," I returned.

"He who seeks may find," Bhutia rejoined.

"But why the snake?" I questioned on a sudden.

For the life of me I couldn't see what the thing had to do with a philosophy of spiritual evolution.

"The serpent is a symbol of wisdom," said Bhutia, fastening his eyes upon me as he spoke. "It is something I use at times to demonstrate the power of mind over matter. I handle it as I will and I live where another would die."

Perforce I accepted his explanation, which I felt did not explain. In everything else he had answered with freedom and ease. In this I could not help the feeling that his mind drew back from my question as the cobra had from his hand.

There had been that look in his eyes, unless I was

mistaken. Still, if he wanted a snake for a pet, it was, after all, no business of mine, and I decided that it would do no good to follow that line of questioning. Instead, I rose and thanked Bhutia for his courtesy, accepted another cigarette at his invitation, and took up my hat. My host struck a gong on his desk with a padded hammer, and almost at once my little man of the yellow robe bobbed in at the door and bowed.

Bhutia glanced at him and at me, and he backed through the door, leaving me to follow, which, after lighting my cigarette, I did. A moment later I was outside, making my way down to the street. Once there I paused and looked back at the place. House of the Ego, or whatever it was, I decided that as a plaything for neurotic women of the fashionable class it was going to be a howling success.

I went back to the *Record* office and saw Smithson.

"Get him?" said he.

I told him all that had happened.

"Sort of a spiritual forcing plant—a darkened chamber for the mushroom growth of souls," he grinned. "You ought to make a cracking story out of that. Play it up big and we'll give it the full page. Go up to the art-room and tell 'em to get a man out there and take a picture of the house and then work out a border with a lot of snakes in it. Make your story as creepy as you like—that's the 'dope.'"

I wrote the story and carried it back to Smithson who marked it for the compositors and laid it aside. And that night I went to see Semi Dual.

I wanted to talk over my latest experience with him and see what he would say to the Swami's elucidation of occult lore.

I walked to the Urania and ascended in a cage, and mounted the stairs to the roof. There was a young moon in the west, and the garden slumbered in the warm night, breathing forth a sweet perfume from its flowers and shrubs. The music of the little fountain came in a soft tinkle to my ears. All at once I pictured the scene of the afternoon in my mind and I smiled.

It might be all right to sit and breathe "Peace" into a superheated darkness, put here in the natural darkness of the night peace itself seemed to dwell as naturally as a dove folds her wings and dreams.

I filled my lungs with the sweetness of the place and trod upon the annunciator-plate. The bells chimed softly on the air. I went up the path, and Henri met me at the door. From long custom he merely smiled his welcome and waved me on into the inner room where I had so many times met Dual.

I crossed the anteroom and pushed the door of that other room inward. My friend glanced up from his reading beside his great desk, and he, too, greeted me with a smile.

"Ah, my friend; it is some time since you have given me the pleasure," he remarked.

I sank into a chair beside the desk and tossed my hat across to the couch on the other side of the room.

"My thoughts have come at least?" I returned.

Dual nodded.

"I have felt them," said he.

As one utterly at home, I opened a drawer of his desk and found myself one of the cigarettes he kept there for me, lighted it, and leaned back in the restful chair.

"I had an odd experience to-day," I began. "I wanted to tell you of it."

Dual closed his book and pushed it aside and smiled.

"I went to see another occult," I continued. "A chap calling himself Swami Bhutia. He has a place on Park Drive which he styles the 'House of the Ego.'"

I saw interest wake in Dual's eyes. He nodded. I went on:

"I had a long talk with him about his beliefs, and he told me a lot of stuff. Dual, what is prana, and what is chitta, if you don't mind?"

"Sanskrit terms for universal truths," said Semi Dual, "translatable into English as forms of energy Prana is energy refracted through material, chitta is energy refracted through mind. Briefly, one is material, the other mental energy. Suppose, my friend, you tell me just what happened today and what this Bhutia said to you?"

I began then and complied. Dual leaned back in his chair and closed his eyes, as was his habit when he wished to concentrate all his mind on something he heard.

I told him of the House of the Ego, of Bhutia, of the little yellow man, and of the class in the darkened room, and lastly of my talk with the Swami and of the snake.

When I was through he sat forward.

"You interest me deeply," he said. "So the cobra sought to elude the man when he attempted to lift it?"

"Yes. If a snake could be afraid I would have said it feared him."

Dual smiled in a somewhat peculiar fashion.

"A good comparison," he observed.

"And what about the rest of the stuff he told me?" I asked.

"So far as his exposition of the truths of Gnani Yoga are concerned, he spoke mainly the truth," Dual replied.

At once he lapsed into silence and sat staring straight before him, yet I was sure that he was not looking at any objective thing. I had the feeling that his eyes were turned inward examining some subjective conception. Presently he spoke:

"It is a clear night, with but few clouds. Suppose you accompany me to the roof of the tower? Let us search for your man in the stars."

I gazed at him in surprise. I had not expected my story to impress him to any appreciable degree beyond a mild interest. Now he appeared as nearly excited as I had ever known him to be. I have told you that he believed in the science of astrology, and I knew what he meant by his words.

He wished to question the fiery units of the sky as to the meaning and purpose of the man I had described. On that first time I had ever worked with him I had come to him one night and found him seeking among them for a man who had taken life. He had found him, and told me where I might do the same in actual life.

Suddenly a peculiar tremor seized me in its grip and carried me away. The circumstances of my meeting with the Hindu all at once appeared portentous in the light of my friend's acute interest. Yet I said nothing as I rose and prepared to follow him from the room.

He led me up a winding stair, and finally we emerged into a broad room at the very top of the tower, whose walls were mainly of glass. Here it was that Semi Dual had his great telescope.

Here at times he sat and swept the heavens for the material for those abstruse calculations of his which had more than once in my experience resulted in bringing the guilty to justice.

Now I stood and watched while he swung the great tube on its bearings and seated himself at the eyepiece. And it was then that he spoke:

"Describe the man to me as nearly as you can. Physically, I mean."

I gave him the details of Bhutia's appearance, and he accepted them with a nod, drew some sheets of paper within reach on a table at his elbow, and fastened his eye to the tube.

I glanced out of the window as he worked. There was no sound high up here in the tower. The city slumbered far below. Nothing broke the silence save the slight sigh of the bearings as Dual moved the great tube.

High above us and all around us gleamed and glistened the pin-points of light in the vault of the sky—and Dual was reading them, as others might read illuminated signs from the streets below. I allowed my glance to come back to him, where he sat swinging his telescope, jotting notes on his paper in a matter-of-fact way.

I considered his broad, strong forehead, his clean, true profile, the pure, firm curve of his lips, the strength of his chin. It was strong, good, open. There was nothing veiled or saturnine or crafty about it. And again, as before, my heart swelled that I could call such a man friend.

Presently he turned from the instrument and began his calculations upon the sheets of paper. Curiosity made me approach the table and stand looking down at the series of signs and numerals he was writing. So far he had not spoken—had worked with complete concentration.

I knew that the matter had proved of deeper moment than I had dreamed it could be. I wondered with a great wonder what he had found in the stars.

He pushed aside the sheets and raised his eyes to mine.

"There is no Swami Bhutia," he said.

"Hold on!" I began. "Has something happened to—"

"There never was a Swami Bhutia," said Semi Dual. "There is a man corresponding to his description in this city pt present, but that is not his name?"

"Then he is an impostor!" I cried.

"I have an idea that he is a very shrewd man," replied Dual. "He knows a great deal of the truth, beyond a doubt—"

"But why should he use an assumed name?" I interrupted. "If he is really an occult teacher, why sail under false colors? Anyway, I felt this afternoon that there was something not quite right about him."

Dual was again studying the sheets of computations he had made.

"Gordon," he began, as I paused, "I have an intuition that there are to be some rather unusual developments in this House of the Ego. Events will transpire there within the near future, not unfraught with danger. So, far as I can tell, they will involve a woman, Bhutia, and—you."

"*Me!*" I exclaimed.

Semi Dual smiled.

"You, my friend."

"Perhaps," I remarked, "I'd better beat it."

Dual's smiled widened.

"The signs—that is, the major ones—indicate that you will be drawn into the affair. Of course, you could exercise your own volition and resist the influences which will operate, but I hardly think that you will. So far as I see at present, the stars will use you as an instrument to their purpose, unless you refuse. I have told you that there will be danger—I have not said there will be death."

He had spoken seriously, for all of his smile. Suddenly I felt my heart swell at his words.

Then what would you advise—shall I go through with the thing?" I asked.

"Play the man's part," said Semi. "And be assured that if at any time you need help I shall come at your call. So far as this and no farther must I advise you. It is not for me to attempt to control a man's free agency, unless he is one who is breaking the universal laws. It is not wise to seek to control others, my friend. Each man should walk alone."

"And you have learned all this from the stars?" I said.

It seemed as wonderful to me tonight as it had the first time I had seen him do it.

"From the stars," he repeated, "and the stars, Gordon—"

"Do not lie," I finished the quotation.

"Exactly, my friend."

"There was a time when I wouldn't have believed it," I told him, "but I believe it now. I have seen it proved too often. I'm glad I came here tonight. Now I think I shall go."

We went back to the room below and I got my hat.

"I may see you again and tell you how things are going." I remarked as I offered my hand.

Dual shook his head.

"Whether you do or not, be assured that I shall be ready,

should you need me," he replied, and gripped my fingers in his.

I went out into the garden and down the stairs and on down to the street. I walked with my head up and my shoulders back. I felt like a soldier going into battle. I didn't know what was going to happen, but I was certain that if Dual said something was coming it would arrive. He was not a man who spoke, from suspicion or surmise.

"Play the man's part," he had said in the room high above me. I nodded to myself as if in assent. If I was, as he said, to be an instrument of fate I resolved to try and be a good one. And back of that resolve, of my entire mood, bolstering it up and making me walk with a new spring of resolution, were the words of my strange friend, who had never failed who had never failed me.

"If at any time you need help, I shall come at your call."

I decided that whatever the House of the Ego held in the way of the unexpected I, for one, would not fail to play my part.

3

A CASE FOR THE DETECTOR

THE EVENTS WHICH Dual had predicted did not, however, develop at once. In fact, several days went by in the usual manner, and my story, of what Smithson persisted in calling the "Park Drive Soul Conservatory," was printed and appeared as the leading feature of the next Sunday's *Record*.

It excited some comment and brought me a modicum of praise, and all the time I went around with a sort of subconscious question as to when the things that were to happen would transpire.

The answer began to take shape two days after my story appeared—on Tuesday, to be exact.

That morning I dropped into the Central police station about ten and nodded to my friend, Sergeant Dan Harrington, who sat back of the desk.

"Top o' the mornin' to ye, sergeant," I greeted. "What's new?"

"Somethin'," said Daniel, "but I don't know what it is. Bryce was tryin' to get you at the *Record* a minute ago. Wait a bit."

He turned to a roundsman loafing back of the rail.

"Get Bryce. He's in the chief's room," said he.

The policeman rose and started off down the hall, and

I waited. Here was news indeed. I wondered what Bryce could want with me. I knew him well, having frequently met him while working on stories for my paper; but I hadn't seen him for some little time.

I imagined that he must have something important on hand to be calling me at the office. But I did not dream at the time that the House of the Ego was in any way mixed up in his desire to connect with myself.

Footsteps came rapidly along the hall and the inspector appeared.

"Hello, Glace," he remarked. "I was tryin' to get you on the wire a bit ago."

"So Dan said," I made answer. "What's up?"

"I reckon," said Bryce, "that that story in Sunday's *Record* about this joint out on Park Drive was your work, wasn't it, Glace?"

I grinned.

"Really, inspector, I cannot tell a lie. I did it with my little typewriter. Anything heinous in the offense?"

Bryce smiled slightly under his short mustache.

"I guess as a piece of writin' it's all right," he replied; "but I don't want to discuss its literary merits right now. You come with me."

"But what's up?" I persisted as he started to turn away.

"You'll find out when we get back to the chief," he told me. "Your Sunday 'feature' may grow into a continued story, from the looks of things, son."

That was enough. I followed him down the hall and paused while he opened the door of the chief's room.

Four people sat there as we came in. Chief of Police Brant I knew, and greeted with a nod. The other three—

two men and a woman—I had never, to my knowledge, seen before. The woman and one of the men were persons briefly described as middle aged, and were palpably people of well-to-do circumstances and seemingly more than usual refinement.

The other man was a well-set-up, light-complexioned chap of somewhere in the twenties, as near as I could judge. One and all, they wore an expression of embarrassment and worry, which seemed to have reached an acute stage.

As soon as Bryce and I had entered and the door was closed, Brant began to speak.

"Mr. and Mrs. Liston and Mr. Andrews, Mr. Glace."

The man and his wife acknowledged the introduction by bows. Andrews, the younger man, rose and gave me his hand.

"Sit down, Glace," said Brant. "Bryce suggested calling you in before we went further with this case, for two reasons: First," he smiled, "because he says he knows from experience that you can keep a close mouth; and secondly, because you wrote that story in the *Record* last Sunday about that Hindu's place out on Park Drive."

My heart began to throb at his words. At that moment I realized that I was now entering the first stage of the thing Dual had predicted. I took a firm grip on my resolve to miss no point in the things which should develop, looked at the chief, and nodded my head.

"You met this chap Bhutia and talked to him, I take it?" Brant went on.

"Yes, chief. I had quite a talk with him."

"And you've had some little experience with this occult

stuff, if what Bryce tells me is correct? You have a friend who believes in it?"

"Yes."

"Bryce thought you might be able to help us," said Brant. "Now, Mr. Liston, suppose you begin at the beginning and tell up as nearly as you can everything which has happened in the affair."

Liston took a pair of pince-nez glasses from his high-bridged nose and held them in his hand as he spoke, tapping them up and down by way of a sort of emphasis. He cleared his throat.

"It has really been a very painful experience for both my wife and myself," he began. "It was only after we had tried all else that we resolved to come to you and see what could be done—"

"We didn't want to incur any police notoriety," interrupted his wife."

"Yes, yes," said Brant; "I understand. Go on."

"Olive has always been of a rather fine drawn nervous type," Liston resumed. "I think her mother bequeathed it to her, myself. I know my brother was very much like myself in his powers of control."

"One moment," arrested the chief. "What is the young woman's name?"

"Olive Liston. She is my brother's only child."

"Very well. Now what happened, if you please?"

"Why, she left home and went to live with that Hindu," exclaimed her aunt.

Brant frowned.

"Mr. Liston," he prompted.

"You see, chief," responded the uncle, "when my brother

died he was a fairly wealthy man, and Olive being his only child, and under age, he made me her guardian and custodian of her wealth. I gave a great deal of time to safeguarding her interests, and she came to us to live, as a matter of course. Under the terms of my brother's will I was to have full charge of her fortune until she reached the age of twenty-one, which was in last February, when I was to turn it over to her, regardless of whether she was married or not. I did so at that time, and I am glad to say that it had increased materially while I had it in my hands. It aggregated nearly a million, over half of which was in actual cash."

Bryce looked at me and grinned. I smiled. Brant was fidgeting in his chair. Now he turned directly to Andrews.

"You were engaged to Miss Liston, I think you said?"

"Yes."

"Do you know the particulars of what caused her to leave her uncle's home?"

"I think I know all about it, chief."

"Then, if you will, tell me about it, as far as you can."

"Briefly," said Andrews, "it was like this. Olive is, as her uncle says, of a highly strung nervous type. She has always been interested in such subjects as metaphysics and kindred lines of thought. Some months ago, when this Swami Bhutia, as he is called, came here and fitted up that house on the drive, a friend of hers went to see him, and afterward retailed to Olive what a wonderful man she thought he was.

"Her stories excited my *fiancée's* curiosity, and she went to the house herself. I don't know all that she saw—that is, I don't know if I do or not—because I went there, once myself with her and I couldn't see anything very unusual except a lot of trick-stage settings, as it seemed to me. But Olive grew greatly interested in the man and his teachings, and finally got so that she went to see him every day. After a time I noticed that she hardly seemed like herself at all, even when she was at home or we were out somewhere together. She seemed to be always dreaming and wishing to go back to this House of the Ego.

"I remonstrated with her about her attitude on several occasions, but without any effect except to cause her to grow greatly excited and accuse me of not wishing her to develop her mind as highly as she might. Eventually she came to a point where she seemed to me to move in a walking dream. That was up to a week ago. At that time she suddenly announced that she had made all arrangements to remove to the house of the Swami and rent apartments there.

"It seems that he has rooms fitted up in the upper story where he takes patients for treatment for various diseases, or those who wish to attain a rapid knowledge of his peculiar tenets of faith. Olive's determination, of course, precipitated a violent resistance both on the part of her aunt and uncle and myself. Our arguments and pleas, however, went without avail. She calmly informed us that she had expected our objections; that she was of age and free to do as she pleased; that one of the chief things in her new religion was to throw aside all things which could hinder her spiritual growth and all old ties and beliefs, and that so far as she and I were concerned, our engagement was at an end.

"I asked her what she meant to do with her life, and she answered that she intended to become a 'teacher of the truth.' Those are her exact words. She left home that night and went to the House of the Ego. Both her uncle and aunt and I have called there to see her. She received us in her room and chatted very pleasantly as long as we made no mention of her returning to us. Any such suggestion resulted uniformly in her reasserting that she was unalterably resolved upon becoming a teacher of the truth. I think that covets the case as far as I am able to speak of my own knowledge."

"And what," asked the chief, "would you say of her mental condition? Would you say she was acting of her own volition in this affair?"

"That's what is puzzling me," said Andrews. "She seems natural enough, except when one tries to get her to give up this life. Then she seems to freeze up and become cold and almost mechanical in her resistance."

"Have you talked with this Bhutia about her case?" questioned Brant.

Yes," returned Andrews. "I have; or, rather, he has talked to me."

"How's that?" Brant leaned forward.

"He asked me a great many questions about her life and her age and such subjects. He asserted that he winded to be sure that she was acting of her own volition. Claimed that the prejudice against his religion was so great that he had to guard himself, and offered to refuse to allow her to remain if we objected; but said that her heart seemed set upon her course."

"And the time you went to the house with her," continued the chief. "What did you see?"

"Nothing much," replied Andrews. "They took us into

a dark room where this chap had a sort of light, in a globe, fixed so that it dimmed and brightened. He gave us a talk and put the class through some breathing exercises, and told us how well and happy we were going to be."

"Don't forget the snake, Richard," Mrs. Liston put in in an excited voice.

"What snake?" snapped Bryce, taking his first part.

"Oh, he had a tame cobra, which stood up and wiggled beside the light globe," Andrews returned. "That's an Oriental trick they all pull."

"Oh, yes. Glace wrote that up," said Bryce;. "Well, I guess a fellow can keep a snake for a pet if he wants to. We can't do nothing about that."

"Does there seem to be any restraint exercised over Miss Liston?" Brant resumed.

"No," admitted Andrews. "She appears to go and come at will, though I don't know if she has left the house since she entered it a week ago."

"Did you ever ask her if she could leave if she wished?"

"I did," said Liston at once.

"And she answered?"

"That she did *not* wish."

"Your niece is of age and absolutely the mistress of her actions and her fortune, then, Mr. Liston?"

"Absolutely, Chief Brant."

"As her guardian you have no longer any control? Have you any power as an agent of her affairs?"

I have given her advice, but I have no legal authority, sir."

"She could do as she pleased with everything she owns?"

"Yes."

"Hum," Brant frowned and turned to Bryce. "It seems

to me this affair resembles that Western matter of a few years ago, where a man posed as a priest of a new cult and got rich from a bunch of dupes. They tried to get him for years before he was landed, and then he made a getaway, if you remember."

Bryce nodded.

"You didn't put nothin' in your story about this soul sanatorium he seems to be runnin'," he remarked to me.

"He didn't mention it," I returned.

I began to see that Swami Bhutia had entertained me with a philosophic dissertation rather than let me into his real affairs.

"What does he charge for board and treatment?" Bryce asked Liston.

"An exorbitant price, as I consider it," he replied. "Olive is paying him one hundred dollars a week."

"Has he got many boarders?"

"Several other women, I believe."

"Shameless creatures," said Mrs. Liston, "living in that house with that Indian!"

Neither Bryce nor Brant paid any attention to her outburst. The chief seemed to be considering the matter.

"These are hard cases for us to handle," he remarked at length. "There is so little to take hold of. If we could prove that your niece was being held there against her will it would be easy to get her away, but the question is, can we? Anyway, we will take the matter up at once. See what you can do, inspector," to Bryce.

The officer nodded.

"You remember, chief, about that fellow you spoke of— he had a boy with him whose folks claimed he was hypnotized by the guinea who was playing the priest; but they couldn't prove it—"

"Hypnotized? Merciful Heavens!" exclaimed Mrs. Liston. "Do you suppose—"

"I ain't supposin' nothin'—yet, ma'am," said the inspector. "I'll get busy and do all I can. I'll go up there and scout around a bit, and maybe I'll see this Bhutia, and if I can I'll see the girl. What does she look like, anyway?"

"I have a photograph," said Andrews. He drew his watch, and opening the back case, handed it to Bryce.

I bent my head to look at the face as Bryce held it. The picture showed a girl with large eyes, set wide apart in a perfectly oval face, of what I should judge to be a brunette type. She was handsome in her way.

Bryce inspected the portrait closely.

"Light or dark?" he inquired.

"Dark—a decided brunette, but with a clear skin," Andrews replied.

The inspector nodded and handed back the case.

"I'll know her if I see her," he declared.

"And see if you can get a line on this fellow," Brant suggested. "See where he came from and if he's left a trail behind him. Maybe he's wanted somewhere or other."

Then, turning to me: "He didn't tell you anything about where he was from, did he, Glace?"

"He said he was a Hindu, educated at Calcutta, and mentioned having studied at Oxford, England," I returned.

Brant nodded.

"All right; we'll do all we can and let you know as soon as we have anything to report, Mr. Liston," he promised. "If we can find out something about this man we may be able to bring pressure to bear upon him. Anyway, we'll take the matter up at once."

"We sincerely hope you may succeed," said Liston, rising and replacing his glasses. "We cannot help feeling that the man is an imposter who has in some way gained control of our niece for the purpose of getting his hands on her fortune. We hope you may be able to prevent his succeeding. Come, my dear."

He held out his hand and assisted his wife to rise.

They left the office, but Andrews still remained after they were gone.

"I can't help feeling that you hit the nail on the head, inspector," he observed, "when you spoke of that boy's case. I believe that this Bhutia uses hypnotic suggestion to control his so-called patients and students. The question is—could he hold several persons under his control at once?"

"Sure he could. Why, I've seen—" began Bryce, and caught my eye.

"Anyway, I've known of its being done," he made an end.

"Granting that it could be, how are you going to prove your specific case?" said Brant.

"I don't know yet," admitted Bryce, "but I'll have a try.

"Do all you can," urged Andrews. "I intended to make Miss Liston my wife, and I hope you can appreciate how I feel. Honestly, gentlemen, I'm afraid the girl's mind is in danger, if not her actual life."

Brant nodded.

"Her life won't be in danger until the fellow has got all he can out of her. By Jove, I ought to have found out about that! Do you happen to know where her money is deposited, Mr. Andrews?"

"I know that a good deal of it is in the Fourth National," Andrews replied. "She has a safety-box in their vaults and keeps her papers there."

"You can find out if she's been drawing put any heavy amounts," said Brant to Bryce. "And now, Glace, have you anything to suggest?"

"Only this," I returned. "If Bryce gets to see the girl I would advise him to draw her into a conversation and notice whether she makes use of any set phrases which she continually repeats. Mr. Andrews, saying that she reiterated that she was to become a teacher of the truth, made me think of that. It is a fact that frequently a person under hypnosis will repeat set formulas consisting of the exact wording in which the suggestion was made to such person during the time the controlling mind was operating upon him or her.

"This might help us to determine whether Miss Liston is actually under this man's control or acting in a voluntary way, merely from hyper-religious fervor, in which case she would be practically in a state of auto-hypnosis rather than under any one's control."

"Good idea," said Bryce.

"And for goodness' sake do all you can. Any expense that is necessary I will most gladly pay," Andrews added with feeling. "I'm sure if Olive were herself she would never remain in that house."

"Then that's all," said Brant. "Bryce! you get on the job and get Glace to help you any way he can. I'll 'tend to getting this fellow's record, if he has one. Better come in to-night."

Bryce, Andrews, and I arose and left the chief's room, going out front. There, after a final request that we do all in our power, Andrews shook hands and left us and Bryce turned to me.

"This is going to be a hard nut to crack, I'm afraid," he declared. "Those fortune-tellers and such ginks are slippery cusses and hard to get anything on. Even if he has got that girl under his control, how are we going to prove it? I wonder if that friend Dual of yours would give us a hand? He's a wonder, that chap. I never saw a fellow in his line who was straight before, but I'll sure stand for him."

"I've already mentioned this matter to him—about the Swami," I informed the inspector, "and he gives me to understand that Bhutia is an assumed name."

"How's he know that?" queried Bryce.

"I should think," said I, "that you'd quit asking that about Dual."

Bryce had met my friend several times and been compelled to admit that he could succeed where the inspector had failed.

Bryce grinned and flushed.

"All right, son," he retorted; "I'll admit the fact, but would he help us, do you think? He ought to know how to get this guinea's goat if any one would, bein' up on that sort of stuff."

"You go ahead and do all you can and let me know what you find out," I told him. "If we get stuck and Dual thinks we need help, we'll get it, I'm sure. In fact, he told me there would be some funny things happen in this House of the

Ego, as long ago as last week, and added that he would be ready if there was any need."

"That's enough for me," snapped Bryce with manifest satisfaction. "I'm as stuck on that Dual as you are, Glace, in my own way. He's white. All right, I'm going on the job. I'll phone you later. You might see Dual in the mean time and tell him about to-day's talk."

"I will," I agreed, and I honestly meant to, but that afternoon a "limited" train struck an open switch some fifty miles from town and scattered death and sorrow amid its ruins. Smithson sent me there for the *Record* and I didn't get back that night.

The most I could do was to call Semi on the phone just before I left, using his secret number, which did not appear in any telephone book. I told him briefly what had happened at the station and gave him the names of the parties concerned. Then, with his low-toned thanks ringing in my ears, I caught a special train which was just leaving for the wreck, and plunged into a scene of horror, which kept me for a night and part of the next day.

When I returned to the office I found a note on my desk asking me to communicate at once with Inspector Bryce.

4

GLACE STARTS AN INVESTIGATION

I CALLED UP the Central Station at once and asked for him. I confess I was as anxious to get in touch as I fancied was he.

All through my work at the wreck I had felt from time to time a growing curiosity as to what was developing in the investigation he was making about the house on Park Drive.

"Hold the wire," came Harrington's voice, as soon as I had given him my name.

"Bryce! Oh, Bryce!" I could hear him yelling. "Here's your man, Glace."

At times I have fancied that one could see at least subjectively over a telephone wire. I could picture the scene in the station as I sat and waited for the inspector to answer— Harrington at the desk, calling to him; his start of attention and movement to respond. Then came the beat of footsteps across the floor, and he spoke to me.

"Hello! That you, Glace?"

"Yes," I responded. "What have you found out?"

"Considerable and not much," said Bryce in a tone of something like disgust. "The trouble is to connect things up. Did you have a talk with Dual before you left town?"

"No," I confessed. "The wreck broke so suddenly that I left on the jump. However, I called him up and had a talk with him while waiting for the relief special to start."

"What'd he say?" Bryce wanted to know.

"Told me to tell you to do all you could and be governed by circumstances," I informed him.

"That means a lot to him, maybe," said the inspector, "but how does it help me? He ought to know I'm no mind reader. He talks like a curved ball looks. What does he mean?"

"Get on the job and stay there I think," I replied.

"I've done that," growled Bryce; "but I'd like to see some results."

"And I think you'll get them if you keep on," I encouraged. "Did you get into the house?"

"Sure!" said Bryce. "Say—Gordon, that is sure some house. Part of it looks like it was trimmed for a Hallowe'en party and part of it looks like the guinea'd swiped it from a museum of antiques. It's some joint."

"See the girl?"

"Yep. Say—what are you going to do this afternoon?"

"What do you want me to do?" I asked.

"I've gotter go out and see them Listons again," explained Bryce. "I sort of thought I'd like you to go along. Think you can make it about four?"

"Let's see—it's three now," I considered. "All right, Bryce. I'll see Smithson and get off. Where'll I meet you?"

"Come, here as soon as you can," he directed, "and we'll go out together. I'll tell that Andrews chap to go out to the house, too. Well—so-long."

I hung up and crossed to Smithson's room, opened the door, and went in.

"Smithson," I began, "I want the afternoon off."

"Funeral or a ball game?" grinned the old man.

"An attempt to clear up something you started," I rejoined.

"I started?" said Smithson.

I nodded, sat down, and told him all about the results of his assignment to interview Bhutia. While I talked I saw his eyes begin to sparkle. Smithson had a keen scent for anything which smelled like a good story. Besides, he knew all about my association with Semi Dual, and had a great respect for my friend's ability in his chosen way of life.

"And Dual thinks there's something shady about this Swami?" he remarked as I finished.

"He said the developments in the House of the Ego would be interesting," I replied.

"And this element of danger—what does he mean by that—danger to the girl or you? Does he think you're liable to get hurt, poking around?"

"He didn't specify."

"Probably it's the girl," said Smithson. "So then you're going out to Liston's with Bryce this afternoon?"

"If you let me off."

"I'll do better than that," said Smithson. "I'll put you on this matter by assignment, till it's cleared up or I call you off."

"Then I'm off!" I reached for my hat.

Smithson grinned.

"Why don't you go out and take some lessons in snake-charming from the Swami?" he suggested. "If there's anything wrong there, the place to look for it is from the inside."

"It might not be a bad idea," I agreed.

"But if you do," he cautioned, "don't let the snake bite you till you've written the story."

"Thanks for your personal interest," I retorted as I started for the door.

"Oh," said Smithson, "I was thinking of the paper! Now remember, I'm looking for a good story. So-long."

What made Smithson say what he did? He thought he said it as a joke, and at the time I accepted it as such and grinned as I left his room, stopped at my desk and stuffed some copy-paper into a pocket. Yet now I can see that even in that those major influences of which Semi Dual had spoken were in subtle operation.

Thus, many of those things which we fondly imagine are the results of our own volition are only added proof of the truth of those invisible forces which shape our lives. Frankly I doubt that without that seeming joke as a casual motive I would ever have done what I did. But once planted in my mind it continued to operate and led me into one of the most peculiar experiences of my life.

I left the office and went straight to the Central Station. There I found Bryce fidgeting about the front office, waiting for me. He saw me as I came up the steps and put my hand on the door, and immediately started to meet me. Seeing him coming I waited until he came out.

"See you made it," said he.

"Better than that," I told him. "I'm on special assignment till this case is cleared up."

"Good!" exclaimed the inspector. "Let's grab a car and get put there right away Andrews said he'd show up."

We boarded a car and rode along in comparative silence, because Bryce said he didn't wait to talk where we might be heard. I told him about my experiences at the wreck, and presently he punched the bell and we swung off on a street which I recognized as Park Drive.

So the Listons lived on the drive also. I marked the fact with interest as indicating afresh that Bhutia's clientele was only from the wealthy class. That point alone seemed suspicious to me. If, as he said, the "Light" shone for all, why should he so carefully cull his pupils from among the well-to-do? It didn't exactly seem consistent to me.

Bryce had turned down the street, and we were walking in a direction away from the House of the Ego. Presently he turned and led me toward a large stone mansion midway of the block.

Mr. and Mrs. Liston were expecting us, and received us in the library of their home. Andrews was also present, and as soon as we had taken seats Bryce plunged into his report.

"I did my first work in the case by trying to find out what was known of this fellow around town. He doesn't seem to have left many trails. I went to see the agents from whom he rented the house he lives in—you know that's the old Pearson home. They told me he came in about six weeks ago and asked what they wanted for the place for six months, with an option of renewal at that time. They told him, and he paid them in gold.

"Then he said he wanted some alterations made, and offered to bear the expense. They said they had made him an estimate, and he had paid for that in gold, too. I asked them what sort of alterations he wanted, and they said he had some partitions run and some electric wiring done in different parts of the house. Then I went out and made a canvass of a lot of employment agencies to get a line on his servants, but as far as I can find he must have brought his own folks with him, as he hasn't hired any in town as far as I could find out. I had a go at tradespeople next, and all I could find out is that he seems to buy most of his stuff wholesale, and pays for everything in gold when he buys it. He's established a good line of credit in town, at any rate.

"I got hold of one or two deliverymen, and they told me the stuff was taken in and paid for by a little fellow in a yellow robe, with a turban on his head, who I reckon is the one Glace saw. I guess he's the Swami's righthand man all right from the looks of things. One of the drivers did say, though, that there was a woman there, too. He called her a nigger, but maybe she's a Hindu. He said he saw her in the kitchen and called her 'mammy,' an' she shook her head and grinned at him, and said something he couldn't understand."

"But, goodness me; didn't you go near the house, Mr. Bryce?" Mrs. Liston interrupted. "I can't see what good it could do to learn that this person pays gold for his provisions. Really, we don't care if he pays at all so long as we get Olive out of his clutches."

"Well, you see, I was comin' to that part, ma'am," the inspector explained in some haste. "Of course I did go to the house. I was just tellin' you what I'd learned about this Bhutia on the outside."

"His personal history is of no interest to me," returned

Mrs. Listen. "I am more interested in what you did toward seeing about helping my poor niece."

"But you see, ma'am, we want to learn all we can about the man to see if we can find any evidence of crookedness about him. Then maybe we could bring that into use as a sort of argument to make him easier to handle," expostulated Bryce, somewhat flustered by her attack.

"Of course," said Liston, "I suppose you know what you are doing, but I really can't see that it matters how he pays his bills or whether he has a negress or a Chinaman for a cook. We are paying you for helping us get our poor Olive back, and no doubt if others find themselves in the same position they will do the same. However, tell your story in your own way. I am merely anxious."

The inspector flushed.

"About that, ma'am, I'm working as a public official," he returned, "an' I'm going to do all I can to help you folks— only I got to work in the way I know how."

"Oh, well, go on," said the lady. "After all, I mustn't expect too much of you."

"I think, from what he says, that the inspector has been doing a lot of work," Andrews came to the rescue. "For my part I am anxious to know *all* that he did."

"Well, then," resumed Bryce, "I went to the house after I'd looked into some other things first, and I asked for this Bhutia. A little fellow in a yellow robe met me and took me into a room fitted up like a palace, and there I met the Swami, as he calls himself. He is a mighty funny man—a chap can't really tell what he means from what he says. I had a talk with him about Miss Liston, and he was as easy as mush.

"He said he was very sorry that her folks had found it necessary to send me to see him, and that if she wanted to leave his house all that was necessary was for her to pack her bag and get out. That sounded reasonable enough, and I asked him if he couldn't order her to do so. He laughed in a funny sort of way and answered me by asking me another question.

" 'My dear inspector,' says he, 'if you were running a hospital or a school, and a person came to you for instruction, and that person was of the age of majority and discretion and her own mistress, and was ready and anxious do pay your charges, would you think it good business on your part to refuse to give what she wished to purchase merely because a distant relative allowed narrow-minded prejudice to cause her to object?' "

"Narrow-minded prejudice!" exclaimed Mrs. Liston. "Well—I never heard of such—"

Bryce grinned slightly. I fancied he had enjoyed rendering that quotation. He utterly ignored the lady's ire and went on:

"I told him that from a business point it wouldn't be liable to make him rich, but that he hadn't answered my question. He grinned a bit at that and said that of course he could order her out, but that he really couldn't see why he should; that she was a perfectly respectable character as far he knew, and deeply interested in the same line of study as he himself. Then right on top of that he asked me if I wouldn't like to talk to the girl herself.

"You bet I grabbed at that chance and told him I would. Then he called this little yellow mutt and had him go fetch the girl. She came back with him, and Bhutia introduced her to me. Then he gets up and says he will leave us alone, and blows out. The fellow certainly seemed to be giving me a free hand."

"He's smooth, all right," Andrews made comment. Bryce nodded.

"Or else he's straight. That's what I'm trying to find out. Well, I sat down and talked with your niece. She was looking all right and a lot better than that picture Andrews had shown me. I told her who I was and she laughed.

" 'My people are making a great amount of trouble over my desire to study this gentleman's religion. I am sorry,' she says.

" 'Why couldn't you study it at home?' I asked her.

" 'To study properly it is necessary to throw aside all dogmas, all old beliefs, all suggested thoughts of childhood, anything and everything which will tend to make the mind less receptive of the truth,' she said. 'The atmosphere of resistance in my uncle's house would be against my best chance of soul development, Mr. Bryce.'

" 'They want you to come back,' says I.

"She shook her head and frowned at that. 'I shall not. I do not wish to leave this house,' she said.

" 'Then, what are you going to do?' I asked her.

" 'I intend to become a teacher of the truth, even as Bhutia is a teacher of the truth,' she says."

"Wait a minute, Bryce," I interrupted. "Those are her exact words to you, aren't they, Andrews?"

"Yes, they are." Miss Liston's *fiancé* nodded an emphatic avowal.

"And her remarks to Bryce about the reasons for leaving her uncle's home are almost a quotation of Bhutia's remarks to me the other day on the subject of his religion. Bryce, how did Miss Liston's eyes look when she was talking to you?"

"Why, her eyes looked all right," said the inspector. "She kept looking straight at me when she talked—almost starin', I might say."

"Were her eyes closed—that is, part way, or wide open?"

"They was wide open, Glace. I know I was surprised how big they looked."

"All right," I told him. "Go on."

"There ain't much more," he admitted. "I asked her if nothin' wouldn't induce her to leave, an' she shook her head right hard. Then I asked her if she didn't want to send any word to Andrews, an' she frowned again an' said that I could tell him she was sorry to give him pain, but that the salvation of the soul of herself and others was a greater thing than a mere physical marriage, and that she had decided to devote her life to being a teacher of the truth."

"There's your basal suggestion," I explained, as he paused. "On top of that is the command to throw aside all dogma and suggested thoughts of childhood. It is those two things which she constantly repeats."

"By George, that's right!" said Bryce. "That's what you told me to watch out for. It's a good thing I remembered just what she said."

"And you left after that, I suppose?" I questioned.

"Almost," he returned. "Just after that, while we was chatting an' I was trying to think of something more to say, she kinder straightened up and looked at a clock on the wall of the room. 'I fear you must excuse me now, inspector,' she says. 'This is the time for my hour of concentration in the silence'—whatever she meant by that.

"I got up, an' she told me to tell her folks that she was well and happy and that they shouldn't worry; that she felt she had a right to do as she was doing, and that if she wanted to use her money to save her soul and that of others she was sure her dead parents would approve. Then she turned round and walked out of the room, an' Bhutia came back while I was wonderin' whether to go or not. I chinned a bit more with him, an' he asked me if I was satisfied that Miss Liston knew what she was doin'. I told him I couldn't see that she acted like she was bein' forced into anything against her will, an' he said that perhaps if you folks would come to see him you could all reach an agreement. Then he gave me a cigar, an' I left."

"Just the same result as when we went to see her," said Liston, sighing. "Almost the same words she used to us, in fact."

"Of course," I cut in. "That's what I hoped they would be. There are three set suggestions as see it now. First, she wants to become a 'teacher'; secondly, she must throw off all adverse influence; thirdly, she is thereby to save herself and others. There you are—motive, means, and result to be obtained. The girl is under Bhutia's power for a thousand any day."

Mrs. Liston began to wring her hands.

"Oh, the poor child," she sobbed. "What are we to do— what are we to do? This man will make her his creature and rob her of all she has, and then cast her aside. Oh, if there is a God, how can he let such things be? Olive's fortune, her good name, even her life are at stake. I feel it. Oh, Gerald"—to her husband—"what are we to do?"

"There, there, my dear Eileen, calm yourself," counseled Liston. "We will do something, of course. Surely here must be some way to reach this parasite. What would you suggest, Mr. Bryce?"

Bryce frowned.

"There ain't much to go on exceptin' Glace's supposition, which ain't proof—" he began.

Andrews had risen and was pacing the room.

"There's got to be a way," he burst out now. "I agree with Glace that Olive is this man's mental slave. She'll do just as he tells her. And I agree with you, inspector, that we haven't any proof. That makes a deadlock. Well—if there isn't any way to break it, I'll break it, and I'll break this Hindu devil at the same time!"

"Nix on that kind of stuff, son," snapped the inspector. "Don't you talk about startin' no rough-house, yet awhile."

"Well, you're up against it, it seems," Andrews flashed.

"Wait a minute, both of you," I said sharply. "Andrews, you want to be careful about using violence. It is just possible that this Bhutia may have given Miss Liston some suggestion which would result in her death if he were harmed—a sort of post-hypnotic command."

He paled.

"My God, can they do that?" he cried, aghast.

"Unfortunately, yes."

"Then What can we—"

"Wait! I commanded.

An idea was forming in my brain. Suddenly as the climax

of the situation had grown a plan had flashed upon me, suggested by Smithson's joking words. I turned to Bryce.

"Did you have a talk with the Fourth National people?" I asked.

He nodded.

"Yes, Miss Liston has personally drawn out five thousand dollars in the last week. She asked for it in gold and they gave it to her, of course. She also instructed them to sell a lot of bonds for her."

"He's robbing her already! Robbing her, Gerald! Do you hear?" shrilled Mrs. Liston.

"Bhutia has not appeared at the bank, then, alone or with the girl?"

"No. She came alone, so far as I could find out. They said they hadn't ever heard of this guinea until they saw your piece in the paper."

Then I took my resolve.

"Bryce," I said, "there's only one way to get anything on this fellow and only one place to hunt for it, unless Brant crossed his trail. Did he?"

"No."

"Then we're up against it unless we can get a man on the inside. He pays coin for all he gets; he has his own native servants. He never appears in public, and he leaves no paper or other trails. He works from the inside altogether, and it's on the inside that anything against him will be found. We've got to get a man inside this House of the Ego and let him get the evidence we need."

"We've got a fat chance, haven't we?" Bryce shook his head. "Not but what your idea's the right one, all right, Glace."

"We must have a man he doesn't know is interested and would not suspect of having an interest," I declared.

"I'd go in a minute, but he knows me," said Andrews.

"I'll go myself," I returned.

"You!"

It was a chorus from every one in the room.

"Why not?" I exclaimed, carried away by my interest and desire to get at the truth of the affair. "I'm on special assignment on this case. I've never seen Bhutia but once, and after that I wrote the *Record* story. I had a long talk with him at that time about his religion, and luckily I told him I would like to go into it further. I can go back and tell him I have decided to study under him for a time. I can rent a room in his house, and I can watch and listen, while I pretend to study. Why not?"

"Good boy!" howled Bryce.

"I think it is very well thought of," said Liston, with a nod.

"Oh, my poor Olive!" gasped his wife, and laid back in her chair.

Andrews drew a check-book and a fountain pen from his pocket and began to write. When he had filled in a blank he tore it out and handed it to me.

"There's a check for five hundred dollars. If at any time you need more it will be ready for you," he told me.

I took it and stood committed to the venture.

Bryce and I rose and made our adieus. Andrews left at the same time. He took us back down-town in his auto, which I had noticed at the curb when we went in. After we had dropped Bryce at the station he took me to the office, and there I told Smithson what I had agreed to do, and got him to cash Andrews's check for me.

I knew it wouldn't do to flash that signature around Bhutia. I took the money in gold. I went to my room and packed a suit-case with such things as I thought I might need, adding an automatic pistol at the last. Then I locked my door, told my landlady I would be gone for some days, and left the house.

That night at nine o'clock I ascended the steps to the House of the Ego and rang the bell.

5

WITHIN THE SHRINE

THE DOOR WAS opened by the same little man in the yellow robe.

"Whom seek ye?" he inquired.

"The Swami Bhutia," I replied, then adding: "I've been here before."

Again he retreated like a crab into the dark-draped hall.

"Enter—please," he hissed.

A hammered brass hanging lamp with perforations through which streamed varicolored ribbons of light threw a subdued illumination over the black-and-gold entry, shining on the diminutive yellow crab, and deepening the shadows along the walls and in the corners.

I stepped inside and set my suit-case on the black carpet. The man straightened and cocked his head upward at me, his beady little eyes staring out of his broad face, his arms and hands held slightly out from his sides like the claws of the creature I have likened him to. As I straightened from setting down the case he opened his slit of a mouth slightly.

"Come wis me," he directed, and scuttered away noiselessly over the black rug. I followed with a sense of disgust for the creature. Seen in the dim light of the black-and-gold entrance, he seemed some way unclean, loathsome, poisonous to me. I felt in that moment as one might do who had invaded a cave and scared forth one of its night-loving denizens, which went clawing and cluttering over the rocks. It seemed to me that there were things in and about this house which would not bear the light of day; things vile, unspeakable, born of evil impulses and hellish determination; which I must find out if was to save the welfare or the fortune of the girl who I was convinced had been trapped and enslaved within its walls.

In that moment I wished that my pistol was in my pocket rather than in my case behind me on the floor.

However, I followed; ain't this time he led me straight to the end of the passage where glowed the amber lamps and, lifting a curtain exactly like all the others, rapped thrice on a door. A voice came from within, speaking a tongue I did not understand. My guide pressed the door inward and waved me to pass beyond him. Crossing the threshold, I found myself in the room where I had talked with the Swami a few days before.

He was seated at the great teak-wood desk and had apparently been reading nothing more exciting than an evening paper. He glanced up as I came through the door and smiled slightly with his lips.

"Oh, Mr. Glace," he greeted, "come in and sit down. Permit me to compliment you upon the article you made from our brief interview. It was well done."

"I am very glad you approve. Swami," I responded. "I tried to put in what you said as well as I could with my understanding."

"You did exceedingly well for an Occidental man," said

Bhutia. "And you handled my philosophy very liberally indeed."

"That brings me naturally to the object of my present visit," I began as I took a chair. "The fact is I have a rather peculiar request to make of you. Our talk of the other day interested me greatly. Although I am a newspaperman I have a little money, and I would like to know if it would be possible for me to take instruction from you?"

Bhutia swung so as to subject me to his full scrutiny and fastened his eyes upon my face. I had been expecting something like that, and I believe I came through the ordeal very well, for despite the boring probe of his black eyes I continued to meet his glance fully.

Presently he smiled, rose, came over, and, thrusting a finger and thumb between my collar and my neck, pressed sharply against my spine. It was as if a hot needle had kissed my skin for an instant, and involuntarily I flinched. Bhutia nodded and resumed his seat.

"As a newspaperman it would be rather hard for you to take regular instruction," he began. "Still—just what was your plan?"

"My idea was that, instead of taking my vacation out of town, I could devote all my time for, say, four or five weeks to learning at least the rudiments of your faith," I told him. "I have heard that you sometimes let people stay here in the house for rapid instruction. If I could—"

"We charge rather highly for that—our rooms are limited," he began.

"How much?" I asked with all the eagerness I could muster, thrusting a hand into my pocket and bringing it out full of gold.

Watching my man, I caught the momentary surprise which swept his features ere he forced them back into a smiling mask.

"We usually charge a hundred of your dollars a week for what you ask," he replied.

"I have five hundred dollars here," I declared. "I will pay you for four weeks to-night if you will let me stay."

"When does your vacation begin?" he questioned, his eyes holding to my handful of gold as to a magnet.

"It began to-day," I made answer, and purposely dropped one of the coins so that it rolled toward him.

It was a double-eagle. He picked it up and laid it on his desk rather than giving it back, and I knew I had won.

"Very well, Mr. Glace, I will consent to your plea," he agreed.

I moved over to the desk and counted out the other three hundred and eighty dollars in twenties. Bhutia took them and, opening a drawer of his desk, dropped them in in a tinkling stream, I saw that the drawer was half full of gold.

It appeared to me that the soul-developing lousiness was a lucrative one, but I kept my thoughts to myself. All the same, I couldn't help comparing the attitude of the Swami Bhutia, with the open desire and willingness of Dual to assist those who needed the help he could give. It seemed to me that this man's claim that the West worshiped material wealth might be extended to cover himself as well.

Bhutia was locking up his drawer of money and now he rose.

"If you will come with me I will show you to your room," he suggested. "As you are to be here but a short time, it will be as well to start your instructions at once—to-night, if you wish."

Well, I was into it irrevocably now, and it behooved me to play the part.

"I would be very glad to begin at once," I absented. "To tell the truth, I brought a suit-case full of things with me and left it in the hall."

Bhutia smiled.

"Ah, you Westerners!" he remarked. "You want to do everything in haste. I understand you are, even using funeral auto-hearses now. What next? Well, come with me. My servant shall bring your luggage."

He struck his gong and ordered the "crab" to get my case and follow us to my room.

We went back into the entrance hallway. Bhutia raised another of the curtains—one at the extreme end this time—and led me through another door. From here we immediately began to ascend the stairs to the second story, and I saw that the original hall had been walled off near their foot and a door masked by the curtain set in. We were now on the main stairway of the original Pearson house. It ascended toward the back and spiraled forward midway, finally coming out again near the front.

Bhutia led me down the upper hall and finally paused at a room, the door of which he opened, and signed that I should enter. Immediately he followed and snapped on a pair of lights in a center cluster dependent, from the ceiling. The crab followed, set down my case, and withdrew.

I glanced about me with interest. The room was slightly longer than wide, and was furnished in quiet taste. Like the lower hall, its walls were draped in black tapestries embroidered in gold thread, which fell from ceiling to floor. A fine specimen of brass bed stood with its head against one wall. A dresser and a small table and a couple of chairs completed the equipment. Save for the draped walls, it resembled the room of an ordinary hotel.

Bhutia allowed me a moment for cursory inspection before he spoke:

"Divest yourself of all clothing and prepare for the bath."

I shot him a questioning glance.

"The bath is symbolic of washing off the taint of the world. The novice must enter the path with clean feet," he explained.

I nodded and began to disrobe. Evidently I was going to get something for my money. I was going to be robbed of none of the trimmings. I was glad, because I felt that the man was taking me in good faith.

The crab came back while I was undressing, and silently laid a bathrobe and a paper-wrapped parcel on my bed, drew back, and waited with bowed head until I had put on the former, when, without a word, he signed me and led me to the bathroom, where a tub of drawn water awaited me.

I bathed, while he stood waiting. When I was finished he seized a towel and hastily dried me, picked up my robe, and held it while I slipped it on. Then he led me back to my room and again disappeared.

Bhutia was still there.

"And now I shall anoint you as a seeker of the truth," he remarked. "Remember that in entering upon the path of attainment you must throw aside all performed religious beliefs."

"I never had any very deep ones," I rejoined.

The Swami smiled.

"A true Occidental," he observed. "However, it will be easier to write on a clean slate."

Suddenly his voice changed and dropped into a monotone.

"Soul, seeking the light, you are about to be accepted as one of those pilgrims who journey along the path toward that light. Free your mind of all unworthy purpose, and vow to walk with care and circumspection. Remember that there is nothing of evil in the plan of the eternal cosmos; that good and bad, light and darkness, are but comparative terms. That which is evil in this life is good in a lower, worse in a higher. It is only as we ascend the scale of existence that we can see clearly and walk unafraid."

He paused. The door opened and the crab appeared with what looked like an immense dish of gold in his hands. Approaching me, he knelt before the Swami and raised this above his head.

"And now," said Bhutia, "I shall anoint ye with the sacred oil. Kneel."

Dipping his fingers; into the dish, he bent forward and touched each eyelid.

"See no evil," he commanded. "Blind your objective eyes to outward seeming evil, remembering that all is good and hence may not be bad."

He touched my cars.

"Hear no evil," he directed. "Close your ears to those; things which shall divert your attention, and open them to the voice of the spirit."

He flicked my lips.

"Speak no evil," he admonished. "Remember that a

spoken word never dies. Use thine lips only to voice the thoughts of the spirit." He drew a double triangle on my brow.

"I draw the six-pointed star on your forehead to remind you that here is all knowledge of the things below and above, and that through harkening to the voice of the soul only can the spirit be heard."

He traced the line of my nostrils.

"Breathe ye the truth."

He touched my hands.

"Work for the truth."

Bending, he swept my naked feet.

"Walk in the path without fear. Thus have I by my rank anointed thee seven times. Arise, thou disciple of the absolute."

I got up I began to see how his trumpery would affect a naturally sensitive or superstitious person, I stood before him and awaited his next command.

"In yonder package you will find a robe and a pair of undergarments," he told me. "They have never been worn by any mortal. Put them on."

I took up the package, opened it, and drew out a long black robe and a pair of knee-length drawers, black also, and nothing else. I turned toward Bhutia.

"Do I have to wear these things while I am here?" I inquired in some surprise.

He nodded.

"But why black?" I wanted to know. The weather was warm, and I imagined I could get along with the trunks and the robe, but the color was not to my liking.

"The color is symbolic of the fact that after darkness

cometh light," said Bhutia. "At present you are walking in the darkness of spiritual blindness. After you have gone farther you will wear a different robe. All novices here wear black. Put on the robe and I will give you your first lesson before retiring."

"And what will that be?" I asked as I slipped into the clothing.

"The first thing a student must learn is the power of mental concentration," said Bhutia. "As I wish you to gain all you can while here I shall begin to teach you that. It is for that that I use the light in the room below which you saw the other day. There is nothing mysterious about the light. It is merely a device for the purpose of riveting and holding the attention. It is exactly similar to the crystal into which seers gaze. They say that they see things in the crystal, but in reality what one sees, while appearing to be in the glass, are but projected pictures of the soul. Come."

I followed him to the door, which he opened. Upon the floor without were a pair of sandals.

"Put them on," Bhutia directed. "You are now setting your feet upon the first stage of the path."

I suppose if I hadn't come there with a firm conviction that the man was a rascal, or if I had been inspired by any true interest in his so-called religion, I would have been impressed. As it was I could compare my reception into the House of the Ego with nothing save an initiation into some secret society, vulgarly spoken of as "riding the goat."

As I stooped and fastened the sandals I breathed a vow that before I left the place the Swami himself would literally be "the goat." Full of that thought I followed him back down the stairs.

At once he led me along the other side of the passage to the curtained doorway, which gave into the room where I had seen the meeting of his class. Now it was totally dark save for the luminous globe of translucent glass upon the dais, which hung like a full moon in a starless sky. Toward this Bhutia led me with a hand upon my arm and as we came closer I saw for the first time that we were not alone in the room. There was a figure seated upon the dais back of the lamp.

As I came closer I strained my eyes to take in its details and saw that it was a woman. She sat cross-legged upon the floor, gazing straight into the heart of the lamp. Her folded hands lay loosely clasped in the lap of her black robe, below the hem of which were two dashes of white which, as I came closer, I saw were her naked feet.

Her hair was unleashed and fell in a cloud as dark as her robe, back of her face and on each side, so that her features gleamed white from its setting. Her eyes were wide open and fastened unblinkingly upon the light. She scarcely seemed to breathe.

With a start I recognized her. She was Olive Liston—the woman whose picture Andrews had shown me in his watch.

She gave no sign that she knew of our presence, and Bhutia did not as much as glance at her that I could see. He waved me to mount the dais, and led me to a spot some four feet from the lamp, where he again signed me to seat myself. After one or two attempts I succeeded in imitating the girl's position in a measure, and Bhutia smiled. The next instant I nearly started to my feet. I had happened to glance around the lamp to the other side and there was Kwali.

He stood staying and swinging to the pulsing of the light. A sudden horror gripped me and I thought of the girl alone there in the darkness with the hooded cobra. It was in my mind to protest, but I remembered that I had a part to play, and choked back the words. Bhutia, however, noticed my start and guessed its cause.

"Free your mind of fear," he said softly. "There is no danger unless there is fear. Remember that lesson. The snake will not strike unless he senses fear in the one who approaches. Behold!"

He walked directly across and literally shoved the serpent aside as though it had been a rag. It hissed slightly, assumed a position midway between Bhutia and the girl, and took up its swaying rhythm again.

The Swami began to speak.

"Gaze into the light," he commanded. "Gaze into its heart and demand that you be given to see what your soul has to tell you. Hold your eyes steadily upon it and your mind fully bound to the seeing of the soul's pictures. Now!"

The last word was slow, soothing, compelling. Almost unconsciously I let my eyes wander to the globe and dwell there. It was an odd thing any way—a clever device. Maybe if I sat and studied I could determine how it was operated in its rhythmic rise and fall—

With a start I caught myself up. Suddenly my soul flashed a warning to my mind. I saw a picture, but not in the globe. It was of Semi Dual in his room, fixing a tiny light so that it flashed and died, flashed and died, and focused its rays on a certain chair where was to sit a man over whom it was necessary that he gain a temporary control in order to save the liberty of an innocent victim.

Hard on the thought came the recollection of his explanation that the light tired the optic nerve and tended to
induce sleep. Hypnosis was a form of induced sleep. Olive
Liston was supposed to be under hypnotic control. So this
was Bhutia's game and the secret of his absolute mastery
of his so-called pupils, in reality his dupes—his victims,
perhaps.

I began to have a keener perception of the antagonist
against whom I played in this game, the stakes of which
were the girl who sat oblivious of my presence beyond me
on the dais. The undertaking upon which I had engaged
took on new aspects in the light of the thing which had
come to me. Unless I guarded myself, well, I too might find
myself in need of help rather than the means of liberating
this other victim of the man.

"What see ye?" came the voice of Bhutia.

I could feel the force of his eyes upon me in a compelling demand.

How far could I go? How far dared I go? I questioned
myself. In keeping with my part I must make some
response. Failure to do so could only result in exciting the
man's suspicions. I decided in desperate haste to simulate
as best I might. It seemed the only possible course.

"Lines—wavering lines and threads of colors which
seem to run and blend together," I faltered, seeking to
throw a sleep-clogged articulation into my tones. "There
seems to be something—but I can't—make it out. It is too
dim—too vague."

For a full moment he made no reply. I feared that already
I was detected as an impostor. Then:

"Doubtless your mind trained to material thought finds

trouble in responding to the inward voices," he made explanation. "I really expected more, however, for ere I accepted you I tested your sensitiveness, as you may remember, by pressing the base of your neck. Still, I predict that ere long you will see wonderful pictures. We will try no more to-night, however, lest we tire you too greatly, and so instead of stimulating, exhaust."

Contrary to my expectations his voice held a note of encouragement and half apology rather than suspicion. He had then accepted my poor ruse at its face value. My heart leaped with satisfaction. As yet I was safe.

But now he turned directly toward Miss Liston.

"Olive," he began, "put forth your hand to the serpent. Let us see how you progress."

Quite slowly the woman raised her arm and extended it toward Kwali where he swayed by the light. The snake expanded its hood and drew back its wicked little head! The extended hand paused, wavered, then remained steady just beyond the snake's reach. Watching it I could see a delicate tremor shake it. Again Bhutia spoke:

"Still the fear lurks in your mind, Olive. Enough. Drop your hand. Until all fear is gone it is unsafe. Cast it out, thou seeker after true wisdom. When all fear is gone there is naught but advancement. Fear is the cause of human sickness and suffering and death. Cast it out."

Without a glance he stooped, caught up the cobra and held it just back of its head. It wriggled and writhed, pendent from his hand. Suddenly he pressed its neck with his fingers and it opened its mouth until I could see its wicked fangs.

Bhutia smiled and, while I sat stricken with horror, slid the reptile up the sleeve of his robe.

"Come," he said.

Once more we went back to my room and the Swami bade me good night.

"To-morrow I will provide you with books and a teacher," he told me, turned to the door and passed out.

I was glad to see him go and take the venomous serpent with him. As Bryce said, if he wanted a pet of that sort he could have it, but personally I breathed easier when the two of them were gone.

For some time I sat on the side of my bed pondering all that had happened; since I came to the place. Then, as one will in a strange house, I rose and approached the door to look out ere locking myself in for the night.

I laid my hand on the knob to pull the door inward, and paused almost aghast. Five minutes before Bhutia had passed through it and I had sat within ten feet of it since. I had heard no sound whatever, and yet the door was locked!

I was locked in! Why? Instantly my fears that Bhutia had seen through my pretense came back to me in an augmented flood. Had he pierced my deception and hence made me a prisoner in my own room? Why was the door locked, and how had it been done?

I put my hand to the key which was sticking in the lock and turned it. It responded readily and I heard the bar engage. So the door had not been fastened with the ordinary fastening at all. There was something else which held it from opening.

In a bound I turned back to my suitcase and dug out the small automatic pistol. If I was discovered, and they sought to do me harm, I resolved in that instant that I would give no mean account of myself.

With the weapon in my hand I crept stealthily back to the mystifying exit from the apartment and got down on the floor. I sought to peer through the crack where it fit into the frame, but it was a well-set piece of work and there was not sufficient space for me to discover what held the leaf to the jamb.

I seized the knob, and placing a foot on the side of the casing I leaned back and pulled. The door never gave a fraction of an inch. Here was a nice pickle indeed. I sat down on the floor in front of the thing and glared at if as though it had had a personality of its own. Then suddenly I took out my penknife and attacked the screws holding the knob-plate to the wood. Perhaps I could see into the socket far enough to discover some cause for the door's obstinacy, I thought.

I forced a blade into the groove of a screw and sought to turn it. The soft brass tore and the blade bent. I persisted. My forehead became dewed with the moisture of work and mental disquiet. Totally engrossed I heard no sound save my own breathing, and then:

"What seek ye?" said a voice.

I whirled and gripped my weapon, half raising it into view. Behind me, between the bed and the door, stood the Swami Bhutia, with a smile upon his face.

Imagine my feelings. I had seen him pass through the door I could not open. I had heard him bid me good night. Now saw him standing behind me, heard his voice raided in question, sensed the veiled amusement of his regard.

And, yet I grinned. Suddenly the whole thing seemed bizarre and almost ludicrous to me and tempered my reply.

"I was seeking to see into that thing," I replied, gesturing to the door. "I was seeking a little light on the subject, if you must know."

Bhutia nodded. His smile grew. He walked across the room to the electric switch by the door and laid his hand upon it.

"If you wish light, why not have it?" he said slowly, pressed a second button and threw on every light in the central cluster, flooding the room with a blinding glare.

Then while I looked straight at him he turned without another word and walked *through the door!*

I saw him lay a hand on the knob and draw it toward him. I saw the door open and the hallway beyond it. I saw his figure pass and the door begin to close. Then with a leap I sprang toward it and seized the knob and shook it in a frenzy of rage and something like terror. For quick as had been my movement, *the door was locked!*

Presently I desisted from my futile efforts and wiped the perspiration from my forehead. I was beginning to see more and more that there were things about the House of the Ego which I did not understand.

6

THE SECRET OF THE DOOR

PRESENTLY AS I stood there, my reason and common sense began to come back. I told myself that I was acting like a child frightened by a nurse's "bogie" story. It was the unexpectedness of the thing which had shaken me.

Men didn't enter locked-rooms without some way of getting there, nor walk through locked doors without unlocking them first. Equally, doors didn't lock and unlock themselves, save by some mechanism deviser by human brains.

I ceased staring about the room like a trapped rabbit and give myself up to a consideration of the incident in detail.

First I had to admit that Bhutia was clever. I could see how his apparent appearance in rooms without warning, his seeming materialization from thin air would affect the average person of nervous type. It bore on the supernatural and must carry its sense of awe. As for myself I was not nervous and my first qualm of surprised amaze was passing rapidly away.

How had he done it? I asked myself.

There was some fact which would prove a clue, I decided. What was it? What had he done? He had walked to the switch and turned on the lights, flooding the room with a blaze. If he had switched off the two lamps then burning, instead of putting on the others, I would not have been surprised.

But his opposite action seemed like a challenge to the understanding, a defiance to one to detect how he performed the trick. Did it hold the germ of the explanation as well? If it did, then the means of locking and unlocking the door was in the switch. I got up from the bed where I had dropped and went over beside the door. The switch was, so far as I could see, nothing more than an ordinary double plate, two buttons of which put on and off the two lamps ordinarily used, the other two controlling the rest of the cluster.

Still—Bhutia had turned on all the lights before opening the door. Was it coincidence or design?

I fell to work. First I put out the extra lamps. Next I turned them on and seized the knob of the door. It remained locked. But I persisted. I tried the lights all on, all off, partly on and partly off; in every conceivable combination. At the end of a half hour I had to confess that I was just where I started, and still securely locked in.

Next it occurred to me that perhaps the Swami's means of entrance might bear a connection with the releasing and relocking of the door. I turned from the baffling barrier and gate my attention to the rest of the room, first putting on all the lights.

My first step was to draw aside the veiling draperies. Behind them I found an ordinary wall of plaster and lath as near as I could judge, with a wooden dado running some three feet up from the floor. It was constructed of small strips of molding set close together and extended entirely around the room.

I attacked this with the butt of my automatic and began a systematic sounding in a circuit of the walls. They rang dully hollow, as do the interior partitions of houses of that type, but there was no place where I could elicit the sharp hollowness which would indicate a panel or door. I spent an hour searching for what I felt rather than knew must be there and then, utterly disgusted, locked my door from the inside, put out the lights, and flung myself upon the bed.

The sun woke me the next morning by shining through my windows and getting into my eyes. The house fronted west and my room was at the back. I rose and looked out upon a garden of flowers and what looked like a glass conservatory, save that I could dimly see chairs and tables within it.

It was a peculiar building, even its roof being of glass. Ranged around it in a circle were six smaller buildings, the sides of which were of brick but which, like the central structure, were covered by domes of glass. I opened my eyes at the sight, for the whole of the rear enclosure was surrounded by a ten-foot wooden wall, and one gained no hint of the buildings from the front of the house.

A covered passage ran from the house itself to the central edifice and smaller ones led from there to each minor building. I immediately began to speculate upon their possible use.

A rap called me away from the window. I crossed, unlocked my part of the door, and admitted the "crab" with a tray containing my breakfast. This he set down on the small table.

"When you 'ave eaten, ze master will see you," he advised me and made his exit.

As a matter of curiosity I followed and tried the door. It was open and responded easily to my touch.

I went back, drew up a chair, and attacked the food. I was in a somewhat peculiar frame of mind, marked mainly by a rising confidence in my venture. Viewed in the full light of day, my experiences of the night before seemed more like the unreasonable figments of a dream than any waking happening.

Still I knew I hadn't imagined the thing, and now that the door was unlocked I wanted to examine it and see what had made it fast. I hurried my breakfast and shoved aside the tray.

It didn't take me long to find the thing which had held the door shut. Sunk into a socket in its edge was what appeared to be an iron bolt, to judge by its visible end. In the casing opposite this was a socket which it palpably engaged. But there was no visible way of operating the device, which still remained a puzzle in its mechanism to me.

While I was still examining it footsteps approached and I had just time to regain my seat at the table when Swami appeared.

"Good morning," said he.

I returned his salutation and immediately carried the conversation to the subject of the night before.

"Tell me, Swami Bhutia," I requested, "why am I locked in my room at night?"

"All novices are locked in nightly until they have proven

their fitness to advance," he replied. "You need not be disturbed by the fact."

That was, in a way, plausible enough and I felt it would not do to raise objections to the procedure. All I could do would be to master the secret of the lock. I nodded my head and asked another question:

"Did I or did I not see you in my room last night after I was locked in?"

"You saw me," said Bhutia quite as a matter of course.

"But how did you get in and how did you get out of that door?" I exclaimed.

Bhutia smiled slightly.

"Patience," said he. "There are many things which you may not hope to know at the first. The free soul goes and comes as it wills. For it there are no bolts or bars."

"Then I've got to be locked in for how long?" I questioned.

"Until you have advanced sufficiently to be in full harmony with the atmosphere of the house," he made answer. "This morning I shall send you some books, marked for your reading. Study them an hour and at twelve be prepared to accompany Ishi when he comes for you. He will conduct you to your teacher. You slept well?"

I assured him that I had and he withdrew, leaving me to my thoughts.

If I was to be locked up like a prisoner how was I to do anything toward reaching Olive Liston, or arranging for her escape from this place? There was only one way that I could think of and that was to master the secret of the door.

The crab, or Ishi, as Bhutia had called him, came back with the books and a robe of orange-colored silk. This latter he threw across the bed and instructed me to don it just before twelve.

I eyed the thing in surprise.

"I must be gaining pretty fast to get out of black into orange already," I threw out as a feeler.

The little yellow man made no direct answer to that, however. "I will return at noon," he told me and scuttered away.

I returned to the window and inspected the back yard again and also the wall below me with a view, to the possible emergency of having to get out by the window. As near as I could judge, I was some twenty feet from the ground and it was a sheer drop. At the worst, however, I figured that I could make a cord of two bed sheets and have not more than eight feet to crop, which would be easy.

Satisfied, I looked at my watch, found it half past eleven, and threw off my black robe, preparatory to putting on the one of orange silk. I was fully decided to play my part and see the venture through, to solve the mystery of the locked door and begin my investigations of the house that night.

Sharp on the stroke of twelve Ishi, the crab, came back and signed me to follow. I felt positively indecent as I stepped out into the hall to obey for my robe came barely to my knees, leaving my feet and legs bare.

It had no sleeves and was cut into a broad "V" both front and back. Still I figured it was all in the game and went with him without a word. I had learned that with him questions did small good.

He led me down the stairs, turned to the rear, and a moment later I realized that we were in the passage to the peculiar building I had seen from the window. The approaches were draped in hangings grading through all shades from black to red, pink, yellow, buff, and orange at the far end where a door gave access to the main structure.

Here Ishi paused and waved me forward. I passed him and entered a circular apartment, flooded with the unobstructed sunshine of the high noon of a cloudless day. All about me were seats; something in the nature of steamer deck-chairs, and in some of them I saw other orange-clad figures reclining. Also I noticed that with the exception of myself they were all women. I paused with a sense of embarrassment as I remembered my rather scanty attire.

Then my glance fell toward the far wall, where a chair was placed, facing me, and on the figure reclining upon it. It was Olive Liston, and I saw that she saw me. She raised a hand slightly and beckoned me to her, and at once I obeyed.

As I drew nearer I became aware that a second unoccupied chair was placed beside hers, and she now signed that should take it.

"Sit down, Mr. Glace," she invited. "I have been appointed your teacher under Bhutia while you are here."

My senses swam. Here was luck!

Or was it luck? I asked myself as I dropped upon the chair and turned my eyes to the girl. Was it not rather another example of the operation of those subtle forces Dual had mentioned? How else might I have hoped to be placed in the position of pupil to the girl I had come to save?

In what other way could I have gained such an opportunity for unrestricted conversation? Surely, the unseen forces were with me in my task. I smiled slightly as I thought that Bhutia had surely made a misplay here.

Then I gave my whole attention to the girl. She was worth it. Like myself, she was not so much clothed as draped in a thin orange robe, cut low in the neck, sleeveless and skirtless below the knees, where her lower limbs gleamed white and tapering in the flood of sunlight.

Each little foot, high-arched and slender, was soled by a sandal, caught over the instep and between the great toe and its fellow by slight bands, united under a boss of dull gold on the arch of the foot. The sheer fabric of the gown clung to her skin until every supple curve and line of her beautiful body lay revealed to my inspection. Rather she seemed to me a woman washed over with a froth of orange foam than one materially clothed. I subscribed to Andrews's good taste in affairs of the heart, and replied:

"I was told I was to have a teacher, but I never hoped for such a pleasant fortune as this. Suppose you begin your instructions by telling me where I am."

Miss Liston smiled—

"That was very nicely put, Mr. Glace," she replied, "and I am yet sufficiently bound to the old life to feel a woman's pleasure in a compliment. In the future, however, talk to me not as to a girl, but as to merely a kindred soul with the same desires and aims as your own."

"That will be hard," I retorted, "and if you are going to try to teach me that I shall ask for a different instructor. Still, I don't know either. I fancy my remark was as sincere as you could wish."

"I fancy I had better answer your question," she said, laughing. "I do not want to be drawn into a conflict of repartee with a shrewd newspaperman, as they tell me you are. We are now in the heart of the sun for the purpose of spending an hour in meditation and the absorption of the life-giving energy of its waves. That is why we wear orange robes of so sheer a consistency. The sunlight penetrates them easily and we breathe it through our skin. The Swami tells me that in his own country where the body is not so taboo a subject all clothing is dispensed with; but with us, of course, he has made this concession to what we are pleased to call modesty, using the orange robes as a partial covering."

I commended her use of the word "partial."

"What do you think of the man, anyway?" I asked.

"He is wonderful!" she cried softly. "I have never met any one like him. He has the most wonderful thoughts and the greatest love for his fellows."

"He also loves their gold," I added, remembering the drawer of yellow metal where Andrews's four hundred nestled with the gleanings from others. "I thought the correct idea was to give freely to one's fellows, rather than charge them a stiff fee."

"Mr. Glace!"

Evidently she was quite shocked at my criticism of her "master."

"The cost of maintaining a place like this is great," she went on. "It is only proper that we who are to profit by it should do all in our power to help bear its expenses. I myself intend to give all I have if need be to the furtherance of this noble work."

There it was. Our conjectures had been right. The girl was to be mulcted. I gritted my teeth and savagely vowed that somebody was going to put a spoke in that wheel of design, and that that some one was I.

"Then you intend to devote your life to this study?" I asked as calmly as I might.

It seemed monstrous to me that so fine a specimen of womanhood should be wasted when the world needed such as she to keep up its standard of life.

"The Swami has promised that I shall become a 'teacher of the truth,'" she told me with a glowing face. "In fact, it was to prove his faith to me that he assigned you to me for instruction. I know very little as yet, but, even so, I may become a master to one who knows less, meanwhile sitting at his feet and increasing: my own knowledge, to give forth again to others. Ah, Mr. Glace, there is so much suffering and pain and sorrow and sin in the world! Surely, I could do no better than devote life and fortune to alleviating it in a measure."

"Well, bless the child!" I muttered as she finished her pure justification of her course.

Equally as my admiration of her grew, my rage at the: man who was prostituting her altruism to his selfish gain increased.

"When you first came here did they lock you up at night?" I inquired.

She nodded. "Yes. It scared me—really. Afterward I learned that they do it to all beginners in the Way. You see, one must prove worthy to advance, and, besides, if one who did not understand were free to wander at will about the house he might intrude upon rites not yet meant for his eyes and become an unsympathetic influence, injuring both himself and others."

So that was it, eh?

"And now?" I asked.

"To-night my door will be unlocked—I have passed my novitiate."

"Did you have to wear black robes, too, Miss Liston?"

"We all do." It is she sign of our spiritual blindness."

She smiled.

"Light cometh after darkness, you know, Mr. Glace. I am beginning to come into the light. To-night I shall receive the gray robe of the teacher. You are my deliverer from the black, since you are my first pupil."

"I'm in luck," I grinned.

"Oh, I hope I can help you greatly!" said she, a quiver of enthusiasm in her mellow tones. "We all want to help others, and he who helps the most gains the most himself. Isn't it beautiful? Truly, it is more blessed to give than to receive."

I wondered cynically whether Bhutia thought so. Also, I noticed the subtle idea of saving herself and others playing its veiled part of suggestion.

Already in the few minutes' chat I had twice stumbled over the basal elements of what I believed was this Hindu's method of binding the woman. He had done his work well. I must think and scheme for a way to undo it. It would take subtlety and time. I must think—hard.

"Don't you find the life here strange—don't you ever grow homesick?" I suggested.

She shook her head.

"It's strange, but I do not," she answered quickly. "You see, Bhutia explained so fully to me that I must cast aside all old dogmas, all suggested thoughts of childhood and preformed beliefs and methods of life that by the time I decided to come here I was in full harmony with the place."

"Ah, yes, I see!" I murmured.

In fact, I saw a lot more than I said. Here was suggestion number three. I had dug up the whole lot. I was satisfied of my ground now. I changed the conversation again.

"What are these other buildings which circle this one?" I said.

"One of Bhutia's wonderful ideas," she told me. "They are the houses of the stars and moon. Each one is so fitted up that it carries out the subtle atmosphere of the planet it represents. In the House of Mars all is red; there are old pieces of armor on the walls and strange instruments of torture of bygone days. In the House of Venus all is blue and gold, with beautiful statues of women ranged about the walls. In that of Mercury everything suggests the intellectual attainments and so on. One day each week a service is held in the building devoted to that star, at the hour when that star's influence on earth is the strongest. Each day at noon we come to the House of the Sun to absorb its light, and on Sunday a special service is held here as well."

"Quite original," I remarked.

"He is a wonderful man," said Miss Liston, and suddenly started slightly.

"Goodness!" she exclaimed. "Here I was to instruct you, and I've been talking about myself and the house. I'm a poor little teacher, I'm afraid, Mr. Glace."

"Instruct me now," I suggested, lying back and letting my eyes sweep her where she lay.

"I am to tell you how to eat and how to sleep," she began. "First, you are to chew every mouthful well, and while you do so hold the thought that all its life-giving energy is leaving its substance and becoming a part of yourself. That sounds easy, but you don't know how hard it is till you try. Then about sleeping: Every night as you retire fill your mind with a desire to grow in the spirit while your body rests, just as the plant grows most at night. In that way you will wake refreshed and invigorated and often be surprised at a new sense of knowledge and power which has come to you in the night.

"You are to read your books and think of them, and if you do not understand any part think of that part when you go to sleep, and the soul will unveil it for you in your sleep. Now I have done my duty for to-day and the hour is ended. If you will follow me I will take you back to your room."

She rose like a golden Venus, and I followed her from the place, back up the stairs, and watched her as she passed down the hall toward her room.

She opened her door, stood framed in its light for a moment, with every line of her beautiful body showing dark against its oblong of light, and was gone.

I went in and sat down. A tray of luncheon was already served on my table. I drew up and ate, and as I ate I concentrated as Olive had directed, only I neglected to fasten my mind on the food. I was lost in amazed admiration of Bhutia and his methods.

Here was a girl hypnotized to the nth degree and yet perfectly normal. Her mind was fully itself, fully able to respond to her volitional control in every way and on every subject save those fields of thought embraced in the three details necessary to keep her subserved to his purpose.

Yer she was as much his slave as a cataleptic body exhibited in a store-window. At his command she would commit any act suggested—short perhaps of murder—and believe herself doing what was right. It was hellish!

My whole concentration was along a method of getting out of my room at night and seeking for what Bryce would call "something on him"—something which we could use as an excuse for arresting and holding him until the girl could be freed.

Again I resolved that I would master the trickery of the lock that night and explore the House of the Ego while its genius was asleep.

That afternoon I attended a public séance in the room of the luminous globe. It was little different from the other save that this time the Swami gave some lessons on the faith of Gnani Yoga, and that Olive was brought in in a beautiful gray robe and ordained as a teacher of the truth.

I don't know how it impressed the others there, but for myself as I gazed upon the pure outline of the girl's face, raised slightly to that of Bhutia, its every feature exhaled with the light of highest endeavor, I could not but feel that I was looking upon the sacrilege of a soul rather than upon its advancement.

The girl was a dupe, yet a dupe who believed and was, as she thought, surrendering all of the natural woman's hopes and ambitions to, as thought, save others who walked in darkness.

Bhutia, with his thin lips and beady eyes of blackness, was to me a ghoul, a vampire, preying upon this creature, who had more light in the glance of her eye than he had in the entire pin-point of his perverted ego.

I had my supper and was locked in. With what patience I

could summon I waited for total darkness, and then turned on my light. Then I attacked the baffling lock.

All at once I wished that I could summon the wonderful ingenuity of Dual to my assistance. I began to wonder if I had not done a foolish thing in coming here without first telling my friend; if the enthusiasm in my venture had not carried me along too fast.

I snapped on the two center lights, waited a minute, and threw on the entire cluster. At the time I did not realize how I did it save that, owing to a somewhat savage mood induced by my thoughts, I drove in the second button until my fingers actually jammed against the plate of the switch as the button went home. The lights flashed up instantly, and coincidentally I heard a faint click. Acting purely upon impulse, I laid a hand on the knob of the door. *It was unlocked!*

I seized it and drew it open. Then I let it close. At once I tried to open it a second time. It was fast.

Well, someway for a moment I had stumbled onto the secret. I looked at the switch and then at my fingers. With a start I noticed that the skin on my index finger was slightly torn. More, it was a fresh tear.

"What could have done it?" was the question which flashed into my mind. I know I had jammed it against the switch, but an inspection of the button socket showed no ragged edges. Then I noticed a screw head in the plate above the button.

Apparently it was partly loosened in the plate and projected slightly. I laid my finger upon it and sought to turn it, but found it resisted. The next second, however, a blinding rush of brains to the head made me press upon it, and I felt it yield.

Instantly came the faint click I had heard before. My hand darted to the door and seized it. *As before, it was unlocked. I had solved the story of the door!*

Like many a thing, it was simple when one saw it unraveled. A soft magnet concealed in the door frame drew an iron plunger or bolt to itself from the socket in the door.

The screw head in the light switch broke the current and recharged the magnet for a few brief seconds, and a spring drew back the bolt until the magnetic connection was again automatically restored. I laughed like a foolish kid as the beauty of the device struck me. With the open door held ajar I searched for an outside operating device, and found it in one of the screws holding a piece of the facing of the door frame in place. With a sigh I let the door close and heard it lock.

I was now perfectly at ease. I could get in or out at will when I wanted. To-night I would ransack the House of the Ego and see what I could find.

I looked at my watch. It was ten o'clock. It wouldn't do to start prowling about as yet. But I was in the nervous elation of having scored my first victory over the mind of Bhutia.

Like Alexander I wanted other fields to conquer. The panel obligingly suggested itself. I had found out how the man got out of my room, why not seek the method of his ingress.

Instantly I set to work. A little thought convinced me that the probable location of any concealed entrance would be in the wall opposite the one where stood the bed.

Rolling up the draperies, I knotted them out of the way,

left all lights burning, and got down on my knees beside the dado, with my open knife in my hand.

I began at one end and worked along the wall, thrusting the blade of the knife between the joining of each strip of molding. I had worked some two-thirds of the length of the side, however, before I felt the blade sink home to the haft.

I let it stand and moved it up and down the entire length of the dado. I was now convinced that here was the door. How to open it was the question next presenting itself.

I probed and pressed and felt over the woodwork, but there was no sign of screw, or knob, or knothole, or other operating device. Still, there was a way I was sure.

The intellect which had devised the panel for the purpose of appearing in his guests' room and leaping out from the concealing draperies upon them would not have neglected an easy way of opening the panel again.

I had examined the entire door; but what of the floor? Here was an idea in truth. I began at the crack I had found and pressed each board where it ran up to the wall, both ways from the crack. So presently I found one which gave slightly.

My pulses bounded. Luck or fate was with me to-night. Rising, I set my foot on that board and bore down with my weight. It sank beneath me and a pressure of my fingers caused a narrow portion of the dado to swing before me.

Without further thought I ducked through the aperture and stood upright in a darkened passage. I put out my hands to locate the opposite wall and gain a sense of direction.

Released by my action, the door in the dado swung shut

with a slight click, shutting out the light. I had unraveled another secret of the House of the Ego and found a hidden passage, but I couldn't determine just where I stood.

7

AT THE END OF THE PASSAGE

I WASN'T EXACTLY afraid as I stood there, locked into the darkness of the unknown passage, yet I trembled with a nervous tremor. I had read many a tale of secret panels and unsuspected stairways in old houses, but I never expected to find one.

I had taken the thrills of the story with due gratitude to the writer whose clever brain had conceived them as a part of the stage setting and let it go at that. Now I was setting a thrill all my own.

Where did the passage lead, and what would I find if I followed its leading?

The spirit of the thing gripped me and led me on. I resolved that I would follow the passage in the walls and explore its mystery. It was probably only the means the Swami had created for the purpose of impressing his dupes by his apparent materializations, but still I might be better able to gain access to his quarters through it than by openly descending the stairs.

I remembered that Bryce had said he had had some partitions run, according to the house agents. Well, this looks like it. Probably every guest's room could be reached from some central point. It was a dandy scheme.

I chuckled softly and got down on my knees to find the catch which held the panel. I wanted to be sure I could get out if I should need to do so.

I found it readily enough. A lever leading from the springing end of the floor board operated a small arm which lifted a catch. All one had to do from the inside was to raise the catch and pull the door in by a handle screwed to its back. I opened the thing and let myself out into my room.

Once there I obtained a box of matches from the pocket of my coat and put out all my lights. Then I went back and passed through the panel for the second time.

I let the door swing to behind me and struck a match. Its rays showed that the passage ended at the house wall beyond me and seemed to end equally at the end of the room joining the wall of the main hall. However, a darker spot in the floor showed me that there a way led down.

I gave a momentary glance at the partition, which from this side showed as constructed of cement hollow squares, and started toward the narrow exit of the place. I now saw that a cement partition had been set in each room, leaving a passage through which one might creep.

Literally, Bhutia had builded a sort of a house within a house, to which the old square architecture had readily lent itself.

The hole at the end next the hall proved to admit the upper end of a ladder, constructed much the same as those means of mounting one used to see in country barns, where boards nailed between two vertide joints led into haymows. Holding a match inside the opening I could see the cleats vanishing downward toward the first floor.

I let the match go out and turning around gripped the edges of the hole and lowered a foot to the first rung of the verticle ladder. I chuckled all alone to myself, there in the total darkness. I fancied that if the Swami could see me now he would have less faith in his bolts and bars and panels.

He had said that to the free soul there *were* no bolts and bars. Surely I must have "advanced," as he would have said, since arriving last night, for here was I laughing at his means of shutting me in and beginning to stalk him through his own house.

Then I laughed again as I thought of Bryce. I could imagine his look of amazed consternation if he could see me, bare-legged, wrapped in a black gown, going down a ladder in a secret passage.

I vowed that some day, after everything was cleared up, I'd take him over the route. And what a story I'd have for Smithson. He would be tickled to death.

My groping foot found bottom. I stepped down and found myself upon a solid floor. Again I struck a match. Before me, as stood, stretched a passage as far as I could see in the flicker of light. I stood and considered a minute before seeking to go forward. As best I could, I cast over the geography of the house.

My room was at the back. I had come to the wall of the upper hall and down the ladder. Therefore, this ladder at the end of the hall would be the one leading to my room. That was the detail I wanted to fix firmly in case I needed to get back in a hurry. So far, I was all right.

Now just where was I? As near as I could see, a new partition had been run along the sides pf the original hallway from front to back to make this passageway in the walls. In support of that, I now remembered that the door into Bhutia's study had appeared that first day to be set into a sort of alcove. That would be explained by the fact that the new wall made the offset.

Feeling confident now that I was right I lighted a new match and went ahead with my exploration. In a moment I discovered another ladder leading upward. Out of curiosity I ascended and came through a hole into a lateral alley, leading along a wall exactly similar to the one in my own room. I went along it as much for practise as anything and searched for the latch of the panel. I found it quickly and opened the little door. Then I slipped out behind the black curtains and peeked through their folds. A little old woman sat in a chair reading. I drew back. She heard nothing. I ducked through the partition and let the door close.

I wondered to myself what that little seeker after light would have thought if the newest pupil had suddenly materialized in her room. I fancied it would have occasioned her surprise.

I redescended the ladder and started onward, passing two more of the cleated means of ascending, and coming at last to another round hole in the floor. I paused beside it and nodded.

I had been wondering how they got by Bhutia's door. Now I saw that one went into the basement. The basement was the central point from which everything else was reached.

I sat down and dangled my legs over the edge of the hole and struck another match. I was enjoying myself. I let the light flare up and looked around. Beyond the hole was another dark opening leading off to the side.

I felt a sense of elation sweep over me as I sat and let the match burn to extinction. I felt certain beyond any doubt that the passage leading off from the end of this one marked the rear wall of the Swami's study, and was the one he used when prowling over the house between its walls.

I grinned to myself. All I would have to do would be to come back here later and let myself out into his study. After all it was going to be easy. Meanwhile I would go on down the ladder and see what other passages I could find and where they led.

Another match and my watch showed me that it was not quite eleven. I had done a lot in the last hour. Without any further hesitation I went quickly down the ladder and found myself in a sort of closet at its bottom among some garden rakes and spades and such implements.

There was a wooden door at one end of this place which opened easily to my touch and let me into the cellar of the house.

More and more I saw how the thing was done. They had run their partitions clear to the floor of the basement, thus providing support and widened them into a small storage room at the ends. A casual inspection would reveal nothing save a lot of tools and such articles in such a place. Directly opposite this room was another, also closed by a simple door of wood. I crossed and opened this and let myself in.

Before me was another ladder which I mounted and made a new discovery at its top. The ladder was loose at its top and could evidently be drawn up. Also there was a trap door to drop over the opening in the floor. I had no doubt that the other side was similarly arranged had I given it sufficient inspection to have seen what was there.

I crawled out into the passage and made an inspection of its length. It was the same as that on my side of Bhutia's study, equipped in the same way, and that was all. I was fully satisfied that I had learned all I could in this direction, and decided that I might as well go back and lie low in the cellar until it seemed likely that the Swami would have retired.

I made my way back to the basement and lighted myself around by matches. Here I found yet another storage closet, containing a ladder, mounted, and found myself in a duplicate of the passage on the other side of the hall. Here was a side passage which I followed and a small door which I opened.

A glance served to show me that I was on the dais, at the back of the luminous globe. Olive Liston sat there, the light of the lamp filtering to me through the nimbus of her hair. Beyond her I caught one glance of Kwali. I shuddered and drew back.

Up to now I had been in a somewhat whimsical mood of amusement lat the trick I was playing on my opponent. Now my entire mental attitude changed. The sight of the woman, the victim of the man's fiendish cleverness, sitting there alone, wasting her time and her life in staring at a trick lamp, her companion a loathsome and venomous serpent, filled me with a deadly rage.

In the light of that fact my mere discovery of some of the mechanical trickery by which he worked seemed childish indeed. I had in no way advanced the mission for which I had come here. The woman was still his slave, bound to him not by any mechanical device for my solving, but by the more subtle chains of his own mental forging.

I might disrupt his entire physical operating plant, and what good would it do this girl? In that moment of self-disgust and realization I vowed to gain my object at any cost. I had brought my automatic with me, and now I thrust a hand into my robe and reassured myself of its presence.

Rising, I crept out of the side passage, turned info the main one, and went down the ladder. My mind was made up. I was going to Bhutia's study and seek for the evidence I must have before I dared call Bryce to my aid.

I found the closet leading to the rear passage on my side and quickly mounted the ladder, crawled through its hole on the far side, and slipped into the lateral alley. Crouching now and choosing each step, I crept along it by the sense of touch, not daring to light any matches, seeking by feeling to locate the exit door.

So step by step I advanced until it seemed to me I must certainly have reached its extreme limits. I put out my hands and groped questioningly along the wall. Nothing!

I took another step and another, while the blood raced and pounded in my ears. Again I put out a questing hand. I caught something metallic and gripped it—the door at last. Then I crouched down, with every nerve tensed to the highest possible tension. I had heard voices in the room.

For a long moment I held my breath, then let it out slowly. My fingers relaxed their hold on the catch. I strained every nerve to listen, sought to concentrate my whole being into the one sense of hearing. Presently made out the individual voices. They were those of Ishi and Bhutia himself.

But I could not hear what they said. At times I could almost catch a tantalizing word, but nothing intelligible to the understanding. Yet I felt that I must hear.

I might never have so good an opportunity to catch the arch-rogue land his lieutenant off guard again. An idea came into my mind and made me actually afraid. Still, I am glad to say I mastered the fear the next instant and decided to take the chance.

My fingers found the catch of the panel once more and I pried it up. Then, very slowly I sought to draw it inward; but found that impossible. I sank to my knees and reversed the process.

I reasoned that if this was the access to the passage from Bhutia's study this door might swing outward. I bore upon it softly and it yielded. By infinitesimal degrees I let it swing until the voices came louder to my ears. Then I braced myself and held it fast. My reward for my daring was instant and made me forget all else.

"You got ze monay?" Ishi was saying.

"Of course," Bhutia replied. "She gave up without the least resistance. Oh, women are easy if one is careful to pick the right sort."

"You are clever, Rama Singh," Ishi told him in a tone of admiration. "Zis making ze sahiba to rob herself, an' bring ze monay to you 'erself, is to me funnay."

"Rather an Oriental form of joke, Ishi," Bhutia admitted with a chuckle."

"Zen," went on the crab, "she ees to become a real teacher of ze truth, yes?"

"She was made a teacher to-day after she got back from

the bank," said Bhutia. "I am undecided about the rest just now."

"Was eet much monay, Rama Singh?" the crab inquired.

"Half a million in cash and half as much in salable bonds," hissed the other.

I quivered there in the darkness as I listened to the two thieves. I saw how it was all working out. Dual, as ever, had been right.

He had said the man's name even was assumed, and here was Ishi calling him by an entirely different one than the one he wore. Moreover, he did it as an equal, and the other responded as of long custom. I could not doubt.

It was all coming as Semi had told me, and the thought gave me courage. I steadied myself and gave my full attention to the sounds in the room beyond.

"Zen 'ad we not bettair leave zis place queekly?" suggested Ishi.

Bhutia chuckled again.

"Good pickin's here, Ishi," he said.

"Lots of women want to pay money to save their souls."

"But zere are reasons," persisted the crab—"othair reasons w'y we should leave 'ere in my estimashun. Eet was of zat I came to talk to you."

"What do you mean, you circumlocutional little devil?"

"Eet is of thees man, calling heemself Glace," Ishi replied.

I pricked up my ears. Things were getting "warm," as we used to say as children playing a game.

All along I had felt a sense of aversion to the little man in yellow, and now he was evidently reciprocating by starting something on me. It began to look as though I had arrived at my present location at the psychological moment to learn a number of things.

"I do not like heem," Ishi declared.

"That grieves me a lot," said Bhutia. "He's small fish, but his coin is good, while it lasts."

"He iss a spy," said Ishi, spitting the word out.

"He's a superstitious idiot," retorted Bhutia with a sneer in the word.

I snarled silently back at him in the darkness and hoped to live to make him eat the word.

At that I wondered how he would feel if he knew where I was.

My soul-teacher went on with a laugh.

"You ought to have seen him when I materialized in his room last night. This morning he wanted to know if it really happened. You've let your dislike warp your judgment, my boy."

"Oh, 'ave I?" exclaimed the other. "Well, zen, look at zat!"

There followed silence while Bhutia plainly examined something the crab had handed to him.

Back of the wall, clinging to the panel, I cudgeled my brains to think what evidence of my real mission in the house the little imp could have found. There was nothing I could think of, strive as I would. Presently there came the crackle of paper and then Bhutia's voice:

"Where did you find this thing?"

"You remembair w'en I made ze search of hees pockets an ze suit-case this morning while he was in ze sunroom? Eet was zen I found zis in a oocket of hees coat wis a lot of blank sheets of paper. You see w'at it say: 'Call up Bryce at once.' You know w'o Bryce ees?"

I remembered, and in the same breath I cursed myself for the fool Bhutia had called me. That day I came from the wreck and found the note to call the inspector I had thrust the paper upon which it was written into the pocket of my coat.

Later, when leaving the office after talking to Smithson, I had filled that pocket with copy paper. Later still, I had purposely brought it along in case I wanted some blank paper.

The note had worked in among the sheets of the copy-pad and had come with me. Bhutia was right. I was an idiot and a fool!

I crouched down to listen, my face flushed with rage and shame.

"Of course I know who Bryce is," said the Swami in a hard tone. "He was that police official who was prowling around here yesterday morning."

"An' w'o found out nuzzing," added Ishi.

"And so they shot this Glace in to pose as a student and keep an eye out. Rather clever," mused Bhutia. "He's playing his part rather well, too."

"You 'ave allowed your work wiz ze girl to make you careless of ze othairs," accused Ishi.

"She was the big fish," Bhutia explained.

"But if we should lose ze monay or our leeberty, pair-haps?"

"We won't lose either," said Bhutia. "This police agent must be taken care of, that's all."

"But zen, ze ceremony set for meednight will be post-pon'?"

"We may postpone it," said Bhutia.

"An' zis ozzer, zall we not end eet queekly?"

"Really, Ishi," observed Bhutia, "while you are a good detective your methods of removing your enemies or opponents partakes singularly of the Occidental methods of gun or club. You ought to be on their police force, my friend."

"But he ees a menace. He ees an agent of zis Bryce. Bryce ees fail. Zis Glace comes. He cannot be allowed to go from here, an' we cannot keep heem prisoner, for hees friend know w'ere he ees. Either way we will 'ave to leave zis city. A body in ze well would remain for some time undiscovered. By zen we are safe."

"Why go at all at this time? Why not give his body to his friends?" inquired Bhutia.

For a moment there followed silence, then I heard Ishi chuckle.

"You are one devil, Rama Singh," he said slowly. "I see. It 'appens an' we are so sorry. Zey may suspect but can zey prove? No, nuzzing at all."

"I'm glad you approve. Stabbing a man or strangling him, or blowing out his brains is risky in this country," Bhutia went on in a tone of amusement. "But the pin-prick of a serpent's fang—that is artistry in murder, my friend."

"Eet ees beautiful!" Ishi exclaimed.

Myself, I couldn't see it. A sense of deadly sickness gripped me in the pit of the stomach. For a moment, as I listened to those two human fiends planning my destruction, I feared that I would lose my grip on the handle of the panel and precipitate myself into the room.

A cold sweat broke out on my brow and I shook and quivered. All the natural man nature, the primal instincts, urged me to leap forth upon them, draw my pistol and shoot, shoot, shoot until my weapon was empty and they lay dead before me on the floor.

Only the thought that my attack might fail in some unforeseen manner, and so leave the woman still in the hands of one or both of the murderous men beyond the thin partition, held me back. Fighting to regain my self-control, I crouched and swayed dizzily in the passage, while I dimly heard Bhutia outline my intended fate.

"I can go to his rooms and invite him, as the Liston girl's pupil, to attend her final ordination as a teacher," he explained. "He will see nothing wrong in that, and in keeping with his part he must accept. The ceremony will be held at midnight, as originally planned before we knew he was to be dealt with—that will be in thirty minutes, to be exact.

"There will be you, I, and this Glace, the girl and Kwali— you out of sight, of course. Only the globe will be lighted. I shall take Glace up on the dais and instruct him to sit down, cross legged. He's awkward at that. Then a shove, unseen in the dark, a stumble against the cobra. Simple, eh, Ishi? The girl herself will testify to the accidental nature of the deplorable occurrence, especially after I have pointed out to her that her poor pupil's demise was undoubtedly foreordained in just that way, even though cobras are not among the fauna of the United States."

"Oh, you devil—you deelightful devil!" gasped Ishi, half choked with admiration. "Eet ees so simple zat already I believe zat is the way eet 'ave 'appen."

"We'd better go up and suggest his attendance, I fancy," Bhutia remarked.

In that instant I woke to one intense desire. It was to get out of my present position, get back to my own room, and be ready to receive these two master villains. I resolved that if they attempted to carry out their scheme I would attend their mock service, and as soon as I was on the dais I would open fire.

First I would destroy the cobra, afterwards, if necessary, Bhutia and Ishi as well. On the other hand, if they did not resist me I would take Olive by the arm and walk out of the house at the point of the gun. Perhaps that was rather melodramatic, but you must remember that I was somewhat excited at what I had heard and ready for almost anything.

Perhaps you will wonder why I didn't try to notify Bryce. To that all I can say is that the only telephone in the house was in the room with the men; that time was short; that to get to any other instrument I would have to leave the house, thus leaving the girl to the mercies of the two dastards, who might do, the Lord knew what, when they found me gone, and that my own plan seemed the best, as one's own plans are apt to.

Fortunately I did retain sufficient common sense to latch the panel before starting away. Then I rose and turned back down the passage, seeking to make as little noise as possible, yet sacrificing a good bit of caution to speed. In fact I sacrificed so much of caution that when I came to the end of the lateral alley I forgot all about the descent into the cellar.

As a result, instead of stepping over the circular hole and continuing toward the ladder at the end of the rear hallway, I walked full into it and fell.

Instinctively as I plunged I threw out my arms. They caught on the edges of the opening, but not securely enough to check my fall. At the same time they broke its force, and after a few sickening seconds there in the darkness I landed at the foot of the ladder, lurched drunkenly against the door of the closet, felt it yield before me, and scrawled full length upon the cellar's floor.

I know that the next day I found both scratches and bruises on my person, but I think that in such moments of stress a man's physical sensibilities become numbed. At that time I felt no pain, and no sooner had I measured my length on the floor of the basement than I was forcing myself up again, groping blindly for the closet door.

I know that at the time my one thought was one of rage at my carelessness, and a wild desire to get back up the ladder to the first floor passage and reach my room in advance of Bhutia and the crab.

I found myself mumbling: "I must get out, I must get out," as I scrambled to my feet and groped in the darkness of the cellar; and then, with one of those ludicrous flashes of irrelevant humor which will at times intrude the most intense situation, I heard myself adding: "This is I surely no place for a minister's son."

I found the door of the closet, which seemed to have swung shut after spewing me out, wrenched it open, groped for the ladder, found it and started up. Just before reaching the top I stopped and listened. There was no sound.

I crawled out into the passage and fairly ran toward the end and the ladder which would take me to the floor above. At last with a great relief I grasped it and swarmed up its cleats. Panting slightly now, I came out in the end of the little lateral which led back to the panel, and darted along it in a few swift strides, guiding myself by my outstretched hands on the walls.

I bent and began a swift search for the latch. My fingers gripped it and forced it up.

I drew the door to me and slipped through. I let the panel close behind me, straightened behind the curtains, swept them aside, stepped into the room and paused aghast.

Not until that moment had I realized that unlike my own this room was lighted; that fate and my, own wits, fuddled by my fall into the cellar, had destroyed my sense of direction and led me through the wrong closet to the opposite end of the house, or that I stood disheveled and blinking in the room of Olive Liston instead of my own.

8

KWALI!

SHE HAD BEEN sitting at her table drawn under the lights, reading a book. At my sudden entrance she sprang to her feet in startled surprise.

"Mr. Glace! What are you doing here? How did you get into my room?" she gasped.

"Through the panel," I told her. "You see, I must have got into the wrong closet. I was trying to get back to my own room. You see—"

I doubt if she did see. It was all very clear to me, but how could she Understand? I don't even think she heard anything but my first words, in fact.

"Through the panel?" she repeated. "What panel are you talking about?"

I lifted my hand and dragged aside the black-and-gold curtain, set my foot on the releasing board and pushed open the panel.

"The panel in the dado—here," I explained. "There is one of them in every guest-room in this accursed House, one of them back of the dais where you sat less than an hour ago with that infernal snake, and one into the study of Bhutia himself."

Miss Liston approached and inspected the opening in

the wall with interest, even bending and seeking to look inside.

"It leads into a passage, doesn't it?" she remarked with wonder. "And you came out of that?"

"Of course," I told her. "How else do you think I get here, or how do you suppose I, who was believed to be locked in my room, knew you were sitting down there with Kwali the cobra, beside that light?"

"That reminds me that you are not expected to wander over the house as yet," she said severely. "I am afraid you are a disobedient pupil. Now I think you had better go back."

"In there?" I inquired.

"It would hardly do for you to run the risk of being seen coming from my room at this hour of the night," she pointed out. "Besides, your door is locked."

I think I should have laughed if things hadn't been so serious. As it was, I decided that as fate had thrown me into her presence I would make one desperate attempt to warn her of the rascality of the two men.

"Miss Liston," I began as earnestly as I knew how, "if you knew that to reenter that passage just now meant my death, would you send me back?"

"Meant your death?" she gasped, starting back and lifting her eyes to mine. "Are you serious, Mr. Glace?"

"Perfectly, Miss Liston."

"Your death from what?"

"From the hands of Ishi and the Swami Bhutia," I replied.

She smiled slightly.

"Something has frightened you," she remarked. "You have had a nightmare or something. The Swami would be the last man to injure any one, my friend. To him all life is sacred. Your words are almost sacrilege to me, but I know you speak from ignorance. Still sit down until you are calmer. After all, you are my brother spirit—remain as long as you need to regain your control."

"Thanks," I said shortly. "After you."

She smiled again and took the chair she had been occupying when I burst in. I took the other, and drew it up to the other side of the table.

"Tell me," said, "has Bhutia ever appeared to you without warning when your room was locked and you thought yourself alone?"

"So that was it, was it?" she asked with a little laugh.

"That was; not 'it,'" I rejoined. "I am no child, Miss Liston, to think my life in danger because a man comes into my room; without rapping. *Has* Bhutia ever so appeared to you?"

She frowned slightly.

"Oh, yes; since you insist. He has done so numerous times."

"And what explanation did he give you of his appearance?"

"He said that the free soul knew naught of bolts and bars," Miss Liston replied.

"Does that appeal to your credulity?" I asked.

Again she frowned.

"Just what do you mean, Mr. Glace?" she inquired, after an interval of straight-eyed scrutiny. "Why do you come here and question me about Bhutia, as well as make desperate allegations against him? I think you had better explain, if you can."

"Suppose," said I, "that, instead of actually manifesting in your room through any occult power, he came through the panel there."

She started slightly and turned her eyes toward the now closed opening in the dado. I could see that, for the moment at least, I had shaken some latent sense of probability within her mind with this suggestion of mine. A moment later, however, she shook her head.

"How do you know that he even knows of the existence of these panels, Mr. Glace?"

"Why, he had them built!" I cried.

"That is preposterous," declared Miss Liston. "He only came here a month ago."

Suddenly she leaned forward, resting her arms on the table and staring straight into my face.

"Just what are you, Mr. Glace?" she demanded. "Even I can now see that you are no person who came here to learn of the Swami's religion. What are you—a spy?"

I wish I could make patent the contempt her soft lips put into the word. Even though I knew I was in the right of the thing, I felt my face flush at her tone. She noticed it and went on:

"I see that touches you, Mr. Glace. It is not a nice word; but, for that matter, its meaning is not nice, either. Come, answer my question. Why do you come here, and why do you seek by your accusations and insinuations to shake my confidence in this man? What is the object? Who sent you? Was it those convention-bound relatives of mine?"

"I think," I said slowly, "that I may say it was the police."

"Then," she flashed with a curling lip, "you are—"

"A spy. Yes. If to come here in order to protect you from

impoverishment and possibly death is the part of a spy, why, call me one. You can believe me or not, Miss Liston; but, frankly, you do not realize your danger?"

She positively laughed in my face.

"No, I do not, because I am in no danger. I have met only courtesy and sympathetic understanding since coming to this house. I have been given a mission to fulfill, and a great work to do, and taken literally into what, in a material world, one might call a partnership with the Swami Bhutia, in his world work of saving souls."

In that instant I actually felt a forced admiration for the arch rascal. Even though I knew that at that minute he was planning my destruction with a chuckle, I could not help marveling at the subtlety of his control of the high-spirited girl before me.

At the same time I began to despair of making her see the real truth, either by material proof or logical deduction. Those basal suggestions of the Hindu were still too strong to be shaken by my lesser mentality.

It would take a stronger brain even than Bhutia's to undo his clever work. Yet I returned to the attack when she paused.

"You were to continue to work with Bhutia, then?"

"Yes. I am to wait until I have sufficiently developed my own self, and then Bhutia and I are to travel from point to point, establishing houses like this for the instruction of the masses who wish to throw off the slavery of old and worn-out traditions and learn the truth. Think what a privilege is to be mine! I, out of all the women he has met and known, he has chosen to be his right hand in his saving labors. Is it not worth any sacrifice of other hopes or ambitions, or money, to gain such an end? What is one life devoted to such an object when compared to the ultimate good to the many?"

"Speaking of money," I remarked, "I suppose your fortune was to be used to finance this undertaking?"

"*Is,*" declared Miss Liston. "I promised the Swami to help him to the limits of my financial power. Could I do less?"

"And to-day you redeemed that promise by turning over the bulk of your money and securities to him," I accused.

Olive Liston started.

"How do you know anything about that?" she asked in surprise. "And I did, what right have you to question me about it? It was mine."

"I know that you went to the bank this afternoon and drew out a half million cash and half as much more in bonds," I replied.

"You seem to be a capable spy, at any rate," she returned, becoming somewhat uneasy, as it seemed to me.

I made no immediate response to her last remark. I was thinking. It seemed to me that suddenly the real meaning of some of the things I had heard through the panel of Bhutia's study was coming out, like a night-worm crawling forth under a pallid moon.

It was there, dimly sensed as something revolting, slimy, cold, half veiled by the darkness, half revealed in a wan light of understanding. A suspicion born of my thought and the men's words raised itself with a writhing insinuation in my mind.

"And what was to follow your turning over of the money-happen to-night, I mean?"

For a minute I thought she was not going to answer me at all. She rose and walked slowly toward the door, turned and came back, her head bowed in thought, to pause beside my chair, "Mr. Glace," she began slowly, "I don't really see where you get your information of what has gone on in this house during the hours of this day, but your questions show that you at least have a partial knowledge of my actions and my plans and those of Bhutia. As a representative of the police I do not know that I have any right to answer your questions, and yet, speaking as woman to man, I feel some way that in your own eyes you feel your course to be justified.

"Of course," she went on," I deem your assertion that my master desires or intends your death as ridiculous. At the same time I can see that he might resent your presence in this house and have done something which made you fancy yourself in danger. It is only fair then that I tell you that I am my own mistress; that by my father's will I have complete control of my own fortune, and that I am of legal age. The whole trouble in my life at present is being made by my uncle and aunt, who do not wish me to devote my life or my money to this cause. However, in the light of what I have told you, you can see that your efforts at changing the situation must fail, because"—she smiled—"I have made up my mind, and I have the right to do as I please. Unless you can change my mental status you must fail. Why not admit it and leave me in peace?"

Well, she had surely stated the situation. Unless I could wake her to a realization of her real position—change her mind, as she said, I would fail of any aid from her, and

I admitted the fact, together with my inability to shake Bhutia's too firmly planted suggestions.

"Still, you haven't answered my question as to what was to happen to-night—at midnight," I said.

She lifted her head and gazed straight over my head. Her face took on its look of exaltation, which it had held at the services of the afternoon.

"I am to be finally consecrated to this life," she declared in rapt tones.

I saw it, and my heart well nigh stopped. In that moment I blessed all the subtle unseen forces which had thrown me into the breach in the nick of time. But for my intrusion into the house some final piece of dastardy would have been perpetrated against this girl. I pressed the subject.

"What form was that consecration to take, Miss Liston?"

"I was to have been given power over symbolic death," she replied.

"Over what?" I half started from my chair.

"Symbolic death. I have at last conquered all fear," she explained.

"In God's name, what do you mean?" I cried, the dread specter of my suspicion crawling farther into the light.

"To-night at midnight," she said slowly, as one repeating a well-conned lesson, "I am to be shown the power of mind over matter, taught how to defy material dissolution through controlling its material incarnation, the snake."

"Good, God!" I exclaimed. Her words tore aside the last shred of concealment from my eyes and I saw the whole terrible intent of the two fiends who had plotted her entanglement, her stripping, and her death.

But for my timely intervention as an unexpected obstacle she, instead of I, would have been the victim of the poisoned fangs of Kwali. My eyes leaped to her face and rested there full of an unspeakable horror. As in a sort of vision I saw her attempt to caress the venomous cobra. I saw her hand and tapering arm extended to it. I saw it draw back and strike. I saw it hang writhing from her out-stretched fingers, its jaws closed on their pink and whiteness. I heard a scream of waking mortal anguish. I saw her body contorted by the fire of the snake's poison, its limbs writhe, straighten, and stiffen and turn cold, the fulness of her swelling bust cease to rise and fall, a slimy froth over the red of her lips, and I turned cold.

I staggered to my feet.

"And they meant that—that!" I cried out in a blind passion of righteous rage which swept all else from my mind except a desire for justice on the pair. "Damn them to hell! Not while I live and can fight!"

"Mr. Glace!"

Olive Liston's voice, full of shocked protest at my words, brought me back and steadied me.

"I beg your pardon," I muttered. "But can't you see it? Good Lord, girl, don't you see what they meant to do to you? *Can't* you see?"

In my great desire to force her understanding I seized her by the shoulders and held her so that her eyes must look into mine.

Her soft warm flesh struck through the thin gray robe to my fingers and nerved me to my purpose, and in that instant I think the intentness of my gaze shook the structure Bhutia had built the least bit.

"To do to me?" she repeated like a frightened child.

"Of course," I said hoarsely. "They meant to kill you. They were done with you. They had stripped you clean. You were to try to control the serpent and it was to bite you. You were to die. There would be no proof that you had been murdered. They would say and repeat that you sought to pick it up; that you tried to force matters; were impatient of your inability to conquer its mastery faster and took a chance with it. There was nothing to show who had your money. You yourself drew it from the bank. Who could prove where it went? Don't you see how easy it would have been for them? Don't you see? Here, sit down and *think*."

Very gently I pushed her into her chair. She rested her elbows on the table and sank her face into the cup of her hands. For a full minute she sat staring before her, then covered her face completely and shuddered.

"Oh, what a picture you have drawn," she breathed.

I leaned across the table close toiler veiled features.

"It is the picture of what would have happened," I said slowly, seeking to drive in each word.

And then her hands came away from her face and she sprang to her feet. She turned upon me almost fiercely.

"Enough of this," she cried. For a moment you unnerved me, but now I am myself again. Leave the room instantly, in any manner you wish, so you go. I shall not endure your vile maligning of my true friends longer. Oh, I was told that all sorts of pressure would be brought upon me to present my following the dictates of my spirit, but I never dreamed of anything like this. Oh, go, go, *go!*"

I had failed. I clenched my hands and swore softly to myself. At the last Bhutia had proved too strong for me in a contest of suggestive power.

I put my hand in my robe and drew my automatic, and smiled somewhat grimly as I did so. I fancied he would not be able to resist its argument, at least. So far as I could see there remained to me but one course, and that was to fight my way to a telephone and get outside help from Bryce or the police.

There was no doubt that by now my absence from my room was discovered and that Bhutia and the crab were doubly on their guard. Well, then, let them have a carb that the hunted did not turn into the hunter.

I would go down to the study openly along the stairs, and if they tried to stop me—it would be just that much the worse for them. Without looking again at the girl, I strode to the door, jerked it open, removed the key from the inside, stepped out and locked the door.

At least I meant to know where she was when I was done with Bhutia and his satellite.

I dropped the key into a pocket in my robe along with the remains of my box of matches, straightened and started for the stairs. I was going down and get at the telephone in the study in spite of all the Hindu fakir in the world. At that moment I felt able to do it, too.

But a slight noise in the hall arrested my attention. I lifted my eyes and let them run down its length, and there was the crab just backing from my own room at the far end.

My heart bounded. Here, at least, was one of the two opponents whom I must overcome, and he had not seen me as yet. I altered my determination of a moment before to fit the new situation, and on the instant I was speeding toward him in a soft-footed rush.

At that he heard me, whirled to see what was coming,

lifted his eyes to mine, and then glanced ground like a trapped thing seeking some burrow into which it might scurry. The next second I was upon him like a whirlwind of vengeance.

My arm went about his neck in a strangle hold which choked a cry before it was uttered. Under the force of my rush he bent backward, doubled at the knees, and sank to the floor. My knee descended upon his soft little paunch and ground it beneath me like the body of the crustacean to which I had compared him all along. His hands clawed futilely upward toward me like its claws.

Holding him with one hand and my knee, I readied up and found the screw-head which unlocked my door, seized the knob, and thrust the leaf inward, rose from his body, gripped him firmly by the collar of his little yellow robe, and dragged him, gasping and clawing, into the room.

There, with a wrench and a heave, I lifted him and threw him toward the center, found the key in the lock, leaped outside, and turned it upon him.

At least I was sure he wouldn't walk through that way, locked as I had locked it, and I figured that it would take him somewhat longer to get into the passage and reach the study than it would me by the stairs. Then, if he did come, after I had called the central station, I didn't care. All I wanted was a good excuse to plug him, in my present mood.

I picked up my gun from where it had fallen in our scuffle and ran swiftly back to the stairs, turned and went down their treads careless of how much noise I was making. All thought of concealment or stealth was gone from my mind, wiped out by the rage which I felt.

I reached the bottom of the stairs and passed through the door into the passage of the amber lamps, where the black draperies hung in their deadly sameness along the walls. Here I had felt I would meet my first check, if any, and I did.

Every single one of those curtains was the same. I knew that one of them masked the door into the study, but what I did not know was which particular one it was. There was only one way to find out, and that was to test each long black fold until I unveiled the door.

Estimating as nearly as I could where I thought the proper curtain ought to be, I attacked the task. One, two, three of the heavy draperies lifted and peered behind them at a solid wall. I seized a fourth and wrenched it aside so viciously that I tore it from its fastenings and it fell, enveloping me in a choking mass of dusty folds.

Gasping an imprecation, I battled with it, threw it off, and glared around me. At any rate, I had at last found what I sought. I sprang forward and seized the knob.

It turned readily in my hand and I tore the door open, leaped through it, and flung it shut behind me. Before me upon the teakwood desk stood the telephone. So far as I could see I was alone in the room.

I crossed to the desk in a bound of elation. At last I was within reach of calling the assistance I knew was but waiting for my voice along the wire. I sank, half sitting upon the edge of a chair drawn, up to the desk, and put out my hand to the phone. My fingers closed around it and drew it toward me until it stood with its mouthpiece in front of my lips. I raised my hand to lift the receiver from the hook.

And in that moment a case full of rare Oriental curios

which stood in the rear corner of the room next the outside wall of the house began to move. Quite noiselessly and with exceeding smoothness it moved out at a widening angle to the wall; and Bhutia, followed by Ishi, sprang into the room.

My hand, gripping my automatic, came up and dropped upon the desk so that the muzzle of the weapon pointed straight at them, as they came out of the wall.

"Stop!" I cried in a voice which quivered with excitement, strive as I would to make it calm. "The jig's up, Bhutia. I happened to be lying in the hole back of you there a half hour ago when Ishi and you were talking. Now I'm calling the police, and if you try to prevent me I'll put a hole in you so quick you won't know what hit you."

A smile of saturnine humor swept the Hindu's face. With a movement so sudden that I could not sense its beginning, he sprang forward in a silent attack. I saw his body leaping toward me and my finger pressed hard on the trigger.

The automatic spat ten shots in rapid succession. I heard them, I saw the stabs of flame from its muzzle, and smelled the smoke. Then, as though he had borne a charmed life, the man was upon me.

I lifted the weapon and sought to strike him with it in his dark, snarling face. A hand gripped my wrist and wrenched it until I thought it was broken. Wedged between the chair and the desk, I could not resist to my full, and, seeking to rise, caught my foot in the leg of the chair. Bhutia's other hand was fumbling at my throat. I heaved and wrenched and could not rise from my half-crouched position. The weight on my wrist increased.

I could feel myself being borne backward. In a final desperate resistance I lost my balance utterly and sprawled on the floor with the chair.

Dimly I sensed that Ishi had circled the room and was waiting to aid his companion if the need arose.

With Bhutia's fingers on my throat I lay and gazed up into his passion-distorted face. Again he smiled in contemptuous fashion.

"If you should live to ever try such a thing again, Mr. Glace," he remarked in quite a casual tone, "permit me to suggest that you first examine your weapon. As it happens, when Ishi discovered your true character to-day he took the opportunity to remove the loads from your clip of cartridges, and so quite neatly converted them into blanks."

"Ishi was right. You're a devil," I said in sullen admission, and he laughed.

"I think you had better go back to your room," he remarked. "The midnight ceremony will have to be postponed. Get up."

He released me and I rose. He picked up my gun and handed it to me. Then he seized me by the arm and led me to the door. Without a word we passed up the stairs and down to my room.

"The key," said Bhutia, and put out his hand.

I gave it to him and he unlocked the door, held it wide, and firmly propelled me through it.

"Good night," he remarked as he might to a friend he was leaving, and locked me in.

In a bound I crossed up the light-switch and pressed it. The light failed to respond. I dashed to the center of the room and sprang up, reaching for the central cluster. My fingers found the empty sockets where the lamps had been.

With a sinking heart I groped to the far wall and sought for the panel, but strive as I would I could not make it work. Either I did not locate it in the dark or they had wedged it from the far side. I ran to the window and threw it open, raced back to the bed and sought for the sheets up twist into a cord. My groping fingers found nothing save a bare mattress—of bedding there was none.

Utterly unnerved, I sat down upon the bed and gave myself up to a sort of despair as I realized that unless I cared to risk the twenty-foot leap from the window into the darkness of the garden, I was trapped.

I heard the click of the lock and whirled. Why I did not spring toward it I do not know to this day, yet I remained where I was, held, as I think, by some subconscious prompting which chained me where I sat. Quite slowly the door opened until I saw a line of light.

A hand and an arm slid slowly inward. For an instant I saw it protruding through the narrow opening then there came a sound as of a soft body dropping upon the carpet, the hand and arm disappeared quickly, and the door was closed.

I sat upon the bed, panting. Cold fear and deadly suspicion were gripping at my heart. With fingers that trembled I drew the match-box from my pocket and sought for a match. There was only one.

Undeterred by that, I drew it out and rubbed its head along the prepared side of the box. It flared into a sudden light. I held it until it was burning freely, then raised it above my head.

My worst fears were confirmed. *Between me and the door, in a mass of slithering coils, lay Kwali, the snake!*

9

THE CALL FOR HELP

I **DO NOT** believe that at any other time in my life has such a paralyzing sickness of fear possessed me as in that moment when I realized my position.

Without means of offense or escape, with all my plans known to the men who had determined upon my death, without even the means of making a light, I was locked into this room with the most deadly of snakes.

I was born with an aversion to serpents. Ever since boyhood the mere kicking out of the weeds of the most harmless garter-snake has made me recoil with a cold shock of horror beyond any seeming ability of mine to control. Now I sat huddled in the exact center of the bare mattress and shivered and shook with a species of mortal terror which made me ashamed.

I could see their entire design. They had counted that I would rush the opening door and meet my fate. Failing that, I might seek in the dark for a way of escape and stumble upon the serpent, with the same result. If not, I would be held there until, overwrought by my terror, I made some desperate endeavor to destroy the living death find met my own. The end having been gained, my body would be carried to the room, below where was the luminous globe.

The girl, creature of Bhutia's will, would be used to give added credence to their tale of my accidental death, even though not an actual witness as planned. There would be no proof of the fact that they lied. So far as my friends or the law was concerned, they were safe.

Presently the sound of a soft dragging across the carpet came to my ears with a fresh terror. Through what seemed like hours of a cold, clammy dread I sat and listened to it creeping, creeping beyond me in the darkness. It seemed to me that it reached the bed and paused. Would it, I asked myself, seek to mount upon it? Was it literally hunting me down? The uncanny idea that perhaps in some vile way of his own Bhutia was able to control the lesser mentality of the snake as he did the greater one of the girl, came upon me, and I fancied that he was directing its course, urging it to seek and find me and sink its fangs into my flesh.

Finally it begin to creep again. I heard it scrape past the foot of the bed and approach the far wall.

Suddenly, as I watched it, it reared itself until its head swayed a horrible silhouette between me and the faint outer light. I think I cried out. I am not sure.

The next conscious thing of which I am aware was a sense of hope. Somewhere in the deeper fastnesses of my soul a voice seemed speaking to my consciousness. It was deep and firm and sincere.

"If at any time you need help be sure I shall come at your call."

It was the voice of Semi Dual, repeating the promise he had given me I days before.

A new sense of power and comfort grew in my soul. Time after time since I had known him my strange friend had, by his peculiar power of telepathy, called me to his quarters in the Urania when he wished me for some purpose connected with our mutual work. Could I, I asked myself, call him to me now in a similar way?

Sorely it seemed to me that I had never needed his help worse than now when, all my endeavors to save another in ruins, I myself was locked in a room to await my own death.

I knew that mental concentration was necessary to the task, but it seemed to me that my very plight must lend power to my cry for help. I glanced at the window where I had last seen Kwali, but he had disappeared.

Then I fastened my mind upon Semi Dual and stared straight before me into the dark.

"Dual—come. Dual—come," was the message I sent. Over and over I threw its two brief word forms forth from my brain, like the waves of a wireless message into space.

In fact, I remember that that was the mental picture I formed as I sat there on the bed like an operator at his key. To my mind my brain became the dynamo from which was generated a vast force which I was hurling into the night. High up on the tower of a distant building was the sensitive brain I was seeking to reach.

"Dual—come," I whispered in final effort, closed my mental key, and sat huddled on the bed.

How long I waited after that I do not know exactly. To my stress of mind it seemed hours. In reality, judging by the time which saw the; whole thing ended, it was not over a comparatively few minutes at most.

Suddenly to my waiting ears there came the sound of a rapidly driven motor, coming up the drive from toward the heart of town. It came on and on, while I strained my ears with listening and my soul with hope. It stopped. Silence came down upon the house.

Then I heard the sound of footsteps coming along the hall. They drew nearer and nearer and paused. The key grated once more in the lock. The door swung entirely open and showed me the Swami Bhutia *and back of him Semi Dual.*

"Gordon," said the voice of my friend.

"Yes," I panted.

The dazzling thread of an electric flashlight in Dual's hands leaped into the room and ran searching about its corners, stopped began a systematic crisscrossing of its floor, stopped again.

Like a great whip, Kwali retired upward and hung swaying in its stream of radiance. The light lowered. The snake followed its retreating shaft.

It crept nearer and nearer the two men, while I watched in a gruesome fascination. Nearer and nearer it followed the light which charmed it, and suddenly I again heard Dual's voice.

"Gordon, come to me."

Released from my nerve-paralyzing terror by that command, I sprang from the bed, darted aside so as to give the serpent as wide a berth as possible, and then, in a final rushing leap, dashed past Dual and the Swami into the hall.

Whirling, I was in time to see Dual close the door and turn the key in the lock.

Bhutia was glaring upon him with a frown.

"Who the devil are you, anyway?" he wanted to know. "By what right do you come to my house, ring my bell, overpower my servant, and force your way into my affairs?"

"By the right of Right," said Semi, smiling upon him. "It is enough."

"Did you catch the crab—the little fellow who answered the door?" I stammered, arrested by the Swami's words.

"Naturally," Semi told me. "At present he is in the hands of the law. I gave him to Bryce after I had picked him up at the door. I fancy the inspector is waiting us below even now. He surrounded the house before I came in."

Bhutia started slightly.

"What do you mean?" he flared out.

"That thy sin has found thee out, Rama Singh," he said quickly "The penalty awaits below, thou renegade. Come!" He gestural toward the stairs.

I don't know just how pale a Hindu may I become, but it seemed to me that the Swami changed color as Dual ceased speaking.

As for myself, my pulses were singing. I was out of the room and the snake was locked in. Dual had received my message. Bhutia was evidently in awe of the man, though trying to bluster. Bryce and his bluecoats were in and about the house.

Olive Liston would be saved in spite of herself, and the world was a fine old place after all. And above all and everything else was the blinding information embodied in Semi's addressing Bhutia by the same name the crab had used.

As I followed the two men down the stairs in procession I turned it over and over. Once more I was given the proof that, while I had thought myself the sole help of the girl in this house of horrors, Dual had kept in touch in his own peculiar fashion. The epitome of it all was, "Dual knew." One could say no more.

We found Bryce nervously pacing the passage of the amber lamps in company with Detective Johnson. They had penetrated that far, and then waited, in accordance with orders from Dual.

"Did you get him?" the inspector burst out as we came through the curtained door from the stairs and surprised him and Johnson with drawn guns.

"Naturally," Dual informed him. "This is he."

He indicated Bhutia with a wave of the hand.

"But before you arrest him, inspector, suppose we go into his study for a few minutes. Where is Mr. Andrews just now?"

"Outside," said Bryce. "I made him wait till we saw how the land lay. He's out there cussin' me to Jerry."

"Suppose you call him in," smiled Dual.

Bryce turned to Johnson at once.

"Tell 'im he can come a runnin' now," he directed, and the detective turned back toward the front door.

The curtain I had pulled loose still lay in a heap by the door of the study. Dual now signed Bryce to take Bhutia into that room. He himself waited until Andrews came in with an eager question in his eyes, when we all followed the inspector and his man.

Our entrance was upon a tirade from the Hindu, who was fiercely addressing Bryce.

"Officer, I tell you this is an unspeakable outrage. There is no reason for this unwarranted breaking into my house in the night, nor for my being subjected to continual police interference. I doubt greatly if even you yourself know the nature of the charge you intend lodging against me, save that I have unwittingly incurred your displeasure, and so must be subject to this sort of disturbance at any and all times."

"That's right. I don't know what the charge is," Bryce told him. "But if this Dual says he 'has something on you,' he has."

Bhutia summoned a sneer and turned toward Semi, who was just closing the door.

"You seem to have convinced your underling of my guilt in advance of any proof," he flashed out. "Do you suppose that I will tamely submit to any such high-handed methods as this? I now demand that you move both yourself and your men from my house at once or I shall be compelled to start proceedings against you for a false entry, verging upon the nature of a malicious persecution."

Dual came as near modern slang in his reply as I had ever known him to do.

"As for proof," he remarked, "I am coming to that. It was for that purpose that I ordered you brought in here. As to starting anything, I do not think that you will long remain in a position to do so. Suppose you sit down?"

"Bryce"—he turned to the inspector—"watch this man, and if he makes any false moves see that he remains here, either alive—or dead."

The inspector grinned and drew his gun.

"Sit down," he directed, gesturing toward Bhutia. "Johnson, get over by the door, and if this Jasper starts any funny plays, plug him. Now, Mr. Dual."

Semi Dual seated himself at the desk and the rest of us found chairs and stools.

"My first connection with this affair," Semi began, "was some days ago, when my friend Glace here came to my apartments and told me of an interview with this man, the Swami Bhutia as he styles himself."

Again I saw Bhutia sneer.

"At that time I was in no small degree interested in what he told me of the man and this place. Particularly was my attention caught by his description of the actions of a serpent—a cobra, to be exact—which was in the man's possession, at such times as the Swami sought to pick it up.

"As Glace told it, the snake appeared to almost fear the Swami's fingers, rather than resent their approach. Such knowledge as I possess of the habits of the cobra made this seem a peculiar action for one of the most deadly of snakes known, and I decided to try and learn more of the affair.

"You, Inspector Bryce, and you, Detective Johnson, have had some little experience of those methods which I at times use in unraveling a mystery, so-called. I will not, perhaps, strain your credulity too far, then, if I tell you that I determined to seek in astrological observation and calculation for some of the information I wished. That night I made such an observation, and I learned at that time that the name Bhutia was assumed.

"In other words, while I could find positive evidence of the presence of a man of the alleged Bhutia's physical description in the city, yet I could find no man who would, under the then existing conditions, be both here and bearing that name, I was then convinced in myself that we had an impostor to deal with.

"My observations, however, carried a little further, also showed me that there would be strange happenings, not unfraught with danger, in this house; also that they would involve this man, a woman, and my friend Glade, provided he continued to interest himself in the affair, as I felt sure he would.

"I told him of this, and told him further that if at any time his need of assistance should require it I would come to his aid. The next day he called me and told me of a conversation between himself, the aunt and uncle of a young woman known as Olive Liston, her *fiancé*, Mr. Andrews here, and the police. I have not heard from Mr. Glace since, nor seen him until to-night.

"But I was confident to let him go forward, for I had told him that I would look into the matter, and I had planted in his mind a suggestion of my assistance, which I knew would operate in case the need arose and caused him to call me to him consciously of otherwise. In the meanwhile I determined to watch the course of events and find out what I could about the self-styled Swami.

"Besides my own means of seeking for information by occult studies, I keep in touch with more material ones. It was easy for me to set investigations in progress both in Oxford, England, and in Calcutta, in regard to a man answering Bhutia's description. As a result I learned some interesting facts. There had never seen man of that name educated at either place who could possibly be the one I was hunting. But there had been a student in both places corresponding exactly with my description of the man who now sits with us in this room.

"I got his records of birth and all other data from the registrars of the universities he had attended, and felt that I was at last on his trail. I went further back. Some time in the past one of the Eastern monasteries of esoteric science, commonly called Yogis, decided to extend the scope of their work by sending certain of their numbers into the Western world. These men, carefully selected for their mental attainments, were sent to various colleges and universities, and educated in the languages and customs of the people they were to approach.

"Most of them, I am glad to say, have either; finished or are still performing their missions in a creditable fashion, but, as in most bodies of men, there was a black sheep among them. Having gained all he could at the expense of his brother disciples, he conceived the idea of using his great knowledge for his own selfish ends. In company with a countryman of his own criminal nature, he started forth on his present career, under an assumed name, changed numerous times. So the renegade of the Eastern Brotherhood became a vampire preying on the public, and worshiping only gold."

"That's your number. I guess, Swami," said Bryce to Bhutia, who sat glowering in his chair.

Dual shook an admonitory head.

"Their visual method was to go to some center and establish a place like this. There they remained until they gained control, by suggestion and actual hypnosis at times, of some woman of great wealth. By their joint efforts, though principally by this man's mental control, they stripped her clean of all property and money, and then arranged for her a fate which, while it might be suspicious, was impossible to fasten upon themselves.

"She might commit suicide, or be run down in a street by seeming accident, or wander from her home at night and fail to return alive. Several died from 'accidental' bites from a trained cobra this so-called Swami possessed, brought on by their own carelessness, as he was able to prove.

"With such data to go on and the birth date of the man, it was easy for me to set up an astrological figure which showed him to be in this city at this time, with all the figures of his horoscope in such a position to those of Olive Liston that he could mean her only evil and eventual death.

"Going further, I saw that the events would come to a climax to-night, and after that I waited for the hour to strike. Knowing the hour of the crisis, all I needed to do was to sensitize my brain to receive the call of my friend Glace when it came, as I knew it must. In the mean time, I called you, Mr. Bryce, and told you to remain at the station after ten, as you will remember, and to get Johnson and your men ready to go with you. I also bade you have Mr. Andrews present, and to bring him with you when I called."

"I know it," said Bryce, "an' I done it. You nearly knocked me off my dip when you called up and began to shoot that stuff into me, Dual. Glace had told me you'd said you'd help it we needed you, but I didn't know you was keeping in touch. He didn't tell me that."

"I didn't know it myself," I exclaimed.

"The deuce! Well, that beats me," grinned Bryce.

"You know the rest, I think," Dual resumed, with a smile. "When Glace called me by his mental appeal I telephoned you and met you as I had arranged. We came here. I came in and handed over the Swami's accomplice to you. I then came back here and induced Bhutia to take me to Glace's room where I found him locked in with this cobra he had mentioned.

"Glace was released and the snake locked in, and we came back here. Now I accuse Bhutia with being an impostor, with having gained control of Miss Liston by an exercise of hypnotic suggestion, and with having intended her death. I may add that his real name is Rama Singh."

"Your deductions and your tracing are clever, Dual," Bhutia remarked, "but I asked you for proof."

"Of what?" said Semi Dual.

"Of any intent of criminality," the Hindu returned.

"There is no proof of that," replied Semi Dual. "We are merely morally sure of it, Singh. You have always been clever enough to conceal any proof which might exist."

Bryce was fidgeting in his chair.

"Then ain't we going to pinch him, Mr. Dual?" he exclaimed, as though in actual pain.

"See here!" I cried, leaning forward. "Dual, I laid in a secret passage in that wall to-night and heard him and his man Ishi plot my own death, at least."

I pointed to the end of the study.

"Could you prove it?" questioned Dual, giving me a straight glance.

Bryce and I both collapsed in a sickening sense of futile failure. The Swami smiled.

"Your perception holds good still, Dual," he observed, quite at his ease. "I suppose this ends the matter, eh?"

"Scarcely."

An inscrutable smile flicked the lips of my friend.

"You see, morally, Rama Singh, I am certain of all I said, and to call this the end would be to deny the truth of the universal retributive law, which must ever exact the penalty for the crime. Besides, I have not yet seen Miss Liston nor secured her release. No, Rama Singh, this is not the end!"

As though the word had been a signal, there rose a wild riot of rushing feet, loudly raised voices, and startled profanity from the outer passage where burned the amber lamps. In a leap Johnson reached the door of the study and tore it open to admit the flushed helmet-crowned face of a policeman who stared into the room.

"Did he come in-here?" he bawled.

"Did who come in here?" demanded Johnson. "What are you talkin' about?"

"That little cuss in the yellow bath-robe," stammered the roundsman. "He gave Jerry and me the slip an' run in here. I was right behind him all the way, and it looked to me like he went right through the wall."

Semi Dual smiled.

"You should have watched more carefully," he said. Then he swung upon me.

"I think you said something about a secret passage, did you not, Gordon?"

"Yes," I cried in excitement. "That's where this fellow has gone. Quick, Johnson, get some of your men into the cellar and we'll catch him. All the passages in this darned house open down there."

Bryce rose with a bound.

"There you are, Johnson. Get a move on," he burst out in direction. "Get Glace to show you the way. Quick now."

"Wait!" said Semi Dual.

Our eyes came to him in surprised question. For the life of me I could not understand what was his reason for delay at such a time.

He went on: "If you will still accept my guidance, Mr. Bryce, direct your men to merely guard the house closely from the outside. I have the feeling that nothing more will be necessary to the end we desire."

The inspector shook a puzzled head, but yielded.

"All right, if you say so," he said slowly. "Callahan"—to the roundsman—"git outside an' see to it that the boys keep a close eye out now. I ought to have you on the carpet for allowin' that getaway but if we get him back I'll forget it this time."

Callahan withdrew in crestfallen obedience, and we sat and waited. There was utter silence in and about the house. For what dénouement Dual was keeping us there I could not possibly guess. I let my eyes turn to Bryce and Johnson and Andrews. They, too, sat stupidly staring at Dual and Bhutia. I turned my eyes back again. Semi was sitting, staring, straight at the Hindu. He opened his lips.

"This, Rama Singh," he said slowly, "is the *beginning* of the end."

The Swami shivered slightly.

"Curse you, Dual!" he snarled.

"As often as you wish—*renegade*," said Semi. "Thy curses are of small avail."

Suddenly I felt an impulse to turn up my head, and I did so. My heart seemed to stop in my breast. For the second time that night the case of Oriental curios swung out from the wall.

In the dark throat of the passage showed the crouched figure of the crab—Ishi. In a bound he was in the room. From his right hand there hung a writhing, wriggling something. He lifted it and whirled it about his head. The lights went out.

I cried but to Dual as I divined his purpose. There was a single sharp hiss and a scream of mortal agony set the darkness aquiver.

And then I heard the voice of Semi.

"Gordon, the door! Lights!"

I understood. In a blind rush I flung myself toward the hole in the wall, collided in the utter blackness with a little figure, and hurled it aside.

My groping fingers found the edge of the door to the secret alley. Trembling with haste, I searched for and found, after what seemed minutes of groping, a little switch. I pressed it and saw that the lights responded, and then I swung around.

The Swami Bhutia was leaning back in his great chair, his eyes wide open and staring, and *from the flesh of his cheek into which it had sunk its fangs hung Kwali, the snake!*

With an oath Johnson flung himself upon the figure of Ishi, who, with his retreat cut off, had crouched down between me and Bhutia. There came the click of handcuffs, and he jerked him to his feet.

"You would, would you?" he yelled hoarsely. "Well, we've got you back again, anyhow, you yellow shrimp!"

I gave the two a glance and turned all my attention to Dual. He had risen to his feet and approached the chair in which Bhutia half lay, half sat.

With entire deliberation he put out a hand and seized the writhing cobra back of its head, pressing inward with his fingers. The serpent released its hold and he lifted it off and held it to one side.

"And this, Rama Singh," he said quite slowly, "*is* the end. It was written, thou one foresworn, and the stars themselves showed a serpent hanging from thy face."

The Hindu opened his eyes widely, closed them again. His body stiffened in its every line and muscle. He shuddered. His jaw dropped. He relaxed utterly in the chair, and sagged down.

Semi swung on his heel and dropped the snake into a lacquered waste-paper basket, throwing a small rug over its top.

He addressed Bryce:

"Ishi made a slight misjudgment of distance in hurling the snake through the darkness, inspector, and so bungled in my intended death. You all saw what he did. It is sufficient. Suppose you call up the Zoo and see if they would perhaps like the serpent for their snake-house. Here is a telephone on the desk."

Without a word the inspector took up the phone and called a number. Presently he was answered, and talked briefly to some one at the Zoo.

"Not on your life!" he broke into sudden expostulation, waited another moment, hung up the receiver, went back and sat down in a chair.

"They seem to be tickled at the chance," he announced. "They wanted me to send it right down or bring it. You heard what I told 'em. They're comin' up. Well, what now?"

"Now," said Dual, "you may as well be taking Ishi along. Also arrange for the disposal of Rama Singh's body. I think the case is clear and complete. Leave a couple of your men in charge of the house for to-night. To-morrow we will take steps to recover such of Miss Liston's fortune as may remain."

"But what of Olive herself?" protested Andrews, rising. "Are you going to do nothing to free her from the devilish control of that hideous creature?"

He pointed to the figure of the Swami.

"Glace said something about post hypnotic suggestions. Will his death free her? What—"

Dual interrupted him, smiling.

"Mr. Andrews, will you not be content to allow me to care for the welfare of Miss Liston?"

"Sure!" nodded Bryce. "Take a tip from me, Andrews, and let Mr. Dual look out for your sweetheart. He's got it over any Hindu fakir seventeen ways from the jack." He approached the handcuffed Ishi. "Come on, you yellow peril," he said.

The door of the study closed behind the crab and his guards, and left Dual, Andrews, and me with the figure in the chair. We sat and waited yet a few minutes until a couple of men sent by Bryce came to us, lifted the dead body, and took it away. Semi turned to me.

"Where *is* Miss Liston now, Gordon?" he asked.

"Locked in her rooms," I told him.

"I have the key."

"Get her quickly," he directed.

I ran from the room and mounted the stairs of the house of horror. Thrusting the key into the lock I opened the door and stepped into Olive Liston's room.

She rose as I entered and stood looking me full in the eye.

"It seems that you persist in your intrusions, Mr. Glace," she observed.

"I came only because I was asked to escort you down-stairs as soon as possible," I explained.

"Down-stairs—"

"A friend of yours is waiting to see you in Bhutia's study—a Mr. Andrews."

"And Bhutia?" she asked.

"Was bitten by Kwali."

She trembled, but caught herself quickly.

"I can hardly believe that of the master. This is all some more of your scheming, I suppose," she accused.

"Very well, I will see Mr. Andrews and afterward I must learn what has really been done to my friend, Bhutia. Come, Mr. Glace."

I trailed back down the stars at her heels and opened the door of the study to admit her.

"Thank you," she said coldly, and swept into the room.

"Olive!"

Andrews rose and stretched out his hands. She gave him one glance and turned interrogative eyes upon Semi Dual, who had risen to his feet.

Instantly he crossed and, bending down, took both of her hands and held them while he spoke. His very action seemed to arrest her with surprised attention and bring her eyes to his.

"Olive, dear soul," he began, "I know all your story, all your desire to advance in knowledge, all the pure innocence of your purpose, and the noble part to which you meant to devote your life."

A smile grew across the girl's lips. They parted slightly her bosom heaved.

"But, dear child seeking light," the mellow tones continued, "in so doing your spiritual eyes have been blinded by a false brilliance. In your manner of seeking to become a teacher of the truth you have fallen somewhat short of choosing the most natural method. In casting, aside all old dogmas all suggested thoughts childhood and preformed beliefs, you have erred in that we should throw aside no knowledge which comes to us, but keep it to compare with new knowledge which we may be given, for in so doing only can we separate the false from the true; in seeking to save your soul and those of others you have walked with a guide whose own light of the spirit was so dimmed by acts of his own that he stumbled blindly upon his death ere he knew it.

"Olive, the Swami Bhutia's fate has overtaken his steps as must the fate of each who seeks to pervert the great truths of life to a purely selfish end. As a result of all those things, thou seeking soul, you have had a strange experience, for while half your soul was awake and seeking knowledge, half of it slumbered in a sleep thrown o'er it by a soul foresworn. Daughter, I say unto you, awake. Throw off the vague dreams of the half truths, and return to the full light of the understanding. *Awake!*"

For a moment the woman swayed before him. Then she lifted her hands and brushed them across her eyes as one awaking from slumber. She turned her head, first to Dual and then about the apartment. Her eyes fell upon Andrews, sitting pale and anxious. Her arms reached out to him.

"Richard!" she cried.

In a bound he was beside her, drawing her into his arms. Dual and I turned away.

I seized his hand.

"You got my message?" I cried from a full heart.

He smiled.

"The message of any soul in need does not go unheeded," he answered—"you played a man's part."

My laugh was a trifle unsteady.

"Just the saline that snake sure had me going," I told him.

Then I looked down at my robe. It was dust stained and rent, and disreputable in the extreme.

"I rather believe I had better get into my room and put on some clothes."

Andrews had led Miss Liston to a carved settee and taken a place at her side. They were conversing in low tones. Now and then I saw that their eyes turned in our direction. Presently the girl rose and approached Dual. Her eyes had lost their staring scrutiny and drooped shyly as she began to speak.

"Mr. Dual, I think I am now quite myself, and I realize all that has happened, and all that both you and Mr. Glace have done to save a very foolish girl in the hands of a wicked man. Mere thanks for such a service seems pitifully inadequate to express my feelings, and yet I want to express them to you both. Only—if there is any way in which—in which—I-can—really show appreciation, I—"

Semi Dual smiled, and stooping once more possessed himself of her hand.

"I understand fully, Miss Liston," he assured her. "And there is way which I am sure will greatly gratify both my friend and myself.

"It is this:

"By remembering that the true House of the Ego, in which dwells the light of the spirit, is your own divine soul, and that it is there we must seek for that light rather than in the darkened mind or the darkened house of any other one."

THE GHOST OF A NAME

1

A CALL AND A CLUE

SOME FIEND OF torment and perversity was ringing a bell in my ear, dispelling those last precious moments of sleep to which a man clings after a wearying day before.

I dug my head into the pillow half consciously and sought escape from the annoyance, but I didn't escape.

Instead I became aware that the shrill sound was of a very material origin, and emanated from that modern rest-disturber, the telephone.

It was, in fact, broad daylight, and the noisy bell was filling all my room with its shrieking clamor. I sat up and reached for the thing.

Even as I did so I wondered what could have happened that I was being roused thus early. I wasn't due at the office for at least a couple of hours, and I hadn't left until two this same morning.

I smothered an imprecation as the bell took another spasm, and lifted the receiver to my ear.

"Hello!" I yelled, none too cordially. Then I forgot the grouch.

Smithson's voice came to me over the wire.

"Glace! Grab a taxi and get out to the residence of Anthony Conrad as quick as you can. There's a murder and suicide story 'breaking' there. Davidson just called me from the central station, and I told him I'd have you cover the story. Beat it, son!"

His receiver clicked up without giving me a chance to ask a question.

I slammed the phone back on its stand, jiggled the hook, and called a taxi-stand for a cab; then I reached for my clothes.

My sleepiness had left me, driven clear from my eyes by that peculiar something which makes newspapermen resemble the trained hound.

Give us a fresh scent and we'll follow the lead till we drop; the desire to be in at the "death," to clear up the mystery if there is one, to win a good story, and score a scoop if possible, finally becomes almost an obsession.

The voice of my city editor, declaring that a story was "breaking," made me forget that I was weary, sleepy, and angry at being waked. Instead I hastened my dressing in every possible way, and was outside on the curb when the taxi drew up.

I went aboard before the driver stopped and flung him the address, with an admonition for speed.

Then I settled down and lighted a cigarette in lieu of breakfast, and thought over what I knew about Anthony Conrad.

He was a retired broker, reputedly very wealthy, and lived on Park Drive, our most fashionable residence street, in a great mansion set in beautiful grounds. A peculiarity of this house was that it was spread over an immense ground area, and was only one story in height.

I had heard that this was owing to the fact that in her

last years Conrad's wife had been practically an invalid, and that he had built all on one floor for her greater convenience.

Now, however, she was dead, and her husband dwelt alone in the place save for his man and his man's wife, who acted as housekeeper, and the servants; and also the son of a brother, who acted in the capacity of secretary to his uncle, and looked out for such business interests as he still kept up.

This nephew's name was, as I remember, Gustav, and so far as was reputed, he was a very decent sort of young fellow, popular, in the younger society set, and recently engaged to the daughter of one of our prominent bankers.

Such, in brief, was all I could recall as I smoked out my cigarette and waited for the cab to get me to my destination.

The cab turned at right angles into Park Drive. Glancing out of the window the tall pile of the Urania Building swept into my range of vision.

I thought of Semi Dual, and I smiled.

Here was I once more in my reportorial capacity, rushing toward the scene of human passions let loose.

No doubt my strange friend was even now rising from his rest and donning his loose robes of purple and white, perhaps breakfasting in his frugal style of cakes and fruit and milk, oddly simple fare for one who dwelt in the midst of luxury.

For Dual dwelt on the roof of the Urania, where he had arranged quarters for himself and one servant in the tower, fitting them with furnishings of rare fineness, and apparatus of marvelous delicacy, devoted to his peculiar investigations into the higher forces of the universe.

I have had people call him a mystic—a fakir; once I myself fancied he might be a charlatan. That, however, was before I met him.

In reality, he was a scientific metaphysician—a man who did strange things in a natural way, and held that nothing in all the universe of worlds was supernatural, because all which seemed so was but the natural effect of the operation of higher laws of nature.

On the roof itself he had constructed a wonderful garden of potted bushes and shrubs and beds of flowers, roofed in winter by a dome of glass, and so kept green the year around.

This realm of his was reached from the twentieth floor of the building by a great staircase of marble and bronze, at the top of which was an inlaid annunciator plate, which rang a chime of bells in the tower.

I had met him long ago, one day when Smithson had sent me to gain an interview for a feature story. That day as I went toward his unusual abode I had fancied that he was some sort of a charlatan preying upon human superstition.

The very name suggested it.

I half expected to have him offer to read my entire life, past and future, for a fee. Instead I found a courteous gentleman, who told me of things of which I had never dreamed, and politely refused to be interviewed for publication.

Since then I had come to call him friend. By aid of his wonderful knowledge I had been enabled to unravel some of the most baffling crimes which had occurred in our city.

I had seen him sit alone in that tower and reach out his hand and point to the guilty, and say "This is the man."

I had found that the man I had suspected of gulling a public was one whose chief aim in existence was to help mankind. So in our ignorance we often misjudge our real friends.

Because of the unusual means which Dual used in obtaining the solutions to seemingly baffling mysteries of crime, Smithson of the *Record* had dubbed him the "Occult Detector."

By a natural association of ideas, I now found myself wondering if this case toward which I was speeding might in any way again throw me into association with my strange friend; if once more I were to see exhibited that almost uncanny ability of deduction possessed by Dual.

So deeply was I engrossed in my own thoughts that I gave little attention to my progress until the taxi turned from the street and began to follow the curving drive which led up to the wide-flung house of Conrad.

Then perforce I lifted my eyes and glanced about.

A long, gray motor, which I immediately recognized as a police-car, already stood at the head of the drive. Almost on the tail of my own machine a second taxi turned into the grounds.

As my own driver came to a stop behind the police-car, this motor also slowed, and from it sprang Jimmy Dean, star man on the *Dispatch,* and a friendly rival of mine.

"Hello, Gordon!" he greeted, smiling. "That was just about a dead heat this time. Smithson must have disturbed your beauty-sleep, old pal."

"And you?" I suggested.

Dean grinned.

"Sweet dreams-sounds of horrid tintinnabulation—dreams shattered. 'Info' that a prominent citizen was I not—gasoline chariot—and now you. What are we waiting for, anyhow?"

We paid our drivers and went up the front steps to the wide porch, side by side. The front door stood open, giving us a view of a wide hall from which doors opened on both sides.

Hovering about the outside of one of these was a woman apparently somewhat past middle age, who, I imagined, was probably Conrad's house-keeper. As it turned out later, I was right.

We walked into the hall, and I accosted her, explaining that we were from the press.

She lifted dazed eyes while I was speaking, and, when I had finished, moved her hand toward the door beside which she was standing.

"In there," she said.

As it afterward appeared, all the sleeping-rooms were on one side of the house and the living-rooms on the other.

Immediately on the woman's words Dean put a hand on the knob, and we walked into what was apparently a suite of rooms.

The first was more a study than anything else, containing a fireplace, some great chairs, and a massive desk, covered with books and papers, and supporting a bracket electric lamp and a telephone.

Beyond this, and separated from it by an arch, draped in heavy silk curtains, was what might be called an alcove bedroom, from which came the sound of voices.

Dean and I crossed and pushed back the curtains, exposing the room to our view, together with some five men who were present, beside the figure on the bed.

Two of these—patrolmen—turned toward tis on our entrance, recognized us, and turned back.

Inspector Bryce and Johnson, the detective, merely nodded and turned back to the fifth man, who was a tall, clean-shaven fellow of somewhere in the fifties, to judge by his looks.

"And you knew nothing of this, heard nothing at all suspicious after you left Mr. Conrad last night?" Bryce was saying.

"No, sir," the man replied. "I went to sleep and slept sound until I came in to awaken Mr. Conrad as was my custom. Then I finds him"—he paused and appeared to struggle for control for a moment—"like this," he finished, and again paused.

"How long have you been with Mr. Conrad, Porter?" asked Bryce.

"Fifteen years, come next month," the fellow stated.

"And in that time do you know of any one's threatening your employer's life?"

"No, sir."

"Mr. Gustav Conrad lived here for the past three years, you say?"

"Yes, sir. He came a month after Mrs. Conrad died."

"And his relations with his uncle were always harmonious?" said Bryce.

Porter paused just a second, as it seemed to me. "Yes, sir. I think you might call them that."

"Mr. Gustav was a good sort, was he, Porter?" Johnson cut in.

"Yes, sir. He was a very nice, steady young man; very polite and considerate he was. He was quite a favorite with us house people, sir."

"Then," said Johnson sharply, "is that why when Bryce asked you if he and his uncle got along well, just now, you hesitated before you answered?"

"Why, no, sir—I—I was just thinking, sir."

"Of what?" snapped Johnson.

"Just a little thing I'd just remembered. Mr. Bryce's words recalled it, sir."

"Well—well," the detective frowned.

"They had some words, sir—last night."

The inspector and Johnson exchanged glances. "What about?" the latter continued.

"I didn't hear them myself," affirmed Porter, visibly ill at ease.

"Who did, then?" Johnson wanted to know.

"My wife, sir. I don't think it really amounted to anything. Mr. Gus was always a prime favorite of his uncle's. I told my wife—"

"Get her," snapped Bryce.

"Yes, sir."

Porter turned away and left the room.

Dean and I gave our attention to the figure on the bed. It was that of a man of about seventy, almost fragile of appearance.

The bed stood so as to face the windows, thus allowing a flood of light to play over the dead man's features, revealing the expression of horror which still clung about them.

Everything about the body and bed spoke of sudden death, accompanied by an unavailing struggle. One leg was drawn up so that the coverings were raised above it, the eyes were wide open, staring and glassy; the lips were drawn back.

The hands, both of which lay above the clothing of the bed, were clenched into tight fists, which had not relaxed after death had occurred. Under the chin, about the shrunken flesh of the neck, ran the purple marks of fingers, plain evidence of how the man had come to his end.

I turned to Dean.

"Smithson said murder and suicide," I remarked, "and this is the murder, clear enough. Wonder where the suicide is."

Bryce got out of his chair and spoke to Johnson.

"Wonder where that doctor is? He ought to be here by now."

I heard and butted in. "What do you want a doctor for?" I asked.

"For the other guy in the second room back," the inspector replied. "He ain't dead yet, though I reckon he's likely to be soon. Shot in the head. Appears to have done for the old boy and then tried to bump himself off. Hello! here's the woman."

Porter came back with his wife, the woman who had been at the door, and the officers gave their attention to her.

"Your husband," said Johnson, "tells me that you heard a quarrel between Mr. Conrad and his nephew Gustav. Tell me just what you heard."

The woman gave a quick glance around before she

answered, dropped into a chair, with her back to the corpse, and began twisting her hands.

"It wasn't much, sir," she began. "It was just before dinner. I came in to announce it, Porter being somewhere about the house, and, just as I come in I heard Mr. Conrad say something about its being final, and that Mr. Gustav could do as he said or he'd change his will. Then Mr. Gustav flared back that he would do as he pleased, and I rapped on the door and they both stopped talking, and when I opened the door Mr. Conrad was red in the face, and Mr. Gustav was very white, and that's all."

"You don't know what the trouble was about, do you?" the detective continued.

"I had an idea it might be about Mr. Gustav's young lady. Mr. Conrad didn't like her pa," Mrs. Porter admitted.

"Then you think your employer may have threatened to cut Mr. Gustav off if he didn't give up this girl?" said Johnson.

"He might have. I know Mr. Gustav expected to come into most of Mr. Conrad's money. Jim and I witnessed his last will."

Again Johnson and Bryce exchanged glances, and Dean grinned at me.

"Did you read that will—when you witnessed it?" said Bryce.

"No, sir—we didn't. Mr. Conrad just called us in and told us to sign the paper, and said it was his will."

"Humph! grunted Bryce. "That's a sample of the old retainer's confidence, Glace."

"Where was the will kept?" he asked, after a moment's thought.

"In the second drawer of the desk on this side," stated Porter promptly.

"Is it there now?"

"I don't know, sir. Shall I look and see?"

"No," refused Bryce, rising. "I'll do that myself."

He left the alcove and we heard him open the drawer in the desk. In a moment he was back with a folded paper in his hands, which he handed to Porter.

"Is that the will you signed?" he asked.

Porter took it and glanced at the signatures at the bottom, then handed it back to Bryce.

"Yes, sir. I am sure that it is," he replied.

The inspector nodded and retired to replace the paper in its drawer. He came back snapping his watch.

"I thought you said you telephoned for your family physician?" he addressed Porter again.

"So I did, sir. His house said he was out, but they would reach him and send him at once."

"Suppose you phone again and see if they got him," suggested Bryce.

Porter left the room, and the inspector walked over to the bed and stood looking down at the body. I spoke to him again.

"Wise me up," I invited.

Bryce smiled slightly.

"Not much necessary, I guess, Glace. We got a wire from this man Porter a little time ago that his employer was dead and the nephew shot and unconscious, with a gun lyin' by his side on the bed. We come up an' found things just about like that. The fellow's story is that when he come in to wake Conrad this morning he found him dead, and on going to the nephew's room to report he found him apparently the same way, but on lookin' closer seen that he was breathin'. So far as we can find out, nothin' was taken, so that it ain't a robbery job, an' you boys heard the rest an' can see how it looks."

"The clock's stopped!" said Mrs. Porter in a voice of shrill excitement.

We turned toward her and beheld her slipped half off her chair.

For a moment I thought her fainting, then realized that she was half bending, half stooping to look under the bed on which the body lay.

In a moment both Dean and I darted around the foot of the bed and stooped over the fallen timepiece. It was an ordinary bedside table clock, and had evidently fallen from a small stand near the right hand side of the bed.

Probably it had been displaced during Conrad's futile struggle with his assassin. Now it lay upon its back, silent, the motionless hands of its face pointing to the accusing hour of two thirty-seven.

I picked it up and handed it across to Bryce.

"Here is a record of the time of the murder," I remarked.

Johnson hurried up and, together with the inspector, examined the clock. After a moment they both nodded, and Bryce made a note of the hour indicated by the hands.

"That fixes it," he declared. "It was knocked off and the jar stopped it, and the murderer forgot to pick it up, or never noticed. If that doctor ever gets here we'll see how he estimates the time Conrad has been dead."

He turned to Porter.

"Do you know if this was running last night?"

The valet, who had just come in from the telephone, nodded.

"Yes, sir, it was. One of my duties was to wind it, and I remember doing so yesterday morning."

"How about the doctor?" asked Bryce.

"They got him, sir, and he's coming right up."

"By the way," continued the inspector, "did your master have any other relatives to whom he might have left his money?"

"He had another relative, but not one as he would have been likely to have left his money to," said Porter.

"How's that?" prompted Bryce.

"Why, sir, he had another nephew, the cousin of Mr. Gustav, a young man by the name of George Mallet, sir. But he wasn't in good with Mr. Conrad, inspector. Mr. Conrad didn't like the way he was living, you see, sir."

"You don't mean George Mallet, the broker?" interrupted Johnson.

"Yes, sir, that's the man, sir. He was Mr. Conrad's sister's child. Mr. Conrad gave him his start in the business a number of years ago."

Johnson whistled and swung around to Bryce.

"Maybe we'd better telephone to Mallet and get him up here," he suggested. "You do it, or shall I?"

Bryce rose.

"I'll do it," said he.

Johnson nodded.

"Tell him we want him at once," he addressed Porter again. "That's all at present. You and your wife can go now. Stay around where we can find you, if we want anything."

"Yes, sir. Come on Annie."

Porter and his wife left the room. We could hear Bryce at the phone. Johnson smiled a thin-lipped smile and lighted a cigar, leaning back in his chair. The two patrolmen had found seats in a wide window, perching upon the sill.

Outside the morning sunshine made all the world bright, and a soft air fanned in through the window the policemen had opened. The smoke of Johnson's cigar curled thin and blue toward the ceiling.

On the bed lay the dead man, Dean hovering at his side, his sharp eyes searching every inch of the surface of pillows and counterpane, now and then dropping to the floor.

"I don't know but I agree with our friend, the deceased," Johnson began, after a moment, gesturing with his cigar. "This Mallet is reputed a rather swift guy. He's been mixed up in some pretty shady transactions and been in several scrapes with women. There's a stripe of yellow in that chap, but he sure is a shrewd money-getter. At that he's more beast than man, from what I can learn. I had to run him in once for beating up a poor girl he got his clutches on. I saw that he squared it, too. 'Course he was drunk, but a gent's a gent, drunk or sober, and George Mallet ain't no gent."

"Too bad he didn't trade places with his cousin and blow off his top piece," said Dean from across the bed.

Johnson shook his head.

"No chance. This was an inside job. I suppose Gus thought he'd fix the old boy before he could switch names in the will, and then after he'd done it he couldn't face it out. Sometimes a feller will kill on an impulse like that, an' then go clean offen his nut after it's too late. So Gus takes a shot at himself, somewheres around three o'clock."

"Funny nobody heard the shot," commented Dean.

"Not necessarily," returned Johnson. "I suppose this Porter an' his wife sleeps in the back, an' this is a well-built house, an' they wasn't expectin' anything, anyway."

Bryce came back into the room.

"Got him," he announced. "He seemed to be pretty completely surprised. Said he'd come up right away, soon's he could call his car. I buzzed him a bit about his whereabouts last night, just to see what he'd say, and his talk was straight as far as I can see.

"He gave a supper in his rooms last night, an' the bunch didn't totter until one this morning. Then he went to bed, and when I called him, his man had to go and wake him up before I could talk to him. I had a talk with the man first, and he tells me he put Mallet to bed himself. Put him to bed is right, too, because he was pretty well saturated before the crowd he was entertaining broke up. Here, Dean, what in thunder are you doing?"

We all turned toward the bed where Dean had been standing.

I saw at a glance that while the sly fox had been keeping Johnson talking and all of us interested in the detective's remarks, he had been quietly putting something over on his own account.

I have stated that Conrad's hands were clenched firmly in his death struggles, and upon this point Jimmy had evidently fastened finally in his own mind.

Very carefully and slowly he had been unclenching those hands, straightening them out one finger at a time.

Now, as Bryce, Johnson, and I sprang to our feet and turned toward him, he had succeeded in completely opening the right hand.

Caught, he merely glanced up and grinned. "Gathering hairs," he remarked with complete nonchalance. "Come over here, you chaps."

There was small need to call us.

We were at the bedside by the time he had ceased speaking, bending to look at the opened hand of the dead man.

Dean smiled and pointed to something which clung to the inner surface of the fingers.

Bryce uttered an exclamation, put out a hand, and carefully picked off half a dozen stiff, reddish-brown hairs, such as might come from a man's mustache!

We opened the other hand and found nothing, but while we were about it Dean moved aside, and the full light again struck upon the dead man's face.

This time I was the one to utter an exclamation and point to the purple marks of the strangling fingers.

For in that last glance I had seen something I had overlooked before!

On each side of the neck of the elder Conrad there was a sharply outlined indentation, in which the skin seemed to be slightly broken!

"They look like the marks of a sharp tooth," muttered Bryce, after he had made an examination.

"Or a long, sharp finger-nail!" I suggested.

2

SEMI DUAL TO THE RESCUE

A MOTOR PURRED up the drive and stopped.

From it hopped a pompous little man, of wide girth, and iron-gray hair, carrying a black surgical bag. Without hesitation this individual mounted the steps and gained the porch.

We realized that at last the belated physician had arrived.

A moment later the door of the outer room opened and Mrs. Porter showed the doctor in. We all made way as he crossed to the bed and bent above the corpse.

Myself, I dropped back beside the woman, outside the now half-open curtains of the alcove.

"I've been thinking," she said slowly, "as how maybe we ought to tell Mr. Gustav's sweetheart, young man."

It was half a statement, half a question. I treated it wholly as the latter.

"I think you had better," I decided. "It's a woman's job. Suppose you wait until we all go into Mr. Gustav's room, as we will now, and then telephone. They have a telephone, of course."

"Oh, yes, sir! If you think best I'll do it. Jim didn't know."

I nodded.

The doctor straightened from examining Conrad.

"He is quite dead," he announced. "I believe, however, that there is a wounded man here—Mr. Conrad's nephew. I will go to him."

"One moment, doctor," said Bryce. "How long has Mr. Conrad been dead?"

"At least six hours," returned the physician promptly. "Perhaps a trifle more, certainly not less."

He came out from the alcove room and turned toward my companion.

"Mr. Gustav in his own room, Mrs. Porter?" he began.

"Yes, Dr. Sommers," she answered, and lifted a corner of her apron to her eyes.

Without further comment the surgeon turned from the room where we stood and passed out of a door near the wall of the alcove. The rest of us trailed along.

We entered another room, furnished, but apparently unoccupied, with a single window opening on the side wall of the house. Crossing this, we passed another doorway and came to the second victim of the night's tragedy.

He was a young man of apparently about thirty, and lay upon his back diagonally across his bed.

His coat was off, and his collar had been removed and lay upon his dressing-table, the tie still in its fold, with a handsome pin thrust through it.

A dark stain of blood had formed on the counterpane of the bed and the edge of the pillow where his head rested. The wound from which it had come was just above the right eyebrow, and from it the blood had poured downward across his cheek.

The wound had evidently been made some time before,

as the blood had ceased flowing and was dried in brownish scales on his skin.

Aside from this gruesome condition the man was a good-looking, well-setup person, with brown hair and a brown mustache. He had a well-shaped head and a good mouth and chin.

I noticed that he was breathing slowly, with a somewhat stertorous sound, aside from which he gave no signs of fife.

Sommers lost no time in beginning his examination.

Calling for warm water he opened his bag and prepared some dressings, washed his hands carefully when the water was brought, and then set about cleansing the blood stains from about the wound.

In so doing he revealed the further fact that the skin surrounding the wound, extending as far down as the upper eyelid, was blackened and stained with powder. Clearly the weapon had been held close to the suicide's head.

Bryce was busying himself with the weapon itself while the physician worked.

When we came in it had lain on the bed, close by the man's hand. Seemingly he had dropped it there after its dreadful work was done. Bryce picked it up and broke it open.

Dean and I hung over his shoulder as he began examining the loads. They were all full except one. In one chamber there remained nothing save the empty shell.

Bryce smiled grimly, closed the revolver and dropped it into his pocket, turned back and watched the doctor at his work without a word. His silence was more eloquent than any words.

In fact, all the elements of the case seemed to speak for

themselves. Even the finger-nails of the wounded man, as I noticed, were long, and on the index finger trimmed into a decided point.

The surgeon finished running a bandage on his patient's head and laid him back on the bed. His fingers went to his pulse.

"What are his chances?" asked Bryce.

"It remains to be seen yet if he has any," replied the physician. "I shall telephone for an ambulance and have him removed to the hospital at once. I shall operate immediately when he arrives there."

"Can you tell what the bullet did, doctor?" I inquired.

Sommers shot me a glance and smiled.

"The ubiquitous newspaperman," he growled. "Well, I can authorize you to say this much: The bullet struck the right frontal bone, pierced its outer layer, fractured the inner table, producing a depression of the fragments, and probably lodged somewhere inside the skull itself. The patient is unconscious, but his recovery is purely problematical upon the amount of internal injury done."

"Have you known your patient long, doctor?"

"Ever since he was a baby. He must have been crazy to have done what it appears he did. I'll phone for the ambulance."

He closed his grip, picked it up, and turned to leave the room.

"Don't disturb him in any way till I return," he cautioned, and bustled out.

I heard him speak to some one in the next room. It was a morning of hurried arrivals it seemed.

Instantly the door he had left filled with another figure—

that of a tall man, little under six feet, brown haired, and wearing a brown mustache, expensively if somewhat flashily dressed. Johnson turned as he entered and nodded.

"Hello, Mallet," he remarked.

George Mallet returned the salutation curtly, entered the room, and came directly across to the bed, where he paused and stood looking down at the silent figure of his cousin.

He was slightly pale, but beyond that completely controlled. Presently, with a shake of the head, he turned away.

"Poor old Gus," he said. "Who'd have thought he'd have ended up like this?"

"When did you see your cousin last?" inquired Bryce.

"Day before yesterday," said Mallet. "Say, officer, if you don't mind, let's go into another room. I'm not very steady this morning after my supper last night."

The lot of us returned to the front room of the suite and found chairs. Sommers was just rising from the telephone, and as we seated ourselves he went back to his patient's side.

"Were you and young Conrad friendly?" asked the inspector as we settled ourselves.

"Quite," returned Mallet. "We were very good friends, indeed. Gus often came to my rooms or my place of business. I seldom came here, however, for the simple reason that our uncle did not approve of me."

"When did you see your uncle last?" Johnson put in suddenly.

Mallet frowned, leaned and dusted a shoe with one of his gray suede gloves and viewed the result before he replied.

"Oh, about a month ago," he said.

"Not last night."

Mallet's habitually almost sleepy-looking eyes widened.

"Is this an examination, Johnson?" he asked in turn. "If it is, I am sorry to inform you that in your own parlance 'you have nothing on me.' When Bryce called up and told me the news after trying to pump my servant, I told him the straight of my story. I was engaged with friends most of the night, and sound asleep when he called. I have not seen my uncle for at least a month."

"Did you know that your uncle had threatened to cut your cousin out of his will?"

"Lord, no!"

There was no mistaking the genuineness of Mallet's surprise.

Johnson nodded.

"Yes! Some trouble about a girl he was going with."

"Not Marian Burton?" cried Mallet.

"Don't know her name," said Johnson. "They had a run-in about it last evening. But I guess you weren't in on the know, all right. I just wanted to find out. What about the girl?"

"I'd rather not say much, Johnson," Mallet responded, after a moment's consideration. "She's a nice girl. Gus was very fond of her. So was I once, till she turned a cold shoulder my way. She was going to marry Gus. She's old John Burton's daughter, you know."

"Burton of the Fourth National Bank?"

"Yes."

"What did your uncle have against her? Burton's all right."

"It was against Burton that he held his grudge," said

Mallet. "In the old days they were business enemies. Uncle Anthony never forgave a grudge, as I ought to know. He disliked the girl because Burton was her father. I know that, but I didn't know that he and Gus had come to a show-down about it. Does Marian know what has happened?"

"Mrs. Porter telephoned to her, I believe," I informed.

"It'll break her all up. She thought an awful lot of Gus," said Mallet.

"Do you want to see your uncle's body?" proffered Johnson.

"Eh?"

Mallet started.

"Good Lord, no!" he went on. "If you chaps are done with me, I think I'll go talk to Porter."

He half rose.

"There'll be a lot of things to arrange while Gus is in the hospital or if he should die," he continued.

"Probably," rejoined Johnson. "By the way, Bryce, what did you do with that will?"

"Put it back in the drawer," replied the inspector.

"Let's take a look at it," suggested the detective. "Since we know Conrad threatened to change it, we ought to find out if he did. We'll examine it while Mr. Mallet is here."

Bryce took the will from the drawer, opened it, and spread it upon the top of the desk.

One and all we crowded about it and ran through its lines. I think they surprised us all, for they were not what we had been led to expect.

It is my desire that my nephew Gustav shall receive from my estate the sum of five thousand dollars, and that my beloved nephew George shall have all of the balance of my property, personal and real, which shall remain after this former bequest of five thousand dollars is paid.

It is my further desire that my nephew shall retain in his employ all of my former servants, and give to them such sums as he may deem fitting as remembrances from their old master. This is my last will and testament, given in my sane mind, and revokes and takes the place of anything heretofore written or in any way purporting to be my will.

Dean looked at me, his jaw hanging.

"Gad!" hissed Bryce, and swung on Johnson. "I guess we know now why Gustav croaked himself after doing for the old man. This drawer was open when I tried it this morning, the first time I had this out to show to Porter. I thought it funny, but now I guess I'm wise. After Gustav had strangled the old boy he came out and looked at the will and found he'd been just an hour or two too late, or may be some months, since this is the will Porter and his wife witnessed.

"Anyway, he finds he's killed the old man, and the will is already against him, and he couldn't stand up under the double shock. It would be fierce to do a thing like that and then find a joker like this played on you by fate. Guess he thought a lead pill was the easiest way out."

Mallet had picked up the will, dropped on one corner of the desk, and was running through the thing again. Now, as Bryce ceased speaking, he stood up, folded the paper and, stooping, replaced it in the drawer.

"Whether Gus lives or dies, I seem to be the chief heir," he remarked as he straightened and began drawing on his gloves. "As I remarked before, if I can be of no further service, I will be going. I expect a busy day at my office, and I am late now. You can find me there at any time, or at my rooms. My man can communicate with me if I am out. I shall inform the Porters that they are to stay on, and you or any one else can call upon me for anything needed for Gus's comfort, or for any information I can furnish. Now if that's all—"

"That's all," said Johnson gruffly.

"Good morning, gentlemen."

George Mallet walked out, stepped into his waiting motor, and was gone.

Johnson sat down and lighted another cigar.

"Well, what do you think of that?" he inquired. "Worst of it is the man's telling the truth. I was taking Dean's tip and tryin' him out to see if I could get a raise out of him. He didn't know nothin'. I wish to hell he did!"

"Oh, it's a clear case enough," rejoined Bryce. "This chap here went crazy over the row and his fear that the old man would cut him off, and took a chance. Don't see how he figured on getting away with it, but sometimes a fellow like that don't look that far ahead. Then, when he realized what he'd done, and found the will was already against him, he blew up and took the shortest road out. Well, what are we going to do now?"

"There doesn't seem to be much left to do," said Johnson. "You can go down and make your report, and I'll stick until the coroner gets here. Not but what his verdict is all ready for him now."

"Going?" suggested Jimmy, reaching for his hat on the desk.

I shook my head. "I want to see the girl," I explained.

"Girl? Oh, Miss Burton? What do you expect to get from her?"

"Human interest, if nothing else," I returned.

"But do you think she'll come?" parried Jimmy. "You're more of a ladies' man than I. Will a girl like that come here?"

"She will if she really loved Gus Conrad," I began, glanced out of the window and then back at Jimmy. "Furthermore, old man, if I'm not wrong, she is coming—now."

An electric brougham had just turned into the drive from the street and was rapidly nearing the house. Dean followed my eyes and nodded agreement.

"Guess I'll stick around," he decided, and walked closer to the window for a better view.

The brougham stopped beside the police car, and from it there descended two women, one evidently a maid, the other, as developed a few minutes later, Marian Burton herself.

I don't care what people say. They may rave about democracy and the equality of men, but there is something in blood, be it animal or human, which tells.

You can tell the thoroughbred at a glance, and you will meet men and women who impress you in the same subtle way. You can't tell what it is, but it is there, none the less—that indefinable something which speaks of breeding.

I noticed it in the woman who followed the maid from the electric motor that day. In every line of her she spoke of fine-drawn blood. There was something in the way she stepped down, something in the pallid control of the sensi-

tive face, which bespoke the woman of culture and refinement, evolved from carefully selected forebears.

As I stood beside Dean I quite agreed with his muttered
expression: "Gad, I don't wonder Gustav couldn't make up
his mind to give up—*that!*"

The two women turned to the porch steps and came
rapidly up them. A moment later I heard the sound of
Mrs. Porter's voice, and then the door opened and admitted them to the room where we were.

Bryce and Johnson had risen and observed, even as had
Dean and I; so that the girl faced a battery of eyes as she
passed the door. She gave us one glance and turned to
Mrs. Porter.

"Take me to him quickly," was all she said, but I knew
then that she truly loved the man she had come to see.

There was that air of possession, half truly female, half
wholly maternal, about her low-voiced intonation which
said more plainly than words: "He is mine and I am his."

Almost without pause she swept across the room, a slender figure in her tailored cleanness of line, restraining her
maid by a silent gesture, and followed Mrs. Porter through
the door.

Instantly Dean darted in pursuit, Johnson and I followed,
so that we came to the door of young Conrad's apartment
as the girl reached the bed.

Sommers glanced up as she came in, but made no
protest, as she passed him by. Rather he stood silent and
observed.

Marian Burton reached the side of her lover, bent above
him, lower and lower, until her fresh lips rested against
his. Her arms went out and encircled his shoulders. So

she stood for a long moment, as it seemed, raised her head slightly, and gazed into his unconscious face.

"Gus," she whispered. "Oh, my boy!"

I took Dean by the arm.

"Come away," I muttered. "This is no place for us, old pal. We're *de trop*."

It seemed like a sacrilege to me that we should crowd upon the woman's grief.

She turned at my words, and a slow curl of her lips expressed her contempt for us. I felt my face flush under her gray-blue eyes.

Without a word she turned away and spoke to Sommers for the first time.

"Doctor—what chance?"

The face, of the pompous little man softened, growing almost tender in a surprising way.

"Now, now, Marian—we'll do all we can. You really ought not to have come, my child."

She made an impatient gesture.

"With Gus like this?" she retorted, motioning to the form on the bed.

"Doctor," she went on, "how long have you known me? Ever since you welcomed me into the world, haven't you, old friend? Do you think you need to evade with me? I want the truth."

Man and woman looked into each other's eyes, then:

"He has a small chance, Marian, but a chance," said Sommers slowly.

She swept to his side and laid her hand on his arm.

"Doctor," she almost whispered, "do you remember how you used to give me anything I wanted when I was a child—how you couldn't refuse me anything—and called me your little tyrant? Doctor—I want Gustav's life more than I ever wanted anything in all the world. Save him for me—"

Johnson seized Dean and me by the arm and dragged us away.

"Ain't you guys got any feelin's at all?" he said gruffly. "I thought maybe I oughter hear what she had to say, but I don't want to now."

Johnson was human after all.

We went back to the other room where Bryce was talking to the maid and endeavoring to understand her Gaelic-English, more to kill time than for information, I suspected.

Presently Miss Burton, escorted by Sommers, came to the door of the room. The maid rose, but her mistress waved her to resume her seat, stood for a moment, and then addressed Johnson and Bryce.

"Dr. Sommers tells me that it is your belief that Mr. Conrad is a murderer and a suicide."

She spoke quietly enough, but I noticed that her hands clenched and unclenched as she talked.

Johnson, evidently ill at ease, replied: "The evidence certainly points that way, miss. Won't you sit down?"

She sank upon the edge of a chair.

"I do not particularly care how your evidence points," she rejoined. "I have known Mr. Gustav Conrad as boy and girl, man and woman, for a long time, and I want to tell you now—before you go any further in this matter—that he is incapable of such a deed."

"I'd like to think you right, miss," said Johnson. "Really

I would. But you see, it's like this: Mr. Conrad quarreled with his uncle, an' the old man made threats about his money. That was last night. This mornin' the uncle is dead, an' Mr. Conrad is lyin' half-dressed on a bed, with a gun by his hand, showin' one empty cartridge and four full ones, and a wound in his head."

"Which proves beyond doubt that he killed his uncle?" flashed the woman. "How? Could not a thief have entered and done these things and laid the gun by Gustav's hand?"

"You see," declared Johnson slowly, "Porter says the gun is Mr. Conrad's."

"Oh!"

Marian Burton bit her lips over the cry. Suddenly she rose and began to pace the room, her self-control visibly breaking. She lifted her hands and shook them clenched before her body.

"I won't believe it—Gus never did it, I am a woman and I feel it. There is some dreadful mistake being made herb."

She swung upon Johnson.

"You are a detective!" she cried. "Why don't you look below the surface—why do you always take things at their face value. You may be mistaken—I tell you you are. Oh, for God's sake, hunt—hunt—until you have found the man who did this thing!"

She paused and seemed to listen. Clear and distinct from the drive came the clang of the ambulance gong.

Marian Burton lifted her hands to her throat and sank back in her chair. Through the windows a long, white car appeared, the red cross blazing forth from its side.

It drew up and paused beside the "greyhound" of the police.

The phone on the desk began to ring. Bryce put out a hand and took it up, spoke into it, and turned to me.

"Glace, you're wanted on the phone."

I took the instrument from him and answered. A voice, rich, deep, vibrant of purpose, thrilled back to me over the wire.

"Gordon?"

I recognized the voice of Semi Dual!

3

THE STARS SPEAK

"YES," I RESPONDED.

Suddenly I felt again that strange thrill which always came to me when my friend intervened in a tangle of human life. The subconscious question rose on the instant and demanded what was to happen now.

How did he know I was here? Why was he calling me over Conrad's wire?

"I got your thought-flash this morning," he was speaking, "and called up Smithson. He told me all he knew, which was enough for a start. Now listen closely. Is there a doctor there?"

"Yes—Sommers," I gasped.

"Tell him that before he leaves he must call me up. Give him my secret number and have him call—be sure he does. Then, my friend, before you do anything else in this matter, come to me. Never mind Smithson—he understands."

I put the receiver back on the hook, fumbling it into its catch. I felt in that instant as though all the room were going slowly around.

Dimly I became conscious that men from the ambulance were passing through the room with a stretcher; that Marian Burton had risen and was standing pale and silent, watching; that Bryce and Johnson had drawn aside and were whispering together.

And over and above everything else was the knowledge that as I rushed here this morning and caught sight of the Urania and thought of Dual, my thoughts had flown straight to him and been sensed by his wonderfully sensitive brain.

Once before I had sent him such a message, in all unconsciousness, and had him respond to it, bringing support and rescue for one near to a woman very dear to me, who was in trouble.

Hence there was nothing in any way beyond my belief in his calling me now. He had caught my telepathic wave and, sensing it, had set about answering in his own peculiar fashion.

That he had done so was enough to prove to me that there was, as Marian Burton had suggested, something beneath the surface here. Dual, as I knew, never interfered unless there was danger of a miscarriage of justice, of the harming of the innocent, the escape of the guilty, and now—Dual was taking hold. Out of it all that one fact remained.

The stretcher came back with Gustav Conrad upon it. With it came Dr. Sommers. I stayed him by a word and gave him Semi Dual's message. He frowned.

"What does he want with me?" he snapped.

"I don't know," I told him. "He said I must see that you called up."

I gave him Dual's number, which was not listed in the public book.

"Humph!" he grunted, and walked to the desk and picked up the phone.

Presently he spoke into it and listened, and as he listened I saw amazement grow upon his ruddy little face.

"I'll do it—yes, sir, I'll do it," he stammered at length and hung up. "Most remarkable," he remarked as he turned toward the door. "Come, Marian, child, you had better go home now."

"I shall go to the hospital," she announced.

"Nonsense," he protested. "I'll let you know everything at once."

"I will be there when you are through," she persisted. "Don't delay, doctor. Marie and I will come on at once."

He gestured and passed out, entered his car and was off after the receding ambulance.

I approached the girl.

"Miss Burton," I began, despite the cold eyes she turned on me at the words, "I am Mr. Glace of the *Record*. Pardon me for interrupting you at this time, but I was impressed by your insistence on Mr. Conrad's innocence a little while ago. You saw me speak over the phone just now, and then send Dr. Sommers to call up a number. Will you believe me if I tell you that something came to me over the phone which makes me hope with you, that you may be right?"

The blue-gray eyes lost their coldness.

"I would believe any man who told me that," she said slowly, "I would worship any man who could prove its truth. Mr. Glace, just what do you mean?"

"Merely that I have a friend, a wonderful detective, who is now working on this matter, and that I look for results," I told her. "I thought you might like to know."

For a moment she made no answer, then:

"You are very kind, and I thank you. God help your friend and guide his brain aright."

She turned quickly away.

"Come, Marie!"

The electric brougham was gone.

The greyhound was gone with Bryce and the two patrol-men. Johnson remained waiting for the coroner who had not yet arrived. Dean and I bade him good-day and went down the steps of the front porch together and took a car for down-town.

"It's funny how women will believe in a fellow in the face of all sorts of evidence," commented Jimmy after we had seated ourselves.

"It's a blamed good thing for the fellows," I returned.

"That girl now believes her Gus is the straight Bayard, *sans reproche.* Gad, what a mess!"

"What if she should be right?" I inquired.

"Huh!" Jimmy turned and looked me over carefully. "The thing's clear enough, isn't it? Why, the old man even had some of the hairs from Gus's mustache in his hand, and the chap's finger-nails were long and sharp. Where's your vaunted sense of perception, Gordon? Don't let your 'human interest' blind your horse-sense."

"I don't intend to," I told him. "I change here. S'-long."

"Where you going?" he asked.

"To get an interview," I responded, ran out and dropped off.

A few minutes later I was on a car which passed the Urania Building *en route.* The last I saw of Jimmy was his nose flattened against the glass of the window, like a blunted interrogation point.

It was eleven o'clock by the clock in the foyer of the Urania when I entered its door and made my way back to the bronze grill of the cages.

I caught an express for the top and watched the floors flit by until the door clanged back on the twentieth floor.

There I left and rapidly mounted the great stairs to the roof and the garden of Dual.

It was bathed in the full flood of the late morning sun, warm, scented with the perfume of roses, blooming in their deep boxes of earth; quiet, peaceful, serene.

I looked up to the blue of the sun-lighted sky where a few fleecy clouds were floating. The tinkle of the fountain in the garden came in a soft damp ripple of sound. A pigeon on the tower cooed as it strutted on a cornice.

I thought of the scene of human passion, grief, and violence from which I had just come, and compared it with this restful seclusion which Dual had created for himself.

I set my foot upon the annunciator-plate and the chimes filled all the drowsy quiet with their soft cadence.

I crossed and went on up the central path toward the tower, where I knew Semi was waiting to take the threads of leading from my fingers and follow them surely and certainly to the end.

A little low sun-dial stood at one side of the path. By the shadow it was but a few minutes after eleven.

Strange characters, symbols of a well-nigh forgotten language, surrounded the outer rim of the dial.

Dual had once told me its translation: "Eternal justice,

eternal right, lie in the hand of God, from Whom comes light."

Some long-dead hand had carved them in the stone, but they were as true in this twentieth century as in the days when they were graven; and in them it seemed to me was expressed the whole atmosphere of the place in which Dual dwelt and worked, and of the man himself.

Semi Dual was the incarnate guardian of right—pure right—right for right's sake, content to sit and wait the appointed hour when justice should strike and that right be vindicated once more, calm in his spirit as his sun-kissed garden, terrible in his ruthless warfare with evil, as that justice for which he worked; content to do his best and leave the issue in the hand of God!

"If I can smooth a path in the slightest, shift or lighten a burden on some weary shoulder, bring a smile of hope to a tired face, a word of comfort to a sick heart, I shall have done my little part and shall not have lived in vain," he said to me once when I came to him.

Such was the man in the tower—Semi Dual.

I shook myself out of the mood, drew a long breath of the warm flower-scented air, and went on up the path.

Dual's servant, Henri, silent, soft-footed, met me at the door and motioned me to the inner room, where I knew Dual was waiting for me. I crossed, pushed open the door, and met his welcoming smile.

He was sitting beside his great desk, in his great chair of carved black oak.

The top of the desk was littered with papers, covered with a vast series of calculations far beyond my comprehension, yet which I knew from past experience were the means by which he determined those questions with which we had had to deal from time to time.

In reality they were the mathematical computations employed in astrology, for among his other accomplishments my strange friend was an adept at reading those planetary influences which all unconsciously to us mortals, sway the course-of our steps through life.

There had been a day when I scoffed at such things. Now I had come to believe in them through proof.

As Dual said, "One believes in anything which is capable of a scientific proof."

According to his usual custom of absolute comfort, which usually took the form of loose robes, Dual had on his flowing garments of white and purple and a pair of low slippers. So garbed in this somewhat exotic fashion, he sat at his ease in the airy room, high-lighted by a brilliant day.

He continued to smile slightly as I found a chair at the end of the desk nearest the door, but not until I was seated did he speak. Then:

"Don't say you were surprised at my calling you, Gordon. You think you were, but below all that you were not, and you'll know it some day, my friend."

"I'm of two minds about it right now," I admitted. "Still—just at first—when I heard your voice, it was a shock."

"Yet you know why?"

"Of course," I nodded. "This morning in the cab I thought of you, very deeply, in fact. You got the thought wave and started to hunt me up."

Dual smiled once more.

"Exactly. You and I are *en rapport*. I can reach you by telepathic suggestion, and equally I can receive your thoughts at times."

"I only waited to be sure Sommers called you, and speak to Miss Burton, and then I came here," I explained.

"Miss Burton?" said Semi Dual.

"The suicide's *fiancée*," replied.

Semi shook his head.

"Suicide is a nasty word," he declared. "The man who murders himself is on a par with the child who shirks a lesson. We are put into this world to learn spiritual truths, gain spiritual schooling. If we play 'hookey'—as you call it—we must be sent back again. One learns his lesson before he advances. That is the law. To accuse a man of suicide is to brand him a coward—which is cruel."

"Well, it's natural to suspect him, under the circumstances," I began.

"It is well not to suspect any one until there is proof against them," said Semi Dual.

"And that from a detective," I laughed.

Dual shot me a glance from his gray eyes.

"Gordon," he began, and laughed in turn, "have I taught you so little that you persist in calling me a detective? I detect *nothing*. I merely read what is written."

"Most of us can't read the writing," I retorted.

"Any one can read if he cares to learn," said Semi. "Come, we are wasting time in discussing what you already know to be true. Here."

He drew a sheet of paper from the array on his desk and handed it to me. I took it and glanced it over. It was covered with letters and words.

First came the name of Anthony Conrad, the letters

written vertically one below the other, down the page. Opposite each letter was placed a numeral, and at the bottom the total of them was written.

Across the sheet the name of Gustav Conrad was similarly treated. Thereafter followed a series of mathematical operations of which I could make neither head nor tail. I shook my head and handed it back.

Dual tossed it aside.

"You remember the murder of Matilda Greenig," he began speaking. "In that I used this same method at the beginning. It is really a rapid form of computation by which we may reach a general conclusion of the main life incidents of a person. I gained these names from Smithson, and set to work. After I had made this page I set up a general figure of the matter and I found out several things more.

"Now give me your detailed account of all which happened while you were on the ground. Unless I have made some error there will be several little things which will point to the truth, in your description, so be careful. It may be that even one word may show us the truth. Go on."

He leaned back in his chair and folded his hands. His eyes closed and he seemed literally to fall asleep.

But that I had seen him thus concentrate all his mental energies to one point before, I would have fancied that I was speaking to a slumbering brain.

Because of my former experience I knew that he focused all his energy upon the sense of hearing by shutting out everything else.

I began to relate the happenings of the morning, speaking distinctly, striving to recall each and every salient point and marshal them before the receptive mind of the silent man beside me.

And as I spoke I knew that he was receiving, arranging, and judging the facts as I gave them, and that upon my care there rested not only justice, perhaps, but perchance the happiness of Marian Burton as well.

When I had finished Dual opened his eyes and reached for a sheet of paper.

"How does this Mallet spell his name?" he inquired.

I shook my head.

"We can find out in the telephone directory," I suggested.

Dual nodded and tossed me the book. I found the name and gave him its spelling.

He wrote it down, vertically as he had written the other names, and began at once to put the numerical equivalent of each letter opposite, finished, and totaled them quickly.

Then, while I watched, he plunged into rapid calculation, reached its end, and threw the paper aside.

"You said that Gustav was shot just above the right eye?" he inquired.

I nodded.

"About the middle of the right eyebrow. The powder spattered the brow and eyelid."

"And he had removed his collar and tie, vest, and coat?"

"Yes, Dual."

"Now, about the older Conrad. I think you spoke of some indentations in the skin of his neck, like the marks of sharp finger-nails?"

"Yes."

"Did this Gustav have such nails?

"His index finger-nails were long and quite sharp," I

replied. "That was one thing which made Bryce and Johnson so sure that he was the murderer."

"And the marks on the neck—were they high up on the
throat or low down?" continued Dual.

"Low down; almost at the bottom of the neck."

Semi smiled.

"That's where they should have been," he remarked, as
though perfectly satisfied.

"Look here!" I cried. "The murderer must have seized
him from above, standing facing the foot of the bed, and
so gouged his nails into the base of his neck."

"Quite a natural deduction," said Semi, and made a
note on the last sheet he had written. "Now, did Johnson
or Bryce examine the rooms or premises for any other
evidence?"

"Not that I know of," I answered. "They hadn't been
there long when I arrived, and they did not afterward.
Everything pointed to its being a clear case, and I think
they accepted it as that. Why, the dead man even had some
hairs from Gustav's mustache in his clenched hands."

Dual turned from his desk and regarded me slowly.

"Do you remember a dead chauffeur who had red hairs
on the catch of his glove?" he inquired.

I sat up.

"Good Heavens!" I exclaimed. "You don't think it could
be another thing like that! The hairs were from some other
face! Dual, what do you mean?"

Semi shook his head.

"Now, about this will," he resumed his questions. "You
said the drawer in the desk was open when Bryce first
produced it for Porter's examination?"

"Yes. Bryce said he thought it was rather odd that it should have been."

"Bryce had a glimmer of common sense. Unfortunately it went out," smiled Semi. "Did you examine the will?"

"I read it over."

"And did you notice any evidences of its having been changed recently? Be careful, Gordon!"

I remained silent long enough to try and visualize the document as I had seen it lying upon the top of the desk. Finally I shook my head.

"I think not," I replied.

"And the writing in all parts of it, save the signatures, was the same?"

"As far as I could see, Dual."

"I used to marvel, and even yet I sometimes am awed, at the manner in which some men's names fit their personalities," Semi mused, without, as I could see, any relevance to the last question. "Parents all unconsciously select names whose letter combinations predicate the characters of their offspring, and the children live up to their names. Give me a man's name and I can tell you much of what will come to him in life. It has been said that a rose by any other name would smell as sweet. It would not—because it couldn't!

"It would have to mirror its name in itself. And so our names are literally the ghosts of ourselves, and the act of a dead man may be safely judged as to its truth by viewing the ghost of his name. Even our names are but added proof of the immortality of justice, which lies in the hand of God. You chose a fitting time to refresh your memory as to the motto on my sun-dial, my friend. Your mind was full of its meaning when you came in a bit ago."

"And you read it, of course," I remarked. "You make me feel as though my head were glass. But what has all this sermon on names to do with this case?"

"Merely that by scanning them aright one may tell whether Bryce and Johnson are right or wrong," said Dual.

"And—"

"Patience," smiled Semi. "The hour is not yet at hand. You mentioned two thirty-seven as the time the clock stopped, did you not?"

"Yes. Bryce made a note of it."

"Suppose," suggested Semi, "that you amuse yourself for a few minutes. Have a cigarette, and look out of the window, or take a stroll through the garden. When you've finished the cigarette come back. I shall be ready to tell you what you must do by that time."

He pulled out a drawer, threw me a box of cigarettes, and took a fresh sheet of paper from a pile by his hand. He glanced at the great clock in the corner.

"Twenty minutes to twelve. The sword of eternal justice shall be unsheathed at noon. Come back then."

I jammed the box of cigarettes into my pocket and left him, went out and to the far end of that garden and climbed upon a platform inside the parapet.

The day was warm and the glass of the dome above the garden was removed. I leaned on the parapet and looked over, lighted a cigarette and tossed the match outward.

It fell flaming downward, went out and dropped, dropped, growing fainter and fainter till it vanished.

The dull noon-roar came faintly up to my ears. A warm, sweet breath from the garden fanned about me. Back there in the tower Dual sat and worked.

As I left I had seen him take a pair of compasses and spin a circle on his fresh page, like a wheel.

The notion came to me as I leaned there and smoked that it was like the wheel of Fate to which our lives are bound. As that wheel turns we rise or fall, and some of us are crushed in its steady whirl.

And Dual had shown that he could read the destiny of a given soul from all the multitude of human atoms clinging to that wheel. I had seen him do it—had seen the fate he predicted come upon that soul of whom he spoke. Odd!

I glanced down again into the cañon of the street. It seemed still more odd that I—reporter on a modern daily, in a modern city—should be standing on the roof of its most modern building, yet surrounded by the atmosphere of the seers and Magi of olden time.

The wheel went round, had been going round all these years, and yet that knowledge, gained when the world was young, still lived. The wheel of Fate—of the Divine Potter, spinning down the grooves of Eternal Time, molding little clay marionettes, which laughed and wept and called themselves men. And as the wheel turned it meted out Eternal Justice, Eternal Right, and the hand of God turned the wheel.

I looked up into the blue of the heavens, where rode those other mysterious worlds we call planets, the units of influence on our mundane life, with which Dual wrought his strange computations as to what the wheel was going to do. Well, what was it going to do?

What time was it, anyway? I looked at my watch. It was two minutes to twelve. What had Dual found out about the wheel in the eighteen minutes since he drew its symbol on a sheet of white paper?

It was time I was going back.

I ground the stub of my second cigarette under my heel and turned again to the garden, walking along a side path to the main one and turning up it toward the tower.

A golden butterfly was waving its wings on the old dial as I passed, and rose and swept upward like a ray of yellow light.

I wondered if its destiny too were bound to the wheel.

Dual's small table, set for luncheon, with crisp lettuce sandwiches and fruit and milk, stood in the room as I entered. He waved me to it.

Sit down and eat before you work," he directed. "Myself I shall not join you, because time presses and I wish to talk. I have called up Johnson, and he will meet you at the Conrad residence in three-quarters of an hour—"

"At Conrad's! Why?" I exclaimed.

"I shall tell you while you eat," said Dual.

I seated myself and attacked the lunch. Dual, opposite me, began to speak.

"You will take a taxi and go to Conrad's. There you will meet Johnson. I got him just as he was leaving. He will get his lunch and return at once. I shall give you a tape measure and a magnifying glass when you return, and when you arrive Johnson and you will make a careful examination of the entire place, inside and out, and in all four rooms involved in the tragedy of last night. Be careful, find out everything, and call me here as soon as you are through. Also have Johnson get hold of Bryce and have him keep in touch so that we can get him when we want him. Tell him to tell Bryce to bring the revolver found with Conrad, and the hairs, if we shall ask him to come to us.

"You will have no trouble. I have told Johnson I believed that there was more to this than appeared, and you will find him ready and willing to cooperate with you. Now, when you have finished you can start."

"But what have you found out? What do you expect me to find?" I cried.

"Everything you can," said Semi. "I shall not hamper you by telling you anything specific. One more thing you must do. Get a sample of Gustav Conrad's writing. Porter can probably find you one; and tell Johnson to get hold of the will."

"The will!" I objected. "Won't Mallet protest our taking that?"

"Not if he doesn't know it," smiled Semi.

I grinned. "All right, I'm ready," I announced.

"And, Gordon," said my friend, "work carefully but as rapidly as you can. A great deal depends upon you."

"And you won't give me a single tip?" I complained.

Semi Dual smiled.

"If it will flick your interest," said he, "I will tell you this much. The stars do not lie in their statements, Gordon, and the stars say that *a double murder was intended last night.*"

4

FINGER-PRINTS

"YOU MEAN—" I gasped.

"That Gustav Conrad was shot before his uncle was strangled," Dual interrupted my stammered amazement.

"And that—"

"You have thirty minutes in which to get a cab, drive to the scene of the crime, meet Johnson, and begin your hunt for material evidence and clues. Here are the tape line and the glass."

He handed them to me.

"And the stars have told you who the real murderer is?" I questioned. Oh, surely, the wheel had moved since twenty minutes to twelve!

"The stars have told me," Dual admitted. "Will you now be about supporting their statement with material evidence for material man?"

My heart leaped. I had dogged him into the admission, and he never said he knew unless he did. I felt my pulses pounding to be off on the trail.

"Will I?" I gloated. "Well—just watch me."

"I shall," said Semi, with a faint smile.

I jammed on my hat and left the tower, passed through the garden, and ran down the stairs to the twentieth floor.

An express had just come up and was disgorging its passengers, and I scuttled in. Swiftly it dropped me back into the roar and surge of every-day life.

It was like waking from a quiet dream. Yet there remained with me those last few words of Dual. He knew already the person who had sought to destroy *two* lives last night.

Alone in his tower he had decided without ever seeing the scene of the crime. And if he said he knew, he did.

Furthermore, he had said that much depended upon me.

I took a long breath and resolved that I would not fail in the trust he was placing in me.

There was a taxi-stand near the building, and I made my way toward it without delay, found a disengaged cab, and sprang in. The chauffeur bent to his crank, leaped aboard, and we lurched away from the curb while I called my destination to him and received a nod of his head.

Now again I had time for reverie.

What, I wondered, did Dual expect me to find? What had the police overlooked? What did he mean by saying that one word might point to the truth of the case?

Yet, with all the questions which whirled through my brain, I could not doubt.

I remembered a time in the winter before when he had sent me to a presumably empty storeroom, even as he was now sending me to this house, and told me to find what I could.

I had gone, and picked up the thread which led straight to the solution of the mystery.

Would I to-day find something like that? Would Johnson be waiting for me? What did Dual mean by saying that we should examine both inside and outside of the four rooms involved in the crime?

I found myself trembling with a species of nervous excitement as the cab rushed along. I was fretted by an impatience to arrive and get to work, demonstrate and justify the faith Dual held in me. And again as before I felt that I was content to work blindly under his guiding hand because I was certain of what the end would be.

Eternal justice, eternal right. Dual was the priest of right and justice, and I was his acolyte—the lesser agent whom he used to bring his ends about.

The cab turned in at the drive and came to a stop at the door. I sprang out and, without exactly knowing why, told the man to drive back to the street and wait.

Then as he let in his clutch and turned his car I began to mount the porch-steps.

Johnson met me at the door, a somewhat quizzical grin upon his thin features.

"Just what is the program, Mr. Reporter?" he asked.

"We're going to play detective and try to detect some-thing," I gave him back.

"What, if you don't mind?" he jeered. "That friend of yours called me up this morning just before twelve, and insisted that I meet you here. I was just leaving, after the coroner had viewed the body and decided not to hold an inquest, as he agreed it was a clear case. But this friend of yours said you was comin' anyway, and I'd better stick around. Now, what sort of a bug have you and him got?"

"It isn't a bug, and we haven't got it yet, anyway," I retorted. "I came here to find it, and I want you to help me, that's all."

"All right, Glace. If you can find anything which will let young Conrad out I won't kick, and from what this Dual said I reckon that's his lay. Lead me to it, son."

"Come along," I told him, and passed on into the larger room.

There I took the glass from my pocket and began to examine windowsills and the floor. Not that I had any hopes of picking out any footprints, save those made during the morning, but I meant to let no chance escape.

Johnson perched on an end of the desk and watched me, grinning.

"You look like a stage detec', son," he jeered as I worked. "Dual thinks this an outside job?"

"I don't know what Dual thinks," I snapped back. "He's a habit of not telling everything he knows."

"Go ahead," said Johnson, and lighted a cigar.

"By the way," I suggested, "get Bryce on the phone and tell him to keep in touch. Tell him to have that gun and those hairs handy when we need them, and to be ready to bring them to us."

Johnson shot me a quick glance.

"Is that from you or Dual?" he inquired. "I was talkin' with Bryce after Dual called me up, and he says the chap's the real stuff. Does he want Bryce to stay close?"

I nodded.

Johnson reached for the phone. While he was talking I went on into the alcove where the body of Conrad had lain and continued my search.

There wasn't a thing I could find. Window-sills, floors, even the panes of the windows, I went over, but they showed nothing which I could call suspicious. Johnson sauntered in as I worked.

"I got Bryce, and he's on edge about the thing," he remarked. "He says I'd better git into the wagon before you boys crack the whip. Is there anything I can do?"

"Not yet," I responded. "I can't find anything here."

I rose and we both went into the unused room between the study of Conrad and Gustav's room. There again I got down and began to examine the floor.

It was close by the window of the end of the room that I found my first reward.

There, as I swept the carpet with my glass, I found something which sent my heart into my mouth. It was a faint outline in the nap of the piling—just the dim outline of a footprint.

But—the toe pointed inward and the outline was plainer at the heel than at the toe.

It was as though some one might have thrown a leg Across the sill and planted a foot on the carpet, rising through the casement, with his full weight thrown upon the heel of his shoe. I bent above it and scanned it through the glass.

There was no mistaking its import.

Some one had stepped there, and about its outline was a fine line of powdered soil, as though particles of earth had clung to the sole of the shoe.

I beckoned Johnson, and he came quickly to my side. I pointed, and he dropped to his knees beside me, glanced at the print, and a second later at me.

"Did anybody stand or sit here this morning?" I asked.

He shook his head.

"I don't think so," he considered.

"The flatties stayed in the room with Conrad, and neither Bryce nor I was here. Sommers might have sat here or stood by the window—where's the other foot?"

I nodded.

"Exactly! Then, Johnson, somebody stepped in through this window, and that somebody had damp soil on his foot, which has since dried. Well—"

"You're right! By the great guns, you're right!" he exclaimed in some excitement "Come on an' we'll see if we can find any more of these."

"Wait a minute," I checked him. "Let's measure this one now. You take notes."

I drew the tape and carefully took the measurements of the print, calling them to the detective, who wrote them down in a book.

"Now," I said as we finished, "we'll look for some more."

We searched, but without success.

There was that single print, pointing inward from the window, and then came the wide path of many other feet leading from door to door across the room, and on into the one where Gustav had lain.

Whatever may have been there earlier in the day was smudged and obliterated by the others which had tracked across them. Once or twice we thought we had found one similar to the first, but we could not be sure.

Johnson swore.

"What a bunch of darned fools we were not to look this morning!" he berated himself and Bryce. "But honest, Glace, the thing looked so clear—"

"That, as Miss Burton said, you never looked below the surface," I finished.

Johnson scowled and wagged his head.

"That's right," he admitted. "But how in time did Dual know the thing was here?"

"I don't know," I confessed, "but he must have had a reason. He never makes a statement unless he does."

"But he wasn't here," puzzled Johnson. "He was miles away, an' he didn't see anything at all, nor know anything at all, and yet—"

"He knew something, all right. You've got to admit that," I took him up.

"It looks that way," he grumbled. "But, good Lord—how?"

I had been thinking. Now, as he paused in confused question, I turned the subject back to the footprint.

"If a man came in through that window he must have laid hands on the sill, Johnson. Come over there and see if we can find any fingerprints."

He started to attention.

"Right you are," he snapped out and reached the window in a bound, bent, and began to scan the wood of the sill with a careful eye.

"Take the glass," I suggested, "and look about a foot inward from each end. He'd reach through, grasp the sill with his hands, and swing his leg between his arms. The footprint in about the middle of the sill if you'll look."

He nodded, took the glass without looking around, and continued his inspection.

"And here they are!" he cried out in sudden exultation.

"See? He did just what you said. Wait! I'll take a print of those. Take the glass."

He literally tossed it to me and reached into his pocket, from which he drew a small package of gray powder, dusting it lightly over the region where the hands of the unknown had rested.

Then with a small sheet of carbon-paper he pressed lightly and smoothly over the dusted outlines and lifted away a gray impress of the telltale marks.

He lifted a face which had grown thinner and more tense.

Glace," he remarked, "we're on the trail of something big and devilish, and we're going to run it down. If this goes like it looks, Gus Conrad was shot by the man who climbed in this window. You can bet I'm going to look below the surface from now on, all right, and I'll get this jasper if it takes ten years!"

Very carefully he put the paper away.

"I reckon we'd better go outside," he added.

We left the house and went into the grounds.

Then we walked around and came down the side, until we were below the window where the man must have entered. There we both went down in the grass and crept carefully toward the wall, scanning the earth for a sign, but not until we were directly beneath the window did we find it.

Then, just where the grass of the lawn ended and left a little bare patch of earth, close to the wall, we came upon another footprint, pressed deep into the damp earth.

Johnson pointed it out with a thin-lipped smile.

"There it is," he said quite calmly. "He stood there and

reached up and gripped the sill. He put all his weight on that foot when he stretched up, and he pressed it in deep. Go on and measure it, and see how it matches up."

I got out the tape, and with hands which trembled I laid it lengthwise and across the well-made print. One by one I gave the measurements to Johnson, and he wrote them down beneath the others from the print inside.

At the end he nodded in satisfaction.

"They tally," he announced. "And see here."

He pointed to a fresh scratch on a brick, broad and smudged, with a bit of mud sticking to it—such a mark as might be made by the toe of a shoe scraping against the wall.

We looked at it for fully a minute; then I turned away.

"Now," I announced, "I've got to see the Porters. Do you know where they are?"

"Somewhere at the back," said Johnson, following along.

We went back into the front hall and walked down it to a door at the rear, where I rapped. Footsteps came from the other side, and it was swung back by the old valet.

"Can you come in front for a few moments?" I requested, and he nodded and stepped into the hall.

Once in the front room, I asked him if there was any way in which I could obtain a sample of the younger Conrad's writing.

He viewed the request with some surprise.

"All the writing done of late was done by Mr. Gustav," he volunteered; "but I rather fancy it would not do to take any of them away, they being mostly business papers and the like."

"I only want a mere specimen," I explained. "Just a word or two."

He knit his brows for a moment.

"How would a small note-book or something like that do?" he asked.

"It would be the very thing," I replied.

Porter turned to Johnson.

"Will it be all right, sir, to let him have it? I was thinking maybe there might be a note-book in the coat-pocket of the suit Mr. Gus was wearing last night."

"Glace is acting with me," reassured Johnson. "If you cm dig up what he wants, get about it quick."

Porter nodded and walked through the door toward Guslav's room. Johnson and I followed.

The coat and vest of the wounded man still hung over the back of a chair, and Porter immediately began an examination of the pockets, presently withdrawing a small book bound in soft red leather, and extending it to me.

"That is a memorandum-book he always carried," he stated. "You can see he's writ his name on the front page himself."

I opened the book and verified his words.

"This is his own writing? You're sure?" I questioned.

"Oh, yes, sir!" declared Porter.

"I'm sure of it, sir."

"And, Porter," I continued, "do you know if the window in the next room was open or shut during last night?"

"It was open, sir. Mr. Conrad always had it open, winter and summer. He liked the air, sir, though he couldn't stand it direct. So he always had this here window open. That was why nobody slept in this room, sir."

"Then it would be easy for somebody to get in that way, Porter?"

"Some one to get in, sir!" cried the man. "Why, yes, sir. But— My Gawd, sir—you don't think that anybody did get in—not last night, sir? I asks your pardon, but just what do you mean by that?"

"We mean that some one came in that window and murdered your master, and tried to murder Mr. Gustav, and thought he had succeeded," said Johnson.

"Then"—Porter's hands were shaking and his lips writhed above the question—"then Mr. Gustav wouldn't have killed the master, sir?"

"No."

"Thank Gawd, sir!" stammered the servant. "I've been thinking—and thinking—and hoping, sir—but I couldn't see it. I'm glad as you can."

"We can't as yet," grinned Johnson; "but you can bet we will."

"Yes, sir," said Porter. "If that's all, sir, I'll be going and tell the wife. She's takin' it hard, sir,"

He shuffled out.

Things were moving. I had the sample of Gustav's writing, and we had two footprints and some finger-marks.

Once more, as before, Dual's wonderful insight into events was being justified as the wheel went round.

All of Johnson's skepticism had vanished. His thin face was eager, tense. There was a look of purpose in his eyes, which I knew would remain until he had run his quarry to earth. No doubt now but that he would continue to look deep below the surface, or rest until he had found the man whose feet and hands fitted those marks.

Like myself, he had witnessed the truth of Dual's methods, and, as in my own case, it was Dual's wonderful force back of him which was now urging him on; though I knew that he did not know it as did I.

As the servant's back vanished into the hall Johnson turned to me.

"Now, is there anything else we were to do?" he asked.

I nodded and I smiled. Even at that time it struck me as rather odd to have this member of the city detective bureau asking me what he should do next. Nevertheless, I did not hesitate about my reply.

"Dual said he wanted us to get hold of the will and be able to produce it when it was wanted."

"Mallet put it back in the drawer," said Johnson. "All we got to do is take it out, I guess."

He drew out the drawer, and lifted the document from it, tossing it upon the desk.

"I wonder why Mallet didn't take it with him, seeing that he's the major heir?"

I shook my head.

"Maybe he meant to come back after it later. He knows he can trust the Porters, and probably didn't want to appear too anxious about it this morning. I'm going to look at the thing again."

I opened it out and spread it upon the desk, pushing back some loose papers to make more room for it, and then I paused, for under the papers there was a spot.

It was nearly circular and slightly raised, higher in the middle than on the edges, and a dead chalky white. It wasn't very large—not bigger in circumference than a large pea—but on the black surface of the mission desk it showed in glaring contrast.

I put out my finger and touched it. It felt dry and yet brittle to the touch.

"See here, Johnson," I exclaimed, "what do you suppose this is?"

He bent down and eyed it, put out his finger and felt it, and finally raised his head.

"It looks like a flake of starch," he declared.

"Take your penknife and scrape it off and add it to the collection, whatever it is," I suggested. "We'll let Dual take a squint at it, anyway. Get it off without breaking, if you can."

Johnson attacked it with the small blade of his knife and, working gently, succeeded in scaling it off the wood. Then he slid it upon a piece of paper and folded it up with exceeding care.

That done we once more turned to the will, and I spread it out on the desk.

Together we read it over, but there seemed nothing in it which could give us a further clue, which shows how a person may look right at a thing and still never see it.

It almost seems at times to carry out the claims of those people who allege that nothing exists save thought, and that what we see is only what we think we see, and isn't there at all.

Just as I was on the point of folding up the will and slipping it into my pocket the light, striking across it revealed something I had overlooked.

I spread it out again, and got out the glass and focused

it on that part of the page where the light had struck. Then I saw it plainer, and I let out a yell.

For, close to the end of the line which the word George appeared, *there was the dim, almost imperceptible outline of a finger-print!*

I gave the glass to Johnson and pointed to the spot. He bent and peered at it as I had done.

"Do you see it?" I asked in some excitement.

He nodded and laid down the glass.

"It's there," he said almost in awe. "If I ever get into a case like this again, where I make so many blamed blunders in the same length of time, I'm going to cut the game and go to driving a milk-cart. The whole trouble was the thing looked so darned simple that it had me hypnotized. I just went to sleep and let anybody tell me anything was true. Well, at all events, this justifies us in taking the will along as evidence. Hand it over, son."

"But Dual wants it," I made protest.

"And he's going to get it!" flashed Johnson. "Good Lord, that fellow's all to the good! He can sit in a chair and beat me at my own game. I'm going to see him before this thing is over. He's got a method I'd like to get next to myself."

I handed over the will, as he desired, and smiled to myself.

I had an idea that Dual's method, as he called it, would take some "getting next" to that Johnson wouldn't be up to, but I didn't tell him just what I thought.

He had drawn the carbon-print he had made of the marks on the window-sill from his pocket, and was scowling at it in deep thought. Presently he put it away again.

"I won't say for sure till I am sure," he began speaking;

"but I've an idea that these marks and that on the will are the same."

"If that's so, the murderer opened this drawer last night and examined the will!" I exclaimed.

"It looks that way now," Johnson agreed.

It seemed to me that we must have accomplished what we had come for, and it was nearly two o'clock.

"Dual told the to call him up," I told Johnson and picked up the phone.

I gave Central Dual's private number, and in an instant he answered my call. I imagined him at the desk, waiting for the ring, ready to guide my course into the next stage of the chase, and I smiled to myself as his voice thrilled along the wire.

"All through, Gordon? Now, listen closely. You have found what you sought, of course? Next, you will go to the St. Mary's Hospital and inquire at the office for anything which Dr. Sommers may have left there for me. He promised to leave it, subject to my call, this morning. After that find a way to get a specimen of Mallet's writing. You have done such things before, and I am leaving it to you. Use your taxi and do not waste time. Also, while you are at the hospital you may as well see Miss Burton and tell her for me that I said her sweetheart is innocent of all wrong-doing, *and that he will live.*

"After you have done this you may go to the *Record* office and report to Smithson, and then come on here. Now, call Johnson to the phone."

5

A MYSTERIOUS ENVELOPE

I LEFT JOHNSON at the phone and went out and down to the street where my taxi still waited, entered it and told the driver to take me to St. Mary's Hospital where Sommers had sent Gustav Conrad for the operation, which it seemed, from Dual's words, was to save his life.

How like Dual was that message, I thought, as I rolled along.

Out of his busy scheming and planning to catch the cowardly assassin who had struck down two men the night before, he could yet find time to give a thought to the woman who lingered beside the bed of one of those men in anxiety and heart-sick fear.

Suffering always appealed to Semi Dual, and he would relieve it if he could.

The golden light of the spring day was dimming. Glancing out of the window I noticed that the clouds in the sky, light and fleecy at noon, had increased in number, and had grown darker in hue.

It looked as though we might be in for a spring rain. I drew back from the window and lighted a cigarette and smoked and thought over everything from the start.

I wondered what it was Dual expected me to get at the

hospital that could possibly bear on the case. Even as I asked myself the question we turned into the grounds of the hospital itself, and slowed down before the main door.

Again telling my man to wait, I went up the great steps to the door and rang the bell. Presently a Sister of Charity came shuffling along the tile floor in her billowing robes of black and set the door ajar.

To her I made known my wants, and with a wordless gesture she turned and led me back through the hall with its faint reek of drugs, its suggestion of nth degree cleanness, to the office, and waved me to enter.

Another sister, fair of skin, round of face, glanced up, and to her I preferred my request for a package or parcel or anything which Sommers may have left. I was vaguely indefinite, for I really didn't know what I had come for.

The sister smiled.

"There was a package left here by Dr. Sommers for a Mr. Dual." She pronounced it in syllables as though slightly puzzled. "Do you come from him?"

I nodded assent.

"Then I shall give it to you," she decided. "Wait just a moment, please."

She rose and passed into a room back of the office and presently returned with a large sealed envelope in her hand.

"This is the package," she said. "Dr. Sommers stated expressly that it was most important, and that some one would call."

She extended the envelope to me.

I took it and thanked her.

"And sister," I requested, "I believe there is a young lady here by the name of Burton, who is waiting until the young man upon whom Dr. Sommers operated to-day shall show signs of recovery or the reverse. Would it be possible for me to see her? I have a message for her."

"I will see," said the woman as she turned to a house phone by her side.

"I will speak to the nurse in charge of the men's surgical department," she explained, and spoke into the phone.

A moment later she turned back to me.

"Miss Burton is in the visitors' parlor on the second floor, at the extreme end of the building. If you will come I will show you the way."

Rising she came from behind the railing and I followed her out to the hall. Everything was very quiet, and I found myself walking on tiptoe as I followed her well-nigh silent flat-footed shuffle.

Every time I put down my heels they clicked and snapped in the quiet of the place, till I felt I must be disturbing the sick inmates. Accordingly I teetered along after my guide.

She took me to a bronze grating, rolled back the door and led me into an elevator which raised us to the next floor.

Then there was another long stretch of hallway with numbered doors on each side. The odor of drugs hung over the place and gripped my fancy.

I found myself wondering what suffering, what sorrow those numbered doors shut in what tragedies of human life. I decided then that I would make a poor member of a hospital force.

The pathos of it would get on my nerves.

But my guide didn't notice. She went steadily down the hall towards a circular room with glass walls at the far end.

Over her shoulder I could see that it was a sort of sun parlor, fitted with wicker tables and touches and lounging chairs, in one of which latter I could see the figure of a woman half reclining.

Even at that distance I could see the droop, the lassitude of tired control in the lines of the figure, and knew that she was the woman I had come to see.

The sister paused at the entrance to the room.

"A gentleman to see you, Miss Burton," she said.

Marian Burton came quickly to her feet and turned toward us.

"To see me—" she began, and catching sight of me, checked herself. "Oh! Mr.—"

"Glace," I supplied, advancing. "I saw you at the house this morning, you remember."

"Yes—I remember," she said slowly, then more quickly. "But why do you intrude on me here? If you wish an interview, I have nothing to say."

"Pardon me," I protested. "I do not wish an interview. In fact, my reason for intruding, as you call it, is to bring you a message."

Her entire face underwent a change.

"A message?" she repeated eagerly, "You have a message for me? Won't you sit down?"

I took a chair and she seated herself nervously upon the edge of another.

I noticed that she looked older, almost haggard, in the light from the western windows, and also that her hands

were trembling as she waited for me to speak. The day had
made ravages on her beyond my expectation.

She was finding it hard to wait.

"My message even, is contingent upon my coming to the
hospital to get something which Dr. Sommers left here for
me. But thinking that you would be here, it seemed a pity
not to see you—"

"Wait," she interrupted. "You say you came here to get
something which Dr. Sommers left for you? Was it something which has a bearing on this dreadful happening?"

"Yes. At least I think so. My friend, of whom I spoke to
you, sent me here to get it, and also told me to see you and
give you the message for him."

"Then," she leaned forward. "He has found out something. Mr. Glace, tell me quickly. What is it that he has
learned?"

She was fairly panting.

I almost began to fear that the reaction which would
follow my words might be too much for her to bear; that
she might collapse utterly when she heard what I had to
say.

Then I steadied myself, for I felt sure that if Semi had
told me to come he must have felt sure that only good
could come from my act. Still, I felt constrained to say a
word to make the girl who sat before me win back a little
of her old poise.

"You must not grow excited," I cautioned. "All I have to
say is good news. If you let go of yourself now it can do no
good, Miss Burton. You—"

"Oh," she rose. "Tell me—I know all those fulsome
things you would say to a girl whose soul is tortured by

fear. Can't you understand that it is my anxiety that is tearing down my control? If your news is good, for God's sake speak it!"

She stood tall and slender against the light from the glassed-in room, one hand on the back of the chair, the other at her breast.

Her eyes were wide, her lips slightly parted. She was breathing how, slowly and deep. There was nothing to do save tell her.

"My friend told me to find you and say to you, that your sweetheart is innocent of all wrong doing, and—that he will survive."

She didn't faint, but she closed her eyes and stood white and silent, with the hand on the chair back gripping the wood until its knuckles whitened and the finger tips purpled, and her figure swayed slightly.

Her lips came together and straightened into a pale line, and the hand against her side pressed inward over her heart. Suddenly the tension broke—she sank into the chair.

"Oh, my God!" She whispered the age-old cry of suffering life and began to weep.

I half rose to go to her, say something to stop the storm of sobs which shook her, and she gave me another surprise. As suddenly as they had come her sobs ceased.

She lowered her hands from her face and sat up on the chair and smiled. And it was as if that flood of tears had washed out much of the worry and terror from her face.

"Do you know," she said slowly, "that my brain feels loose. All day it has felt as though a tight hand were gripping it and crushing it in its circle. Now it feels free—easy."

She shook her head as though to test the truth of her words.

"Who is this friend of yours who sends me such a message, Mr. Glace? How can he know that Gustav will live?"

"His name is Semi Dual," I responded. "He is not a detective in the true sense, Miss Burton, but he is a man who is wonderfully well informed in criminology, and who has before this helped me in solving the problems of several crimes. He is peculiar in that he meets but few people, and will not take hold of a case unless he feels sure that a mistake in the laws of justice is being made.

"He must feel that the side he is working for is right before he will work, but when he feels that, nothing can stop him from laying the criminal by the heels. It was he who called me over the phone this morning, and later talked to the doctor."

"Semi Dual," she repeated. "That is a queer name. How did he know of the case in the first place? I thought you agreed with the police until you told me you hoped they were wrong."

I smiled.

"I can't tell you how he knew," I answered. "It was as much of a surprise to me when he called me as it was to you. But believe me, Miss Burton, Semi Dual has ways of finding out things which neither you nor I fully compre-hend, and which are still quite natural. And he wants to help you and Mr. Conrad in this master, and to see justice done."

"Tell him to spare no effort or expense," said the girl. "Anything he asks I will give if he can make his predictions come true. Is he a doctor, that he thinks Gustav will recover? Oh, tell me! Can't you see I am so anxious to know?"

"Semi Dual does not work for money," I informed her. "He is a man who has all he needs. He takes his reward in doing what he can to help those in trouble or threatened by injustice. He is not a doctor in the sense you mean, and yet he knows more of life forces than most of the physicians of the present day."

"You mean that he is acting in this in a purely disinterested way?"

"Exactly, Miss Burton, in so far as remuneration is concerned, but aside from that he is always interested in seeing right triumph."

"He must be a strange man," she mused. "And he thinks Gustav will live?"

"Knows, is a better word," I amended. "In all the time I have known him I have never had him say a thing like that unless it came true."

She turned her eyes fully upon me.

"Mr. Glace," said she, "do you believe in prayer?"

"Why—I—I—don't know," I stammered.

She smiled.

"It's more used by women than men, I suspect," she said lightly. Then the smile faded and she went on.

"All this dreadful day I have sat here or paced the floor, and I have prayed—prayed—for help. Now I believe that my prayer has been answered; that such a man as you describe, one of whom I never heard, has come to my assistance. Such things don't just—happen, Mr. Glace. They are ordained. Isn't it strange that Dr. Sommers didn't speak of this to me?"

"Sommers doesn't know Dual either," I explained; "I know he was surprised at what he was asked to do. I suppose he didn't want to excite any false hopes in you."

"Possibly," she accepted. "But he left the package for Mr. Dual?"

"Oh, yes. I have it now."

"And how long will it be before this friend of yours is ready to act, Mr. Glace?"

"I can't tell you. Miss Burton," I responded. "He will act when he is ready, and he never delays longer than necessary. He told me this noon that he knew who was the real assassin, and—"

"That he knew?" she fairly gasped.

"Yes."

"But how could he? Nobody knew at that time."

"He did, Miss Burton. He is only waiting now to gather necessary evidence before he accuses the man he believes to be guilty."

"But I don't understand—"

Her brows puckered into a frown.

"You see," I explained, "he is using me to collect this evidence. I have just come from the Conrad house, where Johnson, the detective, and I found enough to assure us that some one entered the house last night. Then I talked to Dual, and he told me to come here and get the package and see you and then find a way to get a sample of Mr. Mallet's handwriting. That will, I fancy, be the last thing he will require before he begins to act. I shall make a try to get it as soon as I leave here."

"But how will you get it?" she questioned.

"I don't just know," I confessed. "I'll have to find a way."

"Could I help?" she asked quickly.

"I don't really see how—" I began.

"Because," she went on, "I'd do anything—anything—to help this friend of yours—help Gus."

"If you care to tell me what you know about Mallet," I suggested. "Don't, if it will give you pain to talk; but it is always well to know something about a man you're about to interview, and I suppose I'll have to go to Mallet in person to get what I want."

"I'll tell you anything I know," she promised instantly. "Ask anything you like. I'll answer. The man deserves no protection from good women."

"What was the real reason for his break with his uncle?" I asked.

"His dissolute habits," Miss Burton replied promptly. "Mr. Anthony Conrad was a proud old man, proud of his name. He did everything for Mr. Mallet until he found that he was living an improper life, and then he still gave him a chance to change, but he would not. After that his uncle cut him from his will, as I understand."

"And yet as the will now reads it seems that he cut Gustav off and left the bulk of his fortune to Mallet."

"Really? Have you seen the will, Mr. Glace?"

"Yes, Miss Burton."

"That was my fault, I suppose," she said slowly. "Mr. Conrad did not like my father, and he was the sort of man who would visit the dislike of the father upon the children. Gus told me last night that he had threatened to do just that thing."

"Last night?" This time I was the one surprised. "You saw him last night?"

"Of course," said Miss Burton. "He was at the house until nearly midnight, when he left to go home. He told me of the trouble with his uncle over his engagement to me, and asked me if I would mind if he failed of his monetary expectations. He seemed very much depressed, and I kept him with me until late, trying to cheer him up."

"Pardon me," I said, for I realized that I was asking a delicate question, "but did he offer you your release from the engagement?"

Miss Burton flushed, then smiled.

"Yes," she made answer. "And I laughed at him and told him that his question was funny; that if he gave me up he would then get the money, and that if he didn't he would get me, and I asked him to choose for himself."

"I can guess his answer," I told her and bowed.

Her flush deepened, but there was a twinkle in her eyes.

"How did he seem when he left you?" I asked.

"We had reached an agreement," she said steadily. "He was to remain with his uncle if Mr. Anthony wished. If not, he was to seek other employment, and Mr. Conrad was to be allowed to do what he pleased about his money."

"Was Gustav friendly with Mallet?" I next questioned.

"On the surface, at least," she replied. "Really, I always felt that it was a mask with Mr. Mallet. I think that below it he hated his cousin, Mr. Glace. You see he felt that Gus had cut him out of a large sum of money, and—" She paused suddenly and bit her lips.

"And also out of your good graces, Miss Burton," I completed the sentence.

"How do you know?" she flashed.

"Mr. Mallet said so this morning," I explained.

"The beast!" said the girl. "He never was in my good graces, Mr. Glace. I always instinctively distrusted the man. Did you ever nearly step on a snake and feel your whole being draw together in a shrinking spasm? That was how I felt toward George Millet, though I'll admit he at one time tried to pose as a suitor of mine."

"Yet he posed as the friend of Mr. Gustav?"

"Yes. I warned Gus many a time of the man, but he only laughed at me."

"What of Mallet's business?"

"He is a broker, Mr. Glace."

"Yes, I know. But is his business solid—prosperous?"

"Oh!" Miss Burton paused and appeared to consider. Presently she raised her head and turned her eyes back to me. "I don't know much about such things, Mr. Glace; but I know that father refused him a loan some time ago. I overheard him tell mother that he had refused to make an extension on a note of Mr. Mallet's, or something like that, because he said he was 'in over his depths.' He also said something about a broker who played his own markets being a fool. Just what would that mean?"

"It would apparently mean that Mallet was needing money pretty badly," I rejoined, grinning. "I quite agree with your father about the speculating broker—they have a habit of going 'broke.' Do you know if he had borrowed much money?"

"I know Gus loaned him a good deal of his own patrimony at times," she responded. "Just last week Mallet was after him for more."

I nodded and rose. "On the whole," I remarked, "I think I had better be going down and see Mallet and try to get a sample of his writing."

"For Mr. Dual?" said the girl.

"Yes; of course."

"What does he want with it?"

"He has a habit of using such things to verify his other deductions," I informed her. "When he tells me to get a thing I just go and get it and ask no questions."

"Wait a minute," she said. "You said just now that you didn't know how you were going to get it. Would you have any objections to obtaining it by a woman's aid?"

"None in the least," I affirmed.

"Just what is the idea, please?"

"Sometimes a woman's strategy succeeds where a man's would take longer or fail," she responded. "Wait. She leaned forward in her chair and knit her brows in an effort at concentration. "Just a line or a word or two would do, would it?"

"Perfectly. Yes."

"Then if I could get him to write a short note—"

"It would be the very thing!"

She smiled and rose to her feet.

"Wait here. I am going to the office for some paper and pen and ink. I will return to you in a few moments." She hurried away down the hall.

I rose again and went to the glass side of the house and looked out. The sky had thickened still more. In fact, sky had thickened still more. There was little doubt that a storm was rising.

Suddenly I felt a desire to get away and accomplish this

last errand of mine and get to the office and back to Dual.
Then I nodded to myself. Once more in the old magical
way the road was smoothing itself before me.

I had come here to see this girl and get the package,
without any idea beyond that. I had even been disturbed
as to the manner in which I was going to get that specimen
from Mallet, and now here was this girl stepping forward
and suggesting the simple expedient of getting him to
answer something which she would write.

It was simpleness in itself. I wondered that I hadn't
thought of it myself. Yet, after all, it was more a woman's
method.

As she had said, feminine strategy would often succeed
where masculine methods might not. There would be nothing to excite any suspicion in Mallet's mind at receiving a
note from his cousin's *fiancée.* Then why should he hesitate
to reply?

And that reply would fall into my hands, and I would
take it to Dual. I wondered if Dual had suspected what
would happen when he told me to see Miss Burton.

No matter, the wheel was going around, and what would
happen would happen.

At least Dual knew what that happening would be. Why
should I worry? After all, I was but an agent who went
where I was sent and did what I was told to gain what I
went for.

Back of all of my work was the greater intelligence of
the man in the tower who directed me in all that I did. I
grinned as I stood.

As a child I had loved to read the "Arabian Nights."
Now the whimsical thought came to me that the relation

of Semi Dual and myself was that of the *Genie of the Lamp* and *Aladdin* reversed.

Dual was the Afrit, all right, with transcendent power, and I was the mortal, but instead of my telling my enslaved magician what to do and when, he was ordering me about. I could imagine Dual's quiet laugh when I should spring that on him in one of our friendly talks.

The click of the girl's returning footsteps turned me away from the window. She entered the sun-room with an envelope in her hand, which she extended to me.

"If you will deliver that to Mr. Mallet by messenger I believe it will gain you what you want," she predicted. "I am sure he will answer it, and you can have the boy bring the answer to you. And, oh, Mr. Glace, I do hope you succeed and that Air. Dual clears everything up quickly. It means such a lot to Gustav and me."

"We will succeed. Dual doesn't fail," I assured her. "I thank you immensely, for this note. I'd have never thought of this way, and it is so easy that it can't fail. Now I'm off."

Quite frankly she held out her hand. "Thank you so much for coming, and good luck," said she.

6

A DECOY LETTER

THE ENVELOPE WAS unsealed. I discovered it after I was back in the cab and speeding down-town, and I grinned to myself.

So Miss Burton had intended that I read what she had written? That being the case, I decided to avail myself of the opportunity to gain an insight into this sample of feminine strategy. I drew the folded page of hospital stationery out of the cover and opened it carefully. Then I read:

Mr. George Mallet,
   City.
Dear Sir:

You will perhaps be glad to learn that your cousin has a chance for his life. Dr. Sommers's operation was in every way successful. At the same time that I send you this I want to take the opportunity to advise you that I have arranged for two special nurses for attendance upon Mr. Conrad, night and day. I hope that you will not deem me overly officious in this, nor as intruding in any way upon your position as present head of the family; but, as you have not been at the hospital today, and I was present, the hospital has naturally referred matters to me. If convenient, could you arrange to meet me at my home, say this evening, for the purpose of discussing all necessary matters regarding your cousin's care?

Awaiting your reply,

Yours sincerely,

Marian Burton.

"Yours sincerely!" I chuckled.

Yes, she was! And yet it was just the thing to make a man like. Mallet seemed to be fall into the trap of writing a reply?

Would he call at her house? Certainly he would. The messenger would be told to wait for an answer, and he would get it. Only that sincerely was rather a joke-or, wait a minute.

Was it? Wasn't it feminine strategy? I rather thought that it was.

I folded up the note carefully and put it back in the envelope and sealed the flap. George Mallet would have no reason to suppose any eyes save his own had read its lines.

I put it in my pocket and glanced at my watch. It was after three. The wheel had been going around for over three hours, and it had developed a lot of things.

I leaned forward and tapped on the glass and signed my driver for greater speed, I wanted to get down-town and send the note to Mallet and then go and see Smithson.

Poor Smithson!

I could imagine his mental state, when Dual had so calmly kidnaped me and used me as his assistant. I wondered who had handled the story of the case for the afternoon edition.

Also, I wondered just what my city editor would say to

me when I did get back, and what Dual had said to him
when he talked with him that morning. I felt almost sorry
for my day's absence.

Say what you will, a reporter grows fond of his paper, and
I experienced a little qualm of regret to think that some
one else had handled the story, even though in the end it
would be myself who would close the tale.

We were getting down-town now, and I told my driver
to take me to a messenger station somewhere near the
Kernan Building, where Mallet had his offices.

A few minutes later he drew in to the curb in front
of a stairway leading down into a basement, where a
district-messenger station displayed its sign, promising
quick and reliable services.

Two or three boys were loafing at the head of the stairs,
but I paid no attention to these, brushed by them, and ran
down the steps into the room at the foot.

There I approached a railed-in space and spoke to a man
at the desk, who looked up at my approach.

"I want a dependable boy who can be relied upon to do
what he's told. It is important that he be quick and intel-
ligent."

I handed the local manager my card.

He glanced at it and tapped a bell twice. A moment
later a well-built youth in uniform came from a room still
farther in the rear and approached the desk.

"This boy will suit you, Mr. Glace," the manager declared.
"Ned, do what the gent tells you and look wise."

The youth came through a gate in the railing and I led
him to one side, drew the envelope which Marian Burton
had given me from my pocket, and handed it to him.

"Do you know the offices of George Mallet, the broker?"
I asked.

He nodded.

"Then take that to him and see him personally. Don't
give it to any one else. Wait for an answer and don't come
back without it. Come back here with it, no matter where
it is addressed. I'll be waiting for you here, and will pay you
for your run when you get back. The quicker you are the
bigger the price I'll stand for. Now, get a wiggle on!"

He grinned slightly, stuck the envelope in his pocket,
and went up the stairs two at a jump.

"He makes a good start, at any rate," I said to the
manager.

"Best boy we've got," he returned, and went back to his
reading of a paper-backed book.

There was a bench outside of the railing, and upon it lay
a rumpled paper. I sat down and picked it up and saw it
was an afternoon edition of the *Record*.

With sudden interest I slipped it back into its machine
folds and turned to the first page. I wanted to see who had
handled the story and what they had made of it.

MURDER AND SUICIDE!

There it was in heavy leads strung clear across the top
of the sheet. Below it in finer type, which dwindled in
size as their statements did in importance, followed the
subheadings:

ANTHONY CONRAD MURDERED BY
NEPHEW

Retired Broker Found Dead in His Mansion—Park
Drive Residence Scene of Awful Crime

Gustav Conrad, nephew of dead broker, found in his own
bedroom with bullet in brain. Evidently attempted suicide
after slaying his relative. Quarrel over rich man's will believed
to be motive for deed. Has not regained consciousness and
physicians say recovery improbable. Elements of mystery in
strange case.

There followed a somewhat lurid article, clearly a revamp
of the original theory of Bryce and Johnson, with a description of the condition of the bodies when found and a mass
of theorization as to the causes leading up to Conrad's
supposed murder of his uncle.

Mallet also had evidently been interviewed by some
one from the office, and was quoted at some length as to
his beliefs and disbeliefs regarding the case. I recognized
Davidson's touch in the main article, and it looked to me
as though Grant had been the man who got the stuff from
Mallet.

All in all it was not the sort of story I would have written, and I felt a fresh qualm of reportorial conscience as
I thought of how I had been chasing around town, while
Smithson and the office force struggled to get out something on the case.

I vowed that when it was settled the old *Record* would
have the best story I had ever written to pay for this, which
almost amounted in my eyes to a "beat."

Still as I thought I read on, and at the bottom I found a
ray of hope in the tail sentences:

We confidently look for new developments in this case. We
understand that there have Actually been new developments,
and as fast as they are obtainable the *Record* will see that they
are printed. Witch for our extra on the streets.

I tossed the paper aside and grinned.

I could imagine that if Jimmy Dean saw that he would
scent a large nigger in the newspaper woodpile. There had
been a question in his eyes when I left him on the car that
morning, and I knew that rather than think the *Record*
bluffing over their lame story, he would be on tenter hooks
of dismayed anxiety.

He would know that I had caught a lead he had not
landed, and would be looking for the *Dispatch* to be
"scooped" again. It was up to me to keep out of his way
until the matter was safely in hand.

Well—the office where I sat appeared pretty safe. Still,
I couldn't see why the boy didn't come back. He had been
gone fifteen minutes, and that appeared long enough to
me for him to have done the errand.

I picked the paper up again and read some more news.

Then I glanced at the clock and got up. I began to get
nervous. What if Mallet wasn't so easy to lead into a trap
as Marion Burton had thought? What if, after all, he only
gave a verbal answer and refused a written one and the boy
had to be satisfied with that?

It was getting late, and if I had to still try for the sample
of his writing, I was going to be in a pretty fix.

I looked up the stairs and watched for a pair of blue-clad
legs to appear at their top. But no blue-clad legs appeared.

Unable to remain inactive for longer, I went out and

climbed the stairs myself and looked down the street in the direction of the Kernan Building, but I could see no sign of my boy.

A hand fell on my arm and I turned with a start to face Tom Grant, one of the regular city men.

"Hello! Why, look who's here!" he greeted, grinning. "Got a job on the messenger force or what, Glace? Ain't you working for us any more?"

"Can that, Tommy!" I told him. "Comedy never was in your line, my son. What's the news?"

"I don't know the answer," said Grant. "Have you seen the *Record's* story? Say, isn't it a beaut'?"

"You ought to know, as you apparently had a hand in its fixing," I taunted. "But if you ask me, it certainly is."

"If you could have done any better with the scraps we had to work with, you'd have been a good one," complained Tommy. "Why, Davidson and I were like a boarding-house keeper, trying to make hash from last Sunday's roast, writing that story. After you left us up in the air and went off on a holiday we had to gather up any sort of crumb that fell from the police-table, and a nice mess we made!"

"You sure did, Tommy," I assented. "How did Smithson like the dose?"

"That's the funny part of the thing," said Grant. "Smithson ought to be frothing at the mouth, tearing his hair, and running amuck, and instead he's smoking a Havana perfecto and smiling like a cat that's just eaten the canary and washed it down with cream. Do you suppose he's knocked silly?"

"I'll go over and see after a while," I replied.

"You've got a nerve," grinned Grant. "It was all your fault."

"Listen, you silly chump!" I stopped him. "I'm working on this case and the 'old man' knows it. Also, he knows it's something big—a lot bigger than any of the printed stories have got it. We're going to put it over 'em all, Tommy! Now, beat it out of here! I'm waiting for some one, and I don't want a crowd attracted by your red hair. And, Tom, if you see Jimmy Dean invite him into a gin-shop and fill him up or lose him, or do something to keep him away from this part of town for half an hour. Let him sympathize with you over the *Record's* story or anything, only close-herd him for a while. Now, git!"

Grant's eyes had opened as I talked, and now he whistled.

"I'm wise," he almost whispered. "Just slip me a tip, Gordon. What's the answer? I won't spill!"

"Double murder," I whispered. "Now, will you go?"

"Yep! I'm gone. I ain't here no more. Oh, Lord"!" said Tommy, and turned down the street.

Still, that infernal boy had not come back. I had been watching the head of the stairs as I talked. I began to have a cold chill.

What if Mallet, instead of writing, had called Marian on the telephone? Neither one of us had thought of that. Well, maybe the girl would be quick-witted enough to send word that she was asleep or something. I had about decided to walk down toward the Kernan Building and watch for the boy there, when I saw Detective Johnson, walking beside the patrolman on the beat and chatting as he walked. I accosted him as he came up.

"Hello, Glace!" he said, dropping out of step with the roundsman. "What you cooling your heels down here for—eh?"

"Same to you and many of them," I came back.

Johnson grinned.

"I'm scouting," he explained.

"Scouting?"

"Yes. That friend Dual of yours didn't seem to be exactly satisfied with all the statements of our friend Mallet. He told me to do a little work about the gentleman's flat and see what I could pick up."

"And what *did* you pick up?" I queried.

"I found a back door opening off his apartments and leading direct to a tradesman's entrance," said Johnson slowly. "That makes two ways in which it would be possible for any one to get out of his flat."

"But it doesn't prove anything at that, Johnson."

"No. It merely settles a possibility. That seemed to be what was wanted." I considered the matter while we stood there.

I wondered just what Dual knew that he had sent Johnson on this investigation, and more than anything else I wondered where my messenger had gone.

"Where are you going now?" I asked at length.

"Nowhere," said Johnson. "I'm just waiting around. I've got a shadow on Mallet, and I'm just watching. Bryce'll be down here before long, and we've a date with your friend at five o'clock. I've an idea things will begin to move shortly after that from what he told me after you left."

A blue-clad figure was coming up the street, dodging in

and out among the pedestrians. I looked again to be sure, and at length I was certain that it was my boy.

I stepped back to the head of the stairs and met him as he came up.

"Sorry to have kept you, mister," he remarked as he drew a sealed envelope from his pocket and gave it to me, "but that guinea kept me an awful time. First I had to wait a long time 'fore I could see him at all, and then after I gave him the note you sent he read it over a couple of times and then he called up some number and had a rag-chew with the folks at the other end and couldn't seem to get the party he wanted. So after that he wrote an answer, and that's it."

I glanced at the envelope I held in my hand.

It was addressed to "Marian Burton" at St. Mary's Hospital. I nodded, and putting my hand into my pocket, drew out a bill and gave it to the boy.

Then I started for the curb where my taxi still waited, when Johnson interrupted.

"What have you got there?" he wanted to know.

"A sample of Mallet's handwriting," I told him, grinning, and hopped into the cab.

Johnson whistled. His face wore a very satisfied smile as the taxi lurched away from the curb.

At last I was on my way to Smithson!

The last step of my task had been taken and crowned with success. Again, as so many times before, the very fates themselves seemed to be working to assist Dual. And he was going to strike!

Johnson had said that he and Bryce had an appointment with Semi for five o'clock. That could mean but one thing to my mind. Dual had said that the sword of justice would be unsheathed at noon.

That was over four hours ago, and the wheel had been going around ever since. At five o'clock he would begin to close in on the guilty. Some time after that the sword was going to fall.

And Dual, sitting in his great room, high above the city, was calmly waiting for the appointed time.

That he knew it I never doubted. On that first case in which he had ever helped me he had set the time of a man's ending to the minute. I doubted them, but now I could no longer doubt. Always I had marveled at the man's wonderful impassivity.

He could look ahead and quietly say at such a time such a thing will happen. More, he could be sure that it would.

And yet, having learned of the fact, he could sit quietly by and give no evidence of excitement, apparently unmoved by the drama of destiny which he could see being played out.

Surely he was a fit priest for the temple of justice.

And with it all Dual was very human. Once or twice I had seen him moved deeply. In those moments the man's unveiled soul had shone forth, pure and tender, above that of any other I had ever seen.

He was human; he understood humanity so well—all its foibles and frailties, and with it all he was so grandly strong in himself. And because he understood so well he could sympathize so fully.

There had been times when I had seen his face glow almost with an inward light, and felt in that room in the tower like one treading the sanctuary of some pure temple, bathed in an atmosphere of pure love—of all the struggling atoms of mankind.

And the wheel of justice was going around.

It seemed to me that each turn was setting the stage for the final climax of the drama of human weakness and selfishness which had caused the tragedy in so many lives.

The light of the day was lessening with each minute. The clouds, light and fleecy at noon, were heavy and black and threatening.

A low rumble of thunder growled across the sky as we drew up in front of the *Record* and stopped, carrying an import of violence, a muttered threat of what was to come.

I left the cab and mounted the stairs to the local room, and passed through it toward the door of Smithson's room at the far end. It stood partially ajar, and I could see that he had switched on the electric above his desk. Its yellow glow shone about the crack of the door.

I crossed the room with a nod to one or two of the boys and tapped on the door.

"Come," snapped Smithson's voice.

I swung the door inward and entered and closed it until its latch clicked, turned and approached his desk.

He glanced up from under his green eye-shade, and a crooked smile twisted his face, but for once he did not expend any sarcasm upon my absence from the post to which he had assigned me. Instead, he reached for a pad of paper, and drawing it in front of him, waited for me to speak.

I sat down by the desk and laid my hat on its top, then I leaned forward and began.

I told him everything from the first to the last, and as

I spoke his pencil raced over page after page of the paper, and the keen interest in his thin face grew and deepened. Writing steadily, he reached into a drawer, found a cigar, thrust it blindly into his month, and struck a light to its end, and wrote on.

I was giving him the final story as it would appear in so far as I could. When the final denouement came it could be quickly set and added to this he was writing.

We had done such things before. At the end he threw down his pencil and nodded.

"It's all ours," he gloated. "I don't think one of the others have a line on it yet. It's a clean scoop, Glace—a clean scoop."

The crooked smile writhed across his lips.

"I don't think any of them will 'reach' Johnson or Bryce; they're working with me," I remarked. "I hated like sin to fall down to-day, but it's going to pay in the end."

Smithson leaned back in his chair and nodded.

"It's all right, son," said he. "You can imagine how much faith I've got in this Dual of yours from my stand to-day. But the man's too much for me. Thirty minutes after I called you this morning he called me and asked me where I'd sent you and what was up. I told him, and he asked for the names. I gave them to him, and in an hour he called me again and told me he wanted you for the day. I kicked. Then he asked me if I wanted a scoop. That got me and I fell for the thing, and here it is."

He tapped the written pages.

"He's going to make good again. But how does he do it? You didn't phone him this morning?"

"No." I shook my head. "But I did think about him. I guess—"

"That he caught your thoughts?" Smithson peered out from under his shade. "Glace, is there something in that telepathy stuff? D'ye mean this Dual, can do a thing like that?"

"He told me to-day that that was what made him call you up."

"I've heard of it, but I always thought it was a fake," said Smithson. "How does he pick your thoughts out of all the others floating around?"

"It's on the principle of the wireless telephone—a harmonizing sensitization of minds," I began.

"Look out," interrupted Smithson, grinning. "You'll choke yourself on a mouthful like that." But he nodded as if he understood what I had meant. "There may be something in it," he said after a moment. "Well, what are you going to do now?"

"I'm going to Dual's. Bryce and Johnson are to come there at five o'clock. Probably I will be able to send you the answer any time after that. I've got some things I must get to him first."

"Meaning the stuff Sommers left for you at the hospital?"

"That and some samples of handwriting."

"What was it Sommers left for you?" he wanted to know.

"I don't know, Smithson," I answered. "The envelope was sealed and I didn't open it."

"Think Dual would care if we did now?" he asked. His curiosity was plainly getting the better of him.

I paused and considered a moment. "Not if we were

careful of it," I finally decided, and reached for the envelope.

Smithson shoved aside the litter of papers on his desk and cleared a space, drawing his chair close to the desk.

With a paper-knife I slit the top of the cover and reached in. Whatever the contents were they were wrapped in blue paper, and drawing the packet out I laid it on the desk.

Turning back the blue wrapper I exposed a couple of folded pads of ordinary surgical gauze, which in turn I unwrapped. Then—

Smithson and I sat in total silence, staring into; each other's eyes across the corner of the desk.

Between its on the pads lay a slightly flattened bullet, some half dozen reddish brown hairs, *and a bit of powder-blackened skin!*

7

A STUDY IN HANDWRITING

STILL IN SILENCE I began wrapping up the two bits of surgical gauze and folded them back in the blue paper. Then I picked up the envelope.

The motion seemed to break the spell.

"What in time?" gasped Smithson, still looking into my eyes.

I shook my head, thrust the envelope into my pocket, and rose to my feet. I stretched out a hand for my hat.

"I think I'd better be going," I observed.

"And for Heaven's sake get the answer in quick!" begged Smithson. "We'll beat the town to-night. I'll have every-thing ready but the head and the tail."

I nodded and opened the door.

Outside I fairly ran through the local room, plunged at the stairs and out to my waiting cab. Its little clock had been eating up money all afternoon, but I knew now that nobody around the *Record* was going to kick when the bill came in.

"Urania, quick!" I called to my driver and yanked open the door.

We were off. The last lap of my chase lay before me. I was going back to Dual.

At the Urania I gave the chauffeur an order on the office and sent him away.

Then I turned into the great entrance and back to the cages, and presently I was walking from the shaft to the great stairs which led up to the abode of Dual.

I came out on the roof and paused a moment, arrested by the awful beauty of the scene.

The great tower rose in its white purity of outline against the darkened west. Back of it the clouds of the oncoming storm were banking and piling in mighty masses, from which came now and then the growl of the thunder.

Yet where I stood all was calm, even quiet with the strange hush which precedes the storm. The flowers and shrubs stood straight and silent in the fathering gloom.

But there was something in the air, a tense electric something which seemed to speak of coming terror, of a horror of earth and air, which created a vague mental discomfort, a dread of what would happen when the fury of the elements was let loose.

Those piling clouds seemed to me almost like the cohorts of vengeance gathering to overwhelm the guilty. And I was come to the place where justice was to be done, and that vengeance struck.

Minute by minute as the wheel turned the setting for the grim ending was evolved. Yonder was no longer the tower of a modern sky-scraper, but an ancient temple of justice, in which I was to behold the sword of that justice fall.

I grossed the annunciator-plate and the bells came thrilling across the dusk.

I passed up the path, and as I neared the little dial I glanced again at its circle. The sharp-pointed spear of steel with which Dual had replaced its former mark no longer cast its shadow across the carven surface.

It stood like a metal finger, pointing to the darkening sky.

The door of the tower stood ajar and I entered. The reception-room was deserted and I went on to the door of the inner room. As I neared it, it opened and Semi Dual himself waved me into the room.

I glanced at him in surprise. He had cast off the suit he had been wearing in the morning and now appeared clad from neck to ankles in a long, loose gown of tawny linen, with short sleeves ending at the elbows, below which his strong, sinewy arms were bare.

He looked like some savant of the Continent at work in his laboratory or clinic, and as I let my gaze sweep beyond him my surprise grew apace. The room itself carried out the appearance of Dual.

It had been completely changed since I left it at noon. Now it might well have passed for the work-room of some wealthy dabbler in the material sciences.

In one end, with its back to the windows, stood a huge camera, its bulls-eye trained upon the room, a large black drape hanging to its tripod. Beside it on a table was a flash-light apparatus and an extra holder.

The great desk had been cleared of books and papers, and its top covered with a slab of thick glass, upon which was arranged a series of bottles of reagents, test tubes in racks, graduated pipettes and droppers, an alcohol lamp, some strips and squares of metal, a test tube holder, and numerous other articles commonly found in the laboratory of a chemical work-shop.

The little table, which slid in through the wall, and had held my luncheon today, was also covered with glass and held a quantity of other apparatus, prominent among which was a large metal plate and some rubber tubing and rings some inch and a half in diameter.

To add to the ensemble, if anything were needed, Dual was smoking a cigarette, a thing he seldom did.

He noted my glance of surprise with a smile of amusement; then, as he did so often, answered the unvoiced question in my mind: "Why is all this?"

He waved his hand about the room.

"Because, Gordon, from now on practically all elements of the higher laws disappear from the case. From now on we deal with hard, cold, material facts, proven truths of science. The higher laws which serve to point the trail have served their purpose, and from now on until justice strikes material proof alone is required."

He crossed and sat down at his desk.

"Let me see what you have brought," he said.

I handed him the note-book from Conrad's pocket, the sealed note from Mallet, and the package from the hospital. Over the latter he raised an interrogative brow.

"Smithson wanted to see what was in it. I opened it," I explained.

Dual smiled.

"Was Smithson satisfied?" he inquired.

"He was only more mystified, and so was I," I answered.

"You'll understand later," said Semi, "and so will Smithson. Now, suppose you tell me what you have done since you left here. Bryce and Johnson and Mallet will be here after a bit, and I want your story first."

"Mallet!" I exclaimed. "Is Mallet coming here?"

"Bryce and Johnson are bringing him here," declared Semi. "Go on with your story."

As in the morning, so now I spoke to his concentrated mind.

I told it all: of the finding of the footprints and the smudge on the wall; of the spot of white on the desk and the finger-print on the wall; of my conversation with Marian Burton and what she had said of Mallet, and her writing of the note to him; of my trip down-town and the sending of the messenger, and even my going to Smithson.

At the end Dual nodded and opened his eyes.

"How high above the ground was the window through which the man entered?" he wanted to know.

"I should judge about five feet," I replied.

Again my friend nodded, reached out and picked up the little red notebook which Porter had given to me. Opening it, he put out his hand.

"Give me the magnifying glass," he required.

I passed it over and he bent above the written pages of the book, scanning the writing through the glass. As he bent that side of his face next to me was in shadow. It was as if I looked at his silhouette against the light from the great windows.

I sat and smoked and watched its pure outline—the strong, high brow; the eyes, deep set and fathomless of purpose; the well-shaped nose, and the firm line of the mouth and chin. Purpose, concentration, knowledge, spoke from every line of it as he bent above the pages of the book.

Presently he put it aside and took up the envelope Mallet had addressed to Miss Burton, opened it, and drew out its contents and spread the page before him upon the glass slab.

Once more he focused the lens upon it, tracing it over the lines, pausing now and then to make a notation on the margin, then going on. And I, who had seen him thus before, knew that, from the lines traced by the fingers of Mallet, he was reading the character of the man's soul.

I had seen some wonderful proofs of his ability as a chirographer. I had known him to allege that a man was a criminal upon such proof alone, and then support the claim by material evidence.

Now I sat and wondered what secrets he was wresting from the written words.

Presently he laid aside the glass and turned to me.

"Names," said he, "are wonderful things. Here we have the written signatures of two men, related by blood, showing largely the same characteristics in more or less degree, and yet each with its subtle difference, which stamps it with the individuality of the man who wrote it.

"Each one of them consists of letters, those little symbols by which we express our thoughts or ourselves. And yet each one of us, as he writes the same lines and curves, fastens upon them some portion of himself which makes them take a distinct personal quality and speaks of their origin.

"Before Bryce and Johnson come here with Mallet, let us see what these specimens of two men's writing have to say of the men. "Here"—he picked up the little red book—"is the personal writing of Gustav Conrad. His name appears on the first page. If you will notice, the writing is firm and strong and steady—the writing of a sane, well-balanced person in good health of body and mind.

Aside from that there is one pre-dominating characteristic which runs not only through the signature but through all the notations in the book. It is that the top of the 'a' and the top of the 'o' are seldom if ever completely closed. At times they appear so to the naked eye, but under the glass there is a gap.

"Furthermore, and with a marked bearing in this case, the loops of the letters which drop below the line, such as the 'g' or 'f' or 'y,' are unusually long. Now, a person who fails to close his letters at the top in this fashion is a person of generous proclivities, free of speech, mind and judgment, usually willing to forgive the faults of others, and slow to condemn.

"Found together with the long lower loops, it would denote an individual with a love for the beautiful in music, art, literature of the highest kind. Taken together with the general strength of the writing, it would denote a man of a high moral tone and type.

"On the other hand"—he laid down the book and picked up the note—"in this writing is exhibited a difference. Taken at first glance, the writings appear similar, as in fact they are, but with an inherent difference which may make their writers' actions entirely dissimilar in kind. Look at the 'o' in George and the 'a' in Mallet. Both of these appear barely closed at the top, but there is a difference.

"Where in the former name the letters are open, the downward stroke leaves the upward stroke in a straight line at an acute angle. In this we are considering there is actually the effect of a loop at the top of the up stroke, very slight, but evident under the glass.

"Also, in the tail of the 'g,' and of other similar letters, there is a difference in the length; those in this writing being proportionately shorter than those in the writing of Conrad. Thus, though similar to the naked eye, these subtle differences mirror a condition which may make a terrible difference in the histories of these two souls, might even lead one of them to heaven and the other one to hell.

"A man who writes as Mallet has written will, on the surface, perhaps resemble the other man whose writing we have here, but in all his acts and thoughts there will appear a sensuousness not apparent in the other. Where the one would be open, free, honest, the other may be expected to be close-mouthed, secretive, dishonest, if the opportunity offers safely. Fond of beauty, in a way, he will lean to its more material expression. He will wish the tangible thing, rather than its suggested essence. He will, in all likelihood, be selfish, cold, and cruel. In other words, this is the writing of the plausible criminal type."

He paused and then went on.

"Such, Gordon, my friend, are names. They are the astral images of ourselves, partaking of all our inherent qualities, expressing in their symbolism those things which we are, and rising at times like ghosts from a dead past to unveil our real selves and confound us. Every letter has an astral quality. Every word has a meaning. Every word we speak, every thought we think, lives as an item in the scale of universal activity as an element for or against us. Every act we do, every cause we set into operation, must under the law produce its effect, which will be good or bad, and leave its record on the tablets of the universe." Again he paused.

"And much study has given me the ability to read these invisible records of things which have been. It is a thing to hold with care. One may do good with it, or harm. But should he do harm he, too, must pay, as all must pay for the wrong he does."

He rose and walked to the great window and looked out.

"See," he said, pointing at the darkened sky, "nature herself is setting a fitting background for the final act in this play of human savagery. A foul crime was committed last night under cover of darkness, and it shall be atoned under a darkened sky. I told you that the sword of Justice would be unsheathed. Look!"

A sudden streak of lightning cut across the dark pall of the clouds.

"He has set a flaming sword," said Semi Dual, his voice ringing throughout the room. "Gordon, the sword is unsheathed and the sword shall fall. Life is of God; His to give and His to take away. It is universal and immortal. He who takes it must pay for the taking. Such is the law!"

He stood tall and straight against the light of the windows, and it seemed to me, in the shadows of the room, that his figure grew and spread as he spoke, until it assumed, the majesty of something heroic.

The deep tones of his voice caught and thrilled me, and swept me out of myself.

I made no answer, but sat and watched as he stood and gazed into the oncoming storm as if in its dark billows he caught a reflection of what was to be.

Abruptly he turned away and came back to the desk,

opened a drawer, and took out another cigarette and lighted it. Over its glowing tip he smiled at me.

"Such things as this affair affect me deeply at times," he said calmly. "Then I feel still, in spite of all I should have learned, the impulse to rush forth and cry from the house-tops those great truths which the world does not care to hear and which each soul must learn for itself. Now I shall again become your old friend Semi Dual."

I felt shaken still by the scene I had just passed through.

"Do you mean," I questioned, "that every thought and word and act which we form leaves a record of itself?"

"Thoughts, words, and actions are only different forms of vibration," said Semi. "Every vibration set into action must continue to act until it meets something to neutralize or polarize itself. Surely, you know that?"

"And why should our names compel us to be certain things?" I pressed.

"Do you remember," he asked, "what I once told you of astrology—how each planet in the earth's universe had a distinct quality? Gordon, every letter equally has a distinct quality which harmonizes with some one of the planetary bodies.

"Supposing a man has a name. Now, the sum of the letters in that name and the mean quality of their qualities will harmonize with the mean influence of certain planets. That man's name is the thing by which he is known, and he must vibrate in tune to its elemental parts and to their combined quality. This, in turn, will follow some definite ratio to the scale of planetary harmony with which it is keyed. The result must be to keep that man's astral self keyed to the same ratio. Do you see, my friend?"

"In a way," I told him. "And so if you were given a name which mirrored certain traits, and could learn which of the planetary influences were operating most strongly upon him at a certain time, you could predicate what his action might be."

"Exactly, my friend," said Semi Dual.

"And that is what you did?"

"Last night," he said slowly, "Mars, the planet of violence, war, bloodshed, was badly aspected toward a certain man in this city. Its influence predominated and overcame that of the other planets. Last night that man stole forth and killed an old man in his sleep and shot another man unawares."

"And you know that man?"

"I know," said Semi Dual. "And because I know I have done all I have done to-day. Once more I am the means to the end, the agent through whom the law will manifest itself, the chosen weapon. And yet mine is not a pleasant task, for I shall be compelled once more to tear aside the veil and leave a poor soul exposed in all its pitiful naked-ness of wrongdoing, with the brand of Cain across its brow.

"It is not pleasant, yet should I hold my hand a greater wrong would follow; an innocent man might be branded with another's crime in the eyes of man, and an innocent woman be cheated of her life's happiness. Therefore, I don the gown of the savant and gather about me the tools of his craft, and with these implements I shall apply the acid test to a human soul and prove it to be not gold, but dross."

"The proof then lies in purely material lines?" I questioned.

"Material proof for material man," said Semi Dual.

"But how," I asked in surprise, "can chemistry prove that Gustav was a victim of another's murderous impulses?"

"By proving that he could not have done what it was made to appear that he did do," replied Dual.

"Then the bit of skin from the wound in Gustav's head is part of the material for your tests?" I cried as the meaning struck me.

Dual smiled.

"You are right, Gordon," he admitted. "The crime was planned to make it appear that Gustav had killed his uncle and then made way with himself. But, as nearly always happens, the criminal made some mistakes. Furthermore, he overlooked or did not know of the strides which scientific criminology has recently made, or that chemistry has come to play a great part in the work of criminologists of late. In this case it will serve to tell the entire story of a crime."

"And the footprints, the fingermarks?" I added.

"Corroborative testimony," said Semi Dual.

"You may be interested," he went on, "to know that there is a fingerprint on the back of this note which you brought from Mallet. He probably made it when he folded the page to enclose it. It is hard for the average man nowadays to escape leaving those traces of his handling."

I was surprised, but then I had had no opportunity to examine the note. I shook my head and smiled.

"Still," I remarked, "I can't see how chemistry is going to solve this crime."

"You will," said Semi, "when the others get here."

"And will Conrad really recover?" I asked. "Sommers seemed to think he had a very slight chance."

"He will recover," Dual asserted confidently. "Furthermore, he will recover with his mental qualities unimpaired. Fortunately, he was shot on the right side of his brain."

"Why fortunately?" I asked in surprise.

"Because," said my friend, "that is what may be called the latent area of the brain of the average individual. Nature in her wonderful foresight has given most of us a vast reserve supply of tissue. We have two lungs, yet we can live with one; two eyes, yet we can see with one; two ears, and most of us use but one to any great extent.

"So with the brain. The average person uses but about one-half of his mental tissue, in the usual case the left half. Judging by his writing, Gustav was right-handed; and, therefore, the left half of his brain is the active half. Even though the bullet wounded the right half, if it did not cause serious hemorrhage his recovery should be perfect."

"And what makes you so sure he will live? Did you question the future as regards his fate?"

"Precisely, Gordon. After I had settled the major questions of the crime, and after you left here at noon, I set up a figure of Conrad's condition. He will recover if we are to believe the stars. Venus is so aspected in his figure that the very attitude of his sweetheart will exercise a holding, strengthening effect on his fate. By sending Miss Burton the message of hope I added to her ability to use that influence for his good."

I shook my head.

"It's wonderful!" I said. "You literally play on the scale of fate, as a virtuoso plays on the keys of his instrument. I'll warrant there isn't much latent tissue lying around inside your skull."

Dual smiled slightly.

"That is a truth and a secret of evolution," he replied. "I am inclined to believe that I still have sufficient unused cells to serve my purpose. I'd be loath to feel that I had reached the limits of my capacity for growth, and yet that is one advantage of rebirth into new lives—we gain new tissues commensurate with our evolution. Those who study deeply and learn gradually call into use more and more of their reserve tissues. However, when I compare what I know to what I desire to learn I am not at all dismayed at the thought."

"And," said I, "when I compare what you know and what I know I am utterly dismayed."

Dual actually laughed.

"That is a sincere compliment and a sign of hope for you in the future," he smiled.

He glanced at the clock in the corner and sobered.

"The hour is drawing near, Gordon, which shall see the wicked confounded. Every pulse-beat, every tick of the clock, is drawing from the little reserve of time which yet remains to them. Soon time shall be ended, its last second spent, and for them naught but eternity shall remain."

My eyes opened.

"What do you mean?" I gasped. "Will justice bring—"

"Justice?" said Semi Dual. "He who takes life must pay—with life. That is the law of man and of God. Why will not man learn to obey the law?"

"A life for a life and a tooth for a tooth and an eye for an eye—Mosaic doctrine," said I.

"Moses was educated by the Egyptian priesthood, at

that time the most advanced cult of students of life in the world," Dual took up my statement.

"Moses only preached the law of cause and effect—of retributive justice, if you like. Hark!"

The chimes rang out from the tower.

In the room the great clock was striking five. In the midst of it all a crash of thunder drowned the lesser sounds.

Dual rose and switched on the lights.

Voices sounded in the next room and a tap fell upon the door.

Semi crossed and set it wide, admitting Johnson, Bryce, and Mallet, and motioning them to seats.

I saw Bryce's eyes open.

The only time he had seen Dual he was wearing his blue-and-white robe. The inspector seemed surprised at the change to the working dress of the chemist. He drew his chair close to mine.

"What has he done with his bathrobe?" he whispered.

Dual's voice interrupted ere I could answer.

"Now, inspector, if you and Detective Johnson will give me the evidence you have we will be ready to begin."

Both men rose and began emptying their pockets. Bryce laid down the gun found beside Conrad and the paper in which he had wrapped the hairs taken from Anthony Conrad's clenched hands.

Johnson turned over the will, the finger tracings, the bit of dried, white substance from the desk, and the notes as to the size of the footprints.

Then the two officers resumed their seats.

Dual took the several articles and laid them with the things I had brought. Then, seating himself at the desk, he glanced at the measurements of the footprints, the tracing of the marks on the window-sill, the fingerprint on the will, turned and picked up Millet's note and scanned its back, nodded, and laid it down.

"And now we are ready to begin," he said.

Another crash of thunder rolled about us.

"Begin what?" asked Mallet when it had died away.

"The scientific demonstration of who intended the double murder at the Conrad house last night," said Semi Dual.

8

SEMI DUAL EXPLAINS

"DOUBLE MURDER?" REPEATED Mallet.

"Yes, Mr. Mallet."

"But I thought my cousin was supposed to have committed suicide? I don't think I understand—"

"I am going to endeavor to make you do so," Dual replied. "Now, if you gentlemen will listen closely I will begin to explain my theory of this case, which, instead of being a murder and suicide as at first stated, proves to be a cowardly and treacherous murder and an attempt at another, which probably failed only because of lack of knowledge on the part of the murderer."

"Do you mean that some one shot my cousin with his own gun?" inquired Mallet, somewhat ill at ease.

"Not at all," Dual returned. "I mean, however, that on the very face of the case your cousin could not have possibly shot himself."

He picked up Conrad's gun and handed it to Bryce.

"Break that and take out all the loads," he directed. "Then hold the barrel to your nose."

Without remark the inspector complied.

"Can you smell fresh powder?" inquired Dual.

Bryce, sniffing, lowered the gun and looked him full in the face.

"No, I can't," he admitted in shame-faced accents. "No, Dual, I can't."

Dual waved him to give the gun to Johnson.

"And you, detective?" he asked.

Johnson shook his head. A dull red crept into his cheeks.

"Yet," said Dual, reaching for the revolver, "a weapon discharged less than twenty-four hours ago should show evidences of powder sediment, should it not? Now, to make sure, suppose we look further."

He took a small, stiff wire and wound some cotton about it and gently swabbed the barrel. It came out very slightly blackened and showing evidences of a slight quantity of oil.

Dual exhibited it and smiled.

"There is the first blunder of the assassin," he remarked. "He should have discharged the gun so as to have fouled its barrel and made it plain that it had been recently used."

"We ought to have thought of that, Bryce," declared Johnson.

"Shut up; we're going to school yet!" growled the inspector. "We're out of it. Let Dual talk."

Semi turned immediately to Bryce.

"Now, inspector," he requested, "look at the bullets which you removed from this revolver just now and tell me what sort of loads they are."

"That's easy," returned Bryce. "They're thirty-twos, ordinary centerfire, soft nose."

"Then they would fit any ordinary thirty-two caliber revolver?"

"Yes, Mr. Dual."

"It is a fact that standard caliber cartridges can be used in all standard weapons, is it not?" Semi continued.

"Yes."

"Now"—Semi picked up the bullet I hid brought from the hospital—"what sort of a bullet is that, inspector?"

Bryce took it and opened his eyes as he turned it in his hand.

"It's a thirty-two, steel-jacketed ball, Dual."

"Yet that is the bullet which Sommers dug out of Gustav Conrad's brain, inspector."

Bryce and Johnson both nodded.

"Now," Dual went on, "look at the mark on the cartridges you hold and tell me what make they are."

"They're Remingtons," announced Bryce.

"And"—Dual took up the revolver and broke it, displaying the back of the empty shell—"this is a Remington, too; only those you have held soft-nosed slugs and this one contained the bullet I just handed to you. Now is it probable that a man contemplating suicide would load his weapon with four soft-nosed bullets and one steel bullet, and then carefully select the latter to fire into his brain?"

"It doesn't seem likely," admitted Johnson.

"In fact, isn't it true that he would have stood a better chance of killing himself at close range with the soft-nosed bullet?"

"Yes, it is," said Bryce.

Dual nodded and laid down the gun.

"All this," he resumed, "is merely leading up to the establishment of a doubt as to the wound's having been self-inflicted. It is necessary to prove the suicide theory untenable before we can confidently declare that murder was attempted, and that is what I am now trying to do.

"Supposing that suicide was not attempted, then we have but one other conclusion to fall back upon. After the murderer had shot Conrad he must have taken one of the loaded shells from Conrad's own gun and replaced it with the empty shell from his own, and then have laid the weapon beside Conrad's hand."

A match crackled in the room.

I glanced up at the sound. Mallet had drawn a cigar from his pocket and was lighting it.

"There is other evidence to support the contention that it was no suicide," Dual went on without noticing Mallet's action. "In all the annals of suicidal deaths there is not one case in which the party taking his own life with a firearm *inflicted the wound in the region of the eye!*

"The probable reason for this is that there is something unnerving even to one courting death, in the view of the barrel of the gun; and further, a horror of putting out the window of sight, which causes them to select some other equally effective point upon which to direct their fire.

"Yet I am told that the wound in Gustav Conrad's head is directly above the right eye, and that the lid of that eye was blackened with powder. Hence, all things considered, I am justified in stating that *Conrad did not commit suicide.*

"And if he did not commit suicide he did not kill his uncle, for that alone was the only logically existing motive which could have driven him to death at his own hands. Therefore, Gustav Conrad is *entirely innocent!*"

Dual paused and looked about the room and smiled.

"And so, gentlemen, as soon as I knew where the wound

was I knew equally that Conrad had been the victim of a dastardly plot. That alone sufficed to start me to searching for the man who crept upon him last night and shot him down with a revolver equipped with a Maxim silencer."

The cigar fell from Mallet's fingers.

I glanced at him and saw that his jaw had dropped, and that surprised horror sat upon his face.

"How," he began—"how do you know that a silencer was used?"

"There was no shot heard, for one thing," returned Dual. "We must remember that the uncle slept only a little way off in a connected suite. He was old, and probably a light sleeper. Had he heard the shot he would undoubtedly have risen and attempted to investigate, but the evidence shows that he was not disturbed, and that he was strangled in his bed. Probably the assassin's hands themselves roused him from sleep."

Mallet had picked up his cigar and now fumbled it into his mouth. He nodded.

"Aside from that," continued Dual, we can learn the same fact from the powder marks. Dr. Sommers described these to me. I have in the past made a careful study of the actions of firearms; I have been with armies in the field, and I have observed various gunshot wounds inflicted in every manner.

"A gun equipped with a silencer makes a peculiar mark, different from one not so provided. The marks on Conrad's forehead and eyelid are those which a weapon so equipped would produce. Yet there was no silencer on Conrad's gun. Here again the assassin's very precaution proves to furnish a clue to the fact that he was there."

"Granting that you have proved that there was a third party who did all this, how does it help to show who it may have been?" said Mallet as Dual paused.

"That will develop as we go along. It is the next step I shall consider, Mr. Mallet," responded Dual.

He reached out and picked up the note-book containing the measurements of the footprints which we had made.

"Briefly," he began again, "we may describe the murderer as a man slightly under six feet, say about five feet eleven inches in height, well built, wearing probably a number eight and a half or a nine glove, of medium complexion, with brown hair and a reddish brown mustache, and quite muscular. I deduce this description from several things.

"In the first place we have the measurements of two of his footprints, which indicate that he probably wears a number eight shoe. Figuring from averages this would give us his probable approximate height. This is also supported by the fact that he entered the house last night through an open window some five feet from the ground. He entered by reaching over the sill, gripping the inner ledge and raising himself by his hands until he could throw a leg over the sill, which we must admit is not the act of a man muscularly weak.

"His height is also further shown by the fact that the foot of the leg he threw ever the sill first struck the floor inside on the heel of the shoe. A smaller man would have reached for the floor with his toe. This, then, may be said to prove his being a tall man.

"Furthermore, when he reached through the window and seized the sill he naturally left the marks of his firmly gripping fingers on the wood. Those marks were found, and here"—he turned and picked up the carbon tracing of the marks Johnson had brought—"is their record taken today by the police."

"And the hairs prove his complexion!" fairly chortled Bryce. "Gad, Dual, this is the best thing I ever listened to. You make me feel like Dr. Watson."

Semi smiled slightly.

"The hairs found in the hands of the elder Conrad certainly prove that the murderer wore a reddish-brown mustache. The picture is plain. The man crept to the bed slowly, stealthily."

Dual's voice became low and monotonous.

"Can't you see him gentlemen—can't you see him with his hands already reddened with the blood of the man he has shot, come slipping into the alcove, pausing at the curtains, drawing them aside, peering at a weak old man in a bed, advancing on tiptoe, his hands out before him, groping for the thin old neck? Nearer and nearer, nearer and nearer, until he stands at the bedside.

"His hands go out, the fingers like reaching claws, they descend and clutch the old man's neck and press and press, their ends digging into the flesh until the nails on them cut the skin of the victim. The old man wakes, he struggles— to what avail—he is as a child in that strangling grip. He reaches up and claws at the cruel face above him and tears a few hairs from a reddish-brown mustache."

It was vivid, gripping, horrible, as his level tones told it. I felt myself chill and quiver.

I glanced at Johnson and Bryce. They sat leaning forward as though viewing the actual scene. I glanced at Mallet and found his eyes staring, his face bloodless, his forehead beaded with sweat which glistened in the light.

As Dual paused he sighed as one coming out from a heavy sleep.

"Could I have a glass of something?" he asked. "I'm a bit shaken by all this. That was horrible, Mr. Dual."

Dual pressed a button for Henri and directed him to serve Mallet with anything he might desire.

He called for whisky, and Henri left the room.

Semi turned to the desk and arranged two papers upon it.

"In order to make sure I had Sommers send me some of the hairs from Gustav Conrad's mustache," he resumed. "These are his."

He laid the hairs from the hospital on one of the sheets of paper and marked them.

"These," he went on, "are those from Anthony Conrad's hands."

He took those Bryce had brought and placed them on the other sheet.

"Viewed through a good glass you will see that the two hairs do not bear the same qualities, though there are some resemblances. However, there is a difference, and that is all we require to prove that they grew upon different lips. Any expert in the line will verify my statements. Thus we see that the hairs Anthony Conrad held in his dead hands were not such hairs as he could have drawn from Gustav's face. Have I made myself clear to you all?"

For the first time he turned his eyes fully upon Mallet.

Mallet nodded and made no other reply. Henri returned with his whisky and he tossed it off at a gulp.

"So now we know that there was a murderer, and that he was a man such as I have described, and we have an actual print of his fingers, and of his foot. It should be easy enough to trace that man from these things. However, it is well to be absolutely sure of all we do and say in a thing like this. While I do not feel that there can be any doubt about the deductions we have made—"

"I should say not! They're riveted!" exclaimed Bryce.

"That we have made," Semi resumed, "still it may be just as well to call in the material sciences to show that they are true, and prove beyond arty question or criticism that Gustav Conrad did not shoot himself. I have prepared to do that before we go any further in the matter of finding the criminal himself. Inspector, come over here by the desk and remove the loads from those cartridges you hold."

Bryce rose immediately, dragged a chair over to the desk and busied himself with digging the bullets out of the shells.

"Be careful not to spill the powder," cautioned Semi.

He himself drew the alcohol lamp to him and lighted its wick, then taking four small steel plates arranged them before himself upon the desk, slipping a sheet of white paper beneath each one.

Next he drew several bottles of reagents toward him and a rack of test tubes, picked up the gun from the desk and removed the discharged shell from its cylinder, setting it upon another sheet of paper open end up.

Meanwhile Bryce had succeeded in unloading the four shells and Dual poured the powder from each into a little pile beside one of the steel squares.

Next he took a thin broad-bladed knife and divided each

pile in two, lifting one portion upon each of the small steel plates, and turned back again to address us.

"It is a proven fact," he began, "that every powder varies in some slight degree from every other, and that the powder used in shells loaded with modern steel-jacketed projectiles is of a slightly different composition from that used in the ordinary shell. It is also a fact that modern chemistry as applied to criminology has found ways to detect those minor differences. Upon those two facts I am basing the further experiments and demonstrations of this crime of last night.

"It is to-day possible to decide positively whether a shell has been loaded with one of a variety of powders by making a chemical test of its remaining smoke settlings, or of its marks upon cloth or other substances, such as skin."

He put out his hand and unfolded the gauze pad which held the trimming from about Gustav Conrad's wound.

"I have here a bit of the blackened skin which Dr. Sommers saved for me when he operated upon Gustav Conrad at the hospital this afternoon. I expect to subject it to tests to show what sort of powder made the mark."

"I see," said Bryce, from his end of the desk, where he was now leaning, his eyes glued on Dual's hands. "An' if the powder mark on the skin matches with the test of that empty shell you've got there, then that's the ball what shot him, an' if those other powders is different, that supports your other idea, eh?"

"That is the salient feature," replied Dual.

Without more words he took up a small dropper, uncorked a vial and drew some of its contents into the glass tip. This he transferred to the empty shell from Conrad's gun, allowed it to stand for a moment and then poured its contents into a test tube.

To this he added water and shook the two together. From there on I lost track of the test.

Dual worked rapidly, without hesitation, and with perfect assurance. Finally, while we all watched, he held the tube over the alcohol lamp and warmed it gently.

Close on the heels of that he took the bit of powder-blackened skin and dropper it into a shallow porcelain dish, subjected it to reagents, and presently poured off the supernatant solution into another tube, which he treated as he had done the former, in the same assured way.

And while he worked we watched.

Bryce leaned forward on his end of the desk, his eyes wide with interest, pursing his heavy lips from time to time, half consciously nodding now and then over something he did not understand. Johnson, thin-lipped, lay back in his chair and smoked in silence and watched Dual's manipulations with complete patience.

Mallet smoked, fidgeted, finally rose and walked about the room, looked out of the window, stopped and read the framed "Noli Me Tangere," started slightly, and turned back to his chair. I found myself grinning at his instinctive start at the words of the motto:

> Beware all ye who would do me wrong, for the curse of an Almighty God shall rest Upon ye. Misfortune will be thine, through all thy life, until the uttermost farthing of thy indebtedness shall be paid. Take heed and curb thy greed lest it destroy thee.

I remembered the first time I had ever read the thing myself. It had given me a distinct shock, until Dual had explained its symbolic meaning and made plain to me that it was no threat, but a warning which it were well for all men to take in their dealings with other men, lest they wish to bring sorrow upon themselves by seeking to overreach or injure others.

To judge by Mallet's face as he came back to his seat, he was inclined to take the words as I had at first. He looked like a man who had sustained a mental shock, and he sighed in a long, unsteady expiration as he sank into the chair.

I became aware that Dual was holding the two tubes he had been working over toward Bryce and pointing.

"By Jove, they're the same!" the inspector cried. "This chemistry stuff is the goods, Johnson. The skin and the shell test up the same."

Dual nodded and set the tubes aside.

Removing the sheets of powder from beneath his plates, he folded up each and laid it aside. Then picking up several other small plates of steel, he held one over the first half pile of powder on the desk and touched it with a lighted taper.

A little puff of blue flame leaped from the lower plate and a thread of white smoke curled upward.

One by one he took other plates and set off the piles of powder on each plate, laying the smoked sections aside as each was made. The succession of tiny spurts of flame ran down the line of plates and died.

When it was ended Semi took the smoked plates and began again upon his series of powder tests.

One by one he subjected the powder-smoked plates to his reagents and washed them into his test tubes, applying his chemicals to each in turn and settling the question as to their constituents.

And as I watched him it came to me that he was literally examining into the spirit of each vanished pile of powder, testing its quality, judging it, weighing it, as ere long a greater intelligence than his might test and weigh the spirit of the one who was guilty of this crime.

Calm, impassive, exact in his motions and his judgment, he was appraising all which each smoke-stain stood for in the history of the case, bending all his faculties upon the one point of learning the truth and nothing more.

The golden apple in the hand of his great bronze Venus glowed with its encased light, and threw a mellow radiance about his head and shoulders as he sat holding the little tubes over the blue flame of the lamp, his eyes fastened upon their transparent contents, noting every degree of change.

So I could imagine the greater power subjecting the spirit of the man to his calm, impassive, purposeful scrutiny, when, as Dual said, its last second of time should be spent.

The last of the tests seemed to be finished. Dual had set his four tubes aside as if satisfied and once more turned from the desk.

"These four specimens react similarly to the same tests and differently from the first two," he stated. "That should indicate that the powder-marks upon Gustav's face and the powder in the shell of the jacketed bullet were of the same nature, and that the load in the-other shells was of a different quality-of powder; consequently, in view of the fact that his gun shows no sign of recent firing, that my deductions are correct and that he was shot as I have suggested."

"That's right," said Bryce. "We can be sure it was murder now, all right. That suicide business is all off after this. I never saw anything like it outside of a book. Mr. Dual, I take my hat off to you."

Dual glanced at the inspector and smiled slightly.

"Professional criminologists are doing this sort of thing every day in the year," he remarked. "The detection of crime is rapidly being put on a scientific basis. One trouble with the methods still employed in this country is the persistence in the habit of forming a theory of a crime and attempting to make the evidence fit, rather than in allowing the evidence to build up the theory. Still, I am gratified that you agree with what I have said."

"No logical mind could refuse the evidence," said Johnson.

"It remains, then, having established the fact that there was a murderer and gained his general description, to find the man himself," Dual resumed.

Johnson nodded.

"That's the one thing lacking," said he. "There may be a hundred men in town answering to the general description; the thing is to fasten it upon one man."

"Before I am done with my work I expect to be able to furnish you with his name," said Semi Dual.

"Then you're not through, Dual?" Johnson smiled, as though well pleased.

"Not nearly. So far I have merely established my preliminary fact, which is that Conrad was shot and could not have shot himself."

Mallet cleared his throat and straightened in his chair.

"And the motive," he remarked. "I'll admit that what you have done is wonderfully clever, Mr. Dual, and apparently indicates that my cousin was, as you say, attacked by some unknown party, but why? There was nothing taken from the house. Even his own personal jewelry was untouched. So far as I know, he had no bitter enemies. If it was a burglar whom Gustav may have surprised—why, after he had shot him, did he not finish his work, and why did he kill my uncle? What motive could he have had?"

"Just so." Dual allowed his eyes to sweep the man's face in a slow glance. "I am coming to the motive, Mr. Mallet."

9

THE GHOST OF A NAME

"MR. MALLET'S POINT is well taken," he went on. "A man does not go to a house, climb in a window, shoot down another man, arrange to make it appear that the man shot has attempted his own life, go to another room and strangle another man without a motive. We really must have a motive. And, because not even the most trivial action is ever performed except from cause, we shall find a motive back of this act."

"And you expect to give us the fellow's name and his motive," said Bryce. "If you can do that, we'll do the rest."

He grinned.

"I expect to give you the man," said Semi Dual, "provided you wish him when we are through with our work."

He spoke quietly, even lightly, and yet I felt myself tremble. For the second time that day I felt the terrible *double entendre* which might lurk in his words. Truly, he had not spoken idly when he said that the sword was going to fall.

He turned to the desk and took up the will and opened its folds.

"This," said he, "is the last will and testament of Anthony Conrad, regularly signed and witnessed. I shall read it to you."

"It is my desire that my nephew Gustav shall receive from my estate the sum of five thousand dollars, and that my beloved nephew George shall have all of the balance of my property, personal and real, which shall remain after this former bequest of five thousand dollars is paid. It is my further desire that my nephew shall retain in his employ all of my former servants, and give to them such sums as he may deem fitting as remembrances from their old master. This is my last will and testament, given in my sane mind, and revokes and takes the place of anything heretofore written or in any way purporting to be my will."

He laid down the parchment and took up the red note-book which I had obtained from Porter.

"In this," he resumed, "we have a sample of the writing of Gustav Conrad. It is his personal memorandum-book. But— The writing of the body of this will is different from the signature of Anthony Conrad, or of the signatures of the witnesses, who were James Porter and Annie Porter, Conrad's valet and his wife. And—the writing in the will is identical with the writing in the note-book. We already know that Gustav Conrad acted as the secretary of his uncle, and we may safely, accept the fact that Gustav's hand penned the main part of this will."

"But wait a minute, Dual," Bryce cut in. "Porter said this morning that Gus was the favorite of his uncle, and that last evening they had a run-in over Gus's girl, and the old man threatened to cut Gus off if he didn't shake the skirt. How in time would that jar Gus if he already knew he was only coming in for five thou of the old boy's money? Why, good Heavens! that was why we thought he'd sure croaked the old man!"

"I am aware of that, inspector," observed Dual. "However, I am speaking of facts, and you are dealing with theories, as ypu will admit."

"But—" Bryce was still inclined to protest.

"I will add that up to last night Gustav also believed himself to be his uncle's chief heir and that he spoke of the quarrel to Miss Burton," Dual proceeded.

"And yet he wrote that will?" Bryce blundered on to a finish.

"So the evidence shows, inspector. Also, if you will recall, when you went to get the will this morning, you found the drawer of the desk in which it was kept unlocked."

"Gad, yes!" cried Bryce.

"We started to look for a motive for the crime of last night," Dual resumed his deductions. "If Gustav Conrad wrote this will, and if Gustav Conrad up till last night believed that he was the chief heir, and if the will, when produced this morning, showed that he was not, but that another was, in fact, what are we to believe?"

"Somebody changed the will," blurted Bryce.

"Such a conclusion might be arrived at," agreed Dual. "It is even supported by the word 'beloved.' It is unlikely that that word would be placed anywhere except before the name of the chief recipient of the donor's will. Yet, if the names had been changed, the person who so changed them might have been unable to change the word or remove it and preserve the form of the will, in fact was so unable, so it was allowed to stand—later to damn by its proof."

His voice rose at the end of the sentence until it grew to a personal accusation in its tones.

"But, good Lord, look what that means!" cried Bryce, aghast.

"We are dealing with facts," returned Dual calmly. "Their implication must fall where it will."

I glanced again at Mallet.

He sat drawn together, his face pale, drawing on his cigar in short, spasmodic puffs, with long intervals between.

"Glace!" Dual's voice roused me. He had risen and was holding the will toward me. "Help me with this."

I took it and followed him toward the great camera near the windows. There he took the holder from the table and, removing its back, fitted the paper into its frame.

Next we moved the table in front of the bull's-eye of the camera and propped it securely.

Semi reached up and drew the heavy silk draperies before the window, shutting out the faint illumination; lifted the black drape from the tripod of the camera and spread it above his head, while he focused the instrument upon the will, then stepped back and began once more to speak.

"I am about to take a photograph of the will as it now stands, for two reasons. First, in case of question, we should have a copy of the will. Secondly, as I shall presently conduct certain experiments with it, it is doubly important to have this record for comparison, in order to prove that the words, presumably changed, are in the writing of another hand than that of Conrad, though one similar on the surface. In reality, however, they correspond to another specimen of writing which I have in my possession, as I shall shortly show you."

He paused and took a plate-holder, loaded and ready, and thrust it into the machine, then handed the flashlight frame to me.

"Johnson, step to the door and turn off the light-switch when I tell you."

He crossed and extinguished the lamp in the hand of Venus, and came back to the camera, picking up its bulb.

"Now, Johnson," he called.

Darkness fell upon the room, as the detective clicked the switch.

"Ready, Gordon," Dual's voice came to me.

I pressed the trigger of the flash.

With a sheet of vivid flame and a roar the apparatus exploded, and in that moment cold fear laid hold-of my heart. Under the intense glare I had let my eyes fall upon the spot where Mallet had been sitting.

It was empty!

Double darkness came down, blinding us for the instant, making it seem after the intense light that we were plunged into a void of black space, until one's head swirled slowly as the eyes refused their function from the effects of the terrific glare.

In that moment I heard a panting exclamation and the sound of a scuffle from somewhere in the room.

"Bryce!" called Johnson, in startled exhortation.

The struggling increased.

I heard Bryce stumble toward the sound, which I now located by the door into the outer room. And all the time I stood stupidly holding the flash-light in my hand.

"Glace, put on the lights."

Dual spoke calmly, almost without haste. The sound of his voice steadied me and spurred me to obedience.

I dropped the flash-light and stumbled and staggered blindly toward where I knew the switch to be, found it, and, with the panting of struggling men close by my side, pressed the button home.

The lights came on.

Blinking, I beheld Bryce and Johnson pinning Mallet against the wall at that end of the room, and realized that he had attempted to get away under cover of the moment when Dual had ordered the room darkened.

It amounted to confession, as he must have known.

Now he stood pale and almost collapsing in the grip of the two men.

Still gripping him tightly, they led him back to his chair. Dual surveyed it all without the flicker of a lid.

"Sit down and wait, Mallet," he said in quiet accents. "The time of your escape is not yet."

Johnson grinned in his prisoner's face.

That was *one* bad break, George," he said softly. "I have been waiting to get you, and I guess I have."

Mallet opened his lips.

"Whisky, for God's sake!" he gasped.

Dual nodded to the detective.

"You'll find my man in the next room, back," he suggested, and Johnson left the room.

We awaited his return in a silence broken only by the labored respiration of the half-fainting man.

It came hard and irregular, rising and falling across the

room in its nerve-racking sibilance, telling more truly than any words of a soul already in torment.

When Johnson returned with a glass of raw spirit Mallet seized it and drained it at a gulp and gave back the glass. "Thank you," he said.

Dual turned back to his desk.

"If my deductions are correct, the names in the will which were changed are Gustav and George. Now, let me call your attention to the fact that George Mallet, of whose writing I have here a sample, writes a similar hand to his cousin, with some exceptions. Among them are that he makes a shorter loop to his small 'g' than does Gustav. Look at the word George as written in the will.

"Although there was an attempt to duplicate the writing of the body of the document, yet that one thing was overlooked, and the 'g' in the word has a shorter loop than any other looped letter in the will. And referring to word 'beloved,' in the light of our knowledge of Mr. Anthony Conrad's attitude toward Mallet, and the fact that he knew of the life which Mr. Mallet has been living, and that he was heavily in debt, that word is sadly out of place."

I thought of Dual's remark of the morning, that one word might serve to point the truth.

Here before my eyes I saw it verified.

"And now," Semi was going on, "let us proceed to prove that we are right before we finally decide. Here"—he took up the scale of white substance which Johnson and I had found on the desk at Conrad's—"is a dried scale of some substance, which was found adhering to the top of the desk in the uncle's study. We will find out what it is."

He laid it upon a piece of paper, picked up a dropper, and dripped one tiny drop of water upon it.

Next he took a small dish and into it poured some quantity of a brownish fluid. "Iodin," he explained.

Lifting the dish, he warmed it gently over the spirit-lamp, lifted the sheet of paper with the dampened scale upon it, and held it over the fumes.

While we sat and watched a change came over the little, dull, white circle. It grew less white, took on a new color, turned blue.

"Starch," said Semi Dual.

The paper about the blue spot had turned brown. Dual noticed my glance and smiled.

"The natural reaction of cellulose to iodin," he explained. "It will occur under similar conditions with any dampened wood-fiber paper."

He picked up the will.

"Now, gentlemen, we will see if this paper upon which Anthony Conrad wrote his last will and testament has been dampened recently. If it has it will turn brown, as this other sheet has done-see?"

He held the back of the will above the steaming iodin in the shallow dish. We waited in a tense anxiety of expectance what would happen.

And as we watched we saw that the same change was coming over the will which had come over the other sheet of paper.

About the first name of Gustav, and the other name of George, the paper was gradually taking on a delicate tan shade, which was deepening with each moment to brown.

But under the names themselves a different thing was transpiring.

Even as in the case of the dampened flake, the surface of the paper upon which those names stood forth was darkening and deepening to a violet hue.

A thin smile flicked Dual's lips.

"Iodin," he said again, "and iodin, gentlemen, means starch when the blue color follows its kiss. Our proof is positive now. We have left theory and confront fact.

"Whoever tampered with this will first erased the original names with a sharp knife or a good eraser, and later transposed the names. To gain a fresh surface upon which to write, and one which would resemble that of the original finish of the paper, this individual made use of a mixture of flour and water. That accounts for the starch, and also for the telltale dampening of the cellulose fibers of the surrounding surface. The violet test proves this."

"Wonderful!" said Johnson. "Why don't we do things like this in this country, Dual?"

"Why," observed Dual, "is a good word. Your question should be answered by every detective bureau in the land. Justice has been said to be blind, but the day is coming when her blindfold will be torn away by science.

"There remains now but one more step, gentlemen, to complete the story of this crime. That is to determine the quality of the ink used in writing the main part of the will, and see whether it corresponds to that used in forming the transposed words."

Reaching out, he drew several vials across the desk toward him and arranged them close to his hand.

"In these," he explained, "I have the various reagents

used in making ink tests. Diluted with water and applied to writing they will upon contact show plainly what variety of ink has been used. The base of most commercial inks is, as you perhaps know, iron, but there are other inks as well. The modern criminologist has to be familiar with all these and their identifying tests. Iron ink, for instance, will vanish utterly under oxalic acid. Vanadin ink would be less affected and probably merely broaden slightly in its outline. Resorcine ink would turn a bright pink. Carbon or India ink would not be affected in the least, either by oxalic acid or any other reagent which we have. Now, in this case I believe from the appearance of the writing that an iron ink was used. I do not wish, to remove it, but only to verify my own opinion; therefore, I am going to use merely an identifying rather than an obliteration test."

He picked up a vial and dropped some of its contents into a tube partially filled with water and shook the mixture.

"Here I have a solution of hydroxid of soda in water. I shall moisten one of the words which Johnson will select with this mixture, and we will see what will happen. Pick your word, detective."

Johnson put out a finger and laid it on the word "dollars."

Dual took a glass rod, dipped it into the solution in the test-tube, and touched the indicated word.

Almost instantly as it seemed its dark lines changed and glowed a deep violent red.

"The base is gallate of iron," Dual declared. "It might have been copper, but if it had it would have run as well as change color. I was right in thinking it was iron instead. Now we will see what we can learn about the names which were written in."

He moistened the first letter of the word "Gustav" with the hydroxid solution.

Johnson and I watched him in breathless interest. Even Bryce, standing beside Mallet, craned forward. But, though we watched and waited, no change occurred.

Dual took up another vial.

"This," said he, "is muriatic acid. It alone of all chemicals will change every variety of ink, save one. You may say I am using a process of elimination in this test."

He made a solution of the acid and, using another glass rod, touched the loop of the small "g" in "George."

As before, we bent to watch the result, without avail. Dual lifted his face to Johnson and me.

"There is still no change," said he.

"Which means—" began the detective.

"That these two words were written in carbon or India ink," replied Semi. "That, as I told you, is the only ink which will not react to an re-agent."

"But just where does that bring us?" Johnson questioned. "Didn't we already have a pretty clear case?"

"We started to find a motive, if I remember," said Dual in answer. "If Anthony Conrad had actually made Gustav his heir, and Mallet, whom we know to have needed money badly, and to have hated his cousin for, as he believed, winning a woman whom he himself was in love with, had changed the will to read as it does, we would have found it, I think."

"Oh, my God!" Mallet half started from his chair and sank back, gasping.

Dual turned his eyes slowly upon him and held them for

a moment, while over his face fled an expression of what I felt was pity, a great, embracing compassion for the man.

Every line of his noble face in that moment spoke of the sympathy of the pure soul. I thought of what he had said to me of the painful duty which was to be his, and I knew that he was suffering, too, in the pain he caused.

Suddenly his voice came deep and full as a bell.

"Patience! The end is soon."

"The fact that iron ink was used by Conrad," he went on in a moment, "enables us to follow the case to the end. All iron inks penetrate the paper upon which they are used, sinking through the surface into the very fiber of the substance, so that, once applied, there will always be some trace remaining. We have a photograph of the present form of the will for future reference, so that now I may properly remove the transposed names."

He set some water to warming over the alcohol-damp, crossed and took the large metal plate from the smaller table, together with a couple of the rubber rings and a short rubber tube equipped with a spray nozzle.

Bringing these back to the desk, he laid the will upon the plate, face downward, placed one of the rings around each of the names in question, and fastened them in place with rubber bands.

Taking the now boiling water, he poured it into an atomizer and fitted the spray-tipped tube to its spout. With this he sprayed the paper surrounded by the rings.

Presently he set down the atomizer, took a piece of blotting-paper, and absorbed the excess moisture from the back of the will, unfastened the rings and turned the will over.

The two names had disappeared!

He picked up a fresh vial from the desk and took out the stopper.

"This," he observed, "is sulfid of ammonia. I will now moisten the paper where the words were written, and we shall see."

With a thin rod he dipped into the liquid in the vial and touched it to the dampened spots.

Both Johnson and I leaned forward to watch.

And as I watched I became aware that in those blank spaces dim lines were forming before my eyes—forming and growing, seeming to spread, and run toward each other until their lines met other lines and formed a definite something—letters—and at last words.

And—in that space where the name of Gustav had stood the name of George stood forth, and where George had once been written *the name of Gustav now appeared!*

Dual leaned back from the desk and raised his face to us.

"There, gentlemen," said he, "is your motive. It lies in the ghost of a name."

Neither one of us spoke, and presently he went on:

"And, like the ghost of a dead past, it rises to confront and confound. That at which you are looking is in reality the spirit of the dead Conrad's will."

"That ought to settle it," began Johnson.

"Wait!" said Semi Dual. He swung completely around in his chair so as to face Mallet.

"George Mallet," he spoke slowly, "I now formally accuse you with the murder of your uncle, Anthony Conrad and the attempted murder of your cousin, Gustav Conrad. Driven to desperation by your financial troubles, your inability to make loans, your knowledge that your uncle would cut you off, and your hatred of your cousin as your uncle's favorite and the *fiancé* of a woman you loved, you planned this crime.

"Last night you left your apartment and went to your uncle's house, entering by a window which you knew to be habitually open. You met your cousin and engaged him in conversation. When he was off his guard you shot him in the head with a weapon which you had previously equipped with a silencer. You then placed him on his bed and laid his own revolver beside him, after substituting the discharged shell from your gun for one of those in his weapon. You believed him fatally wounded, and left him for dead. You then went to your uncle's bedroom and there strangled him in his bed. This was at two-thirty-seven, as shown by a clock which was knocked to the floor by your struggles.

"After you had done this you went into the study and broke open the drawer in which the will was kept. You erased the name of yourself and that of your cousin, and in order to cover the traces of the work you resurfaced the paper with a mixture of flour and water. In so doing you dropped a spot of this on the desk, and either overlooked it or forgot to wipe it off. You waited until the paper was again dry, and wrote in the erased names in reversed order, thereby changing the will to your favor. You used an India ink, not knowing that it would be possible for any one to detect the difference or failing to remember the fact. You then left the will in the drawer and went home.

"In preparation for all of this, and to establish an alibi against possible suspicion, you gave a party at your rooms last evening. That lasted until one this morning. After the

guests had gone you feigned drunkenness and had your
man put you to bed. When he had gone, you slipped from
your room and left your apartment by a rear door opening
upon a tradesman's stairway. After you had committed
the crime and arranged, as you believed, to have it appear
as suicide on the part of your cousin, you slipped back to
your bed in the same manner and remained there until
your man called you to answer the phone call of Inspector
Bryce. But—

"The clock found on the floor beside your uncle's bed
shows the time of his death, and not even your servant
can testify to a positive knowledge that you were in your
room after possibly one-thirty this morning; so that your
alibi has no value in the face of the other evidence which
we have.

"Furthermore, in holding the paper of the will to erase
its names, you left a finger-print on its margin. That finger-
print corresponds to the marks found by Detective Johnson
on the window-sill of the room where you entered—and
also to a print upon the back of a note which you to-day
wrote in your office and addressed to your cousin's fiancée!"

Mallet sat relaxed in his chair, seemingly but half
conscious of Dual's words. Yet now as Semi paused he
very slowly nodded as one resigned.

After a long moment Dual went on.

"There is one thing more. Besides the marks of fingers
on your uncle's neck there are the indentations of two deep
gouges in the flesh, one on each side of the neck—low
down. The police believed those to be additional evidence
against your cousin, because the nails on his index-fingers
were long and sharp.

"But if that had been true the strangling hand must have been gripped about your uncle's throat from above downward, and because of the other evidence we know that your cousin did not kill your uncle. Had you crept into the room as you did, you would not have paused or delayed to turn so as to face the foot of the bed in which he lay, but would have reached for his throat at once. Therefore the marks of the nails in his flesh were not made by the nails of the index-finger, but by those of the little finger. George Mallet—*hold out your hands!*"

For a moment we waited. Then Bryce reached downward and gripped the hand of Mallet nearest his own—the left—and dragged it into view.

The nail of its little finger *was long and sharpened to a point!*

And in that moment Mallet acted. His figure came out of his chair as though shot by a spring. His right hand came up and caught Bryce squarely on the tip of the chin. The inspector grunted slightly and measurer his length on the floor.

In a bound Mallet crossed Bryce's body and flung himself at the door.

Seizing its knob with one hand, he dragged a small black weapon from a pocket and leveled it upon us.

"Stand back—all of you," he panted, "or I'll send you to join the rest!"

He jerked the door open and was gone!

Johnson hurled himself in pursuit.

I followed his lead.

"Yet I remember that as I sprang forward I glimpsed

Dual. He was sitting calm and impassive beside his great desk.

The detective and I gained the outer room in time to see Mallet's back vanish into the garden, and we raced in pursuit, Johnson drawing his police revolver as we ran.

A dull twilight met us at the tower door. Before us along the central path appeared the figure of Mallet. Instantly Johnson lifted his gun and fired over his head.

"Come back here, Mallet!" he bellowed. "The next shot will be to kill!"

The figure wavered in its stride, faltered, and turned to dash into the screening plants of the garden; turned and struck against the base of the old sun dial, and, clawing at the empty air, sprawled downward across its face.

Johnson and I rushed forward.

Yet even as I ran I wondered at the stillness of the figure across the dial—wondered that it made no move to struggle upward and make good its attempted escape.

But I did not comprehend, and I am sure that Johnson never suspected. Not until we stood beside him and bent to raise him and saw his head hanging on a limp neck across the edge of the dial did I understand and feel my heart contract with horror as we sought to lift him and found a resistance greater than that Born of his weight.

Then I knew that the sword of justice had fallen.

The sharp spear of the marker had gone straight to his heart.

Its length was stained a dull crimson as we lifted him off, and about its base was a little pool of dull red.

Panting more from the shock than the effort, Johnson

and I freed the body and laid it on the path, its head to the dull, stormy crimson of the west.

Rising, I became conscious that Dual had come out and was standing beside us, and, lifting my eyes, I gazed again into his face in which naught but compassion remained.

"Eternal justice," said Semi Dual, "lies in the hand of God."

ABOUT THE AUTHOR:
DR. J.U. GIESY

BORN NEAR CHILLICOTHE, Ohio, August 6, 1877. That makes me a Buckeye, and some people have suggested that I was a nut. Of my actual birth I have no recollection. So this is mere hearsay evidence. When I was eight months of age my parents removed to southeastern Kansas and took me with them, as I was still unable to shift for myself.

When I was thirteen we again removed to Utah, where I received my common school education in common with other youngsters of a similar age. In 1895, I entered the Starling Medical College, Columbus, Ohio, and received my medical degree from that institution in 1898.

Returning to Salt Lake, I served an interneship in a local hospital and have practiced medicine in that city ever since, with the exception of the time I spent in the United States service during the World War as a captain in the Medical Corps. As regards the Army I am still a major in the Reserve, attached to the Division Surgeon's Office of the 104th Division. In 1916 I was instrumental in organizing the first Plattsburg camp ever held in the State, starting the movement and acting as secretary of the general committee which put it over.

I began to write in 1910. Unlike many well known writers, I have had rejections since. At the same time I've found a lot of editors who liked my work. I have written as an avocation ever since. At present I am associate editor for Utah on the staff of *California and Western Medicine,* and the staff of the *Archives of Physical Therapy X-Ray and Radium.* Because of the latter fact I am a member of the American Medical Editors Association.

I am also a member of the Salt Lake Chamber of Commerce, and a life member of the American College of Physical Therapy, which I have served as an officer for several years. My ancestors made me a Son of the American Revolution, and I have made myself more or less of a nuisance to a lot of people all by myself.

I was married in San Francisco, to Juliet Galena Conwell, in December, 1904, and the marriage took. Personally I think they did better work along those lines, that long ago. Anyway we're still living in the same apartment, with no intentions of divorce.

Just why the editor should want to print this confession I really can't imagine. But that's his business. He's asked for it and here it is!

ABOUT THE AUTHOR:
JUNIUS B. SMITH

I WAS BORN at Salt Lake City, Utah, September 29, 1883, at approximately 3:55:27 P.M., right ascension of the mid-heaven (for the benefit of my astrological readers) 16 hrs. 27 min. 57 sec., or 246° 59' 15"; position of planets, Neptune 20° 45' ret. Taurus, Saturn 10° 6' ret. Gemini, Mars 22° 10' Cancer, Jupiter 0° 26' Leo, Moon 22° 24' Virgo, Uranus 24° 34' Virgo, Sun 6° 27' 23" Libra, Venus 8° 52' Libra, Mercury 20° 31' ret. Libra. Declinations: Sun 2° 34' south, Moon 0° 7' south, Neptune 16° 13' north, Uranus 2° 50' north, Saturn 20° 2' north, Jupiter 20° 18' north, Mars 22° 25' north, Venus 2° 20' south, Mercury 11° 17' south.

With this meager astronomical data, the astrologians will know more about me than I could write in a volume.

For the benefit of you other readers:

I am an attorney at law and practiced for many years, paying my office expenses in the lean years by writing. I never had the bitter experience of having to write years before anything sold. At the beginning of my writing career, Dr. J.U. Giesy and I joined intellectual forces, and our first joint effort was submitted to *Argosy* way back in 1911. It sold, first time out. Rapidly we "dashed" off more and they sold also. We each write separately as well as jointly, at such times as we cannot get together.

Early in life I took up astrology as a hobby and lived to see it recognized in judicial decisions as a science. That I have helped, in some measure, to brush away the misconceptions in the minds of many people regarding this much maligned subject is perhaps testified to by my election to Fellowship in the American Academy of Astrologians, an organization that one can't get into for the asking.

I've wasted enough time playing checkers to have built one of the Egyptian pyramids single-handed. Another hobby is shorthand, which has fascinated me for thirty years. I understand several systems. I can sling a wicked toe on the dance floor, but only dance when my weight crowds two hundred. One year I spent the summer on the desert drying out, where my own cooking, plus the heat, effected a material reduction. But I come honestly by it: my father weighed two hundred and sixty in athletic condition— three hundred when not.

And speaking of ancestors: My grandfather was a brother of Joseph Smith, who founded the Mormon Church, which probably explains why I was born in Utah.